RELUCTANT ASSASSIN

RELUCTANT ROYALS: BOOK TWO

MONTANA ASH

RELUCTANT ASSASSIN

Published by Paladin Publishing
Cover design by Laura Social-Clarke, Covers By Aura
Formatting by Montana Ash

RELUCTANT ASSASSIN

RELUCTANT ROYALS: BOOK TWO

MONTANA ASH

DEDICATION

This goes out to my Scottish sprinting buddy and fellow author, Eve L. Mitchell. Thank you for sharing in my delirium at 3am as we worded the words.

And to my alpha-beta-nit-pickers. Honestly, you guys are the best. I appreciate you all the way to Purgatory and back. Thank you.

PREFACE

Dear Liz,

I am writing to you personally because I understand you took exception to my ability to 'thrust continuously for 30 minutes straight'. I am very sorry that this hasn't been your experience with men in the past. It sounds like the quality of your bed partners has been rather poor. Likely because you are on the Earth plane and humans have very little stamina and imagination. I, however, am a mighty demon from Purgatory. I am a direct descendant of Cerberus himself. My ability to thrust is the stuff of legends.

Now, unfortunately, I am already spoken for by a rather possessive angel assassin. But I am positive I can rustle up another demon, or perhaps a vampire or two, who would be more than happy to assist you with this sad state of affairs.

Please contact me using the below email if you would like assistance finding a 'thrusting buddy' who has endurance. Please include 'supernatural thrusting buddy wanted' in the subject line so the email won't get lost.

abraxis.thrusts.like.the.demon.he.is@gmx.com

Wishing you a fun-filled 30+ minutes of pounding very soon.

Yours truly,

Brax
(Current King and Demon Horde General of Purgatory)

PROLOGUE

The first thing she remembered was the blue of the sky. Blinking in confusion, she stared at the rooftop of the world, watching white fluffy clouds pass slowly overhead. She was on her back on the ground, and although she wasn't uncomfortable, she still sat up quickly.

Looking around, she found herself in a small clearing. There was green grass underneath her, that pretty blue sky above her, and a dense forest of trees to her left. To her right, however, there was a huge white building with dozens of windows. It gave the impression of wealth but not of home. In fact, she shivered a little as she took in the fancy house.

Something rustled behind her, and she gasped. Grabbing onto all the red, she yanked it around so she could see the feathers more closely. They were shiny, a startling crimson colour, and attached to her back. *Wings,* she thought. *These are my wings.* She promptly gave a mental order for them to recede into her skin. She didn't know how they fit, given their sheer size, but accepted it for the magic that it was. Her memories were fuzzy, and she was very confused, but she knew her wings were supposed to be kept hidden.

Standing up, she looked at the house again. Her stomach roiled a little, but she nonetheless set off in that direction. She didn't get far. Two men rushed out of a door, menace in their expressions and weapons held high. She paused but was oddly unafraid.

"Stop where you are, kid," a tall, burly man demanded.

She didn't point out that she had already stopped. Nor that she wasn't a kid. Or was she? Looking down, she discovered that she *was* rather low to the ground and that the two men in front of her *did* tower over her. Holding her hands out, she saw that they were very small – almost delicate. She huffed, feeling irritated. It appeared she was indeed a child. She didn't feel like a kid. Every second brought new information as her brain and memories caught up with being thrust through the veil. Brain fog was sometimes a thing, especially in the very young. And especially when one had been created rather than born.

She rolled her eyes at herself, knowledge and awareness returning even faster now. No wonder her memories were few as well as vague, she didn't have a lifetime of stored memories in her head. Merely the few years since she had been handmade in the Heavens themselves. Her body had moulded into its shape, her feathers painstakingly arranged one at a time in precise order. She didn't personally remember that, of course. There had been no awareness at that time. Not until she had been imbued with Grace and her wings had spread wide, changing from the cream of creation to the crimson of resurrection.

An angel. I'm an angel, she told herself, knowing it down to her very bones. She had not been birthed by a body but had been created deliberately. A mission had been set for her before she'd even taken her first breath. She was a tool, a weapon.

She was a guardian.

"What are you doing here?" The fierce, brute of a man demanded.

She took a step back, wondering how fast she could run. She couldn't quite recall. "Sorry," she muttered, unable to answer the question because she had no idea where 'here' was. The big guy went to reach for her, but the other man stopped him, drawing her attention.

"What's your name?" The blond, handsome man asked. He had a kind face and warm brown eyes.

"Isrephel," she promptly replied, knowing it was true.

The blond man went very still, piercing eyes travelling over her from head to toe. Greed and excitement flashed over his face before he carefully schooled his expression. "Isrephel, huh? That's an angelic name."

"Yes," Isrephel replied. The two men looked at each other, and she could easily see the calculation in their eyes. She disliked them immensely but stayed where she was for now.

"I am Carlisle," the seemingly nicer man said. "And this is my humble home and my place of business." He gestured to the mansion behind him. "Tell me, Isrephel, who gave you that name?"

"My mother," she didn't hesitate to reply. She knew instinctively not to reveal that she had been created. To not reveal she was a guardian.

"Ah," Carlisle said, looking disappointed. "And where is your mother now?"

"We were attacked," Isrephel explained, quickly weaving a story. "She was killed. It's just me now. I'm lost. I'm afraid ..." She added a small whimper, wrapping her arms around herself. Most of it was an act, but not all. She *was* lost and would continue to be until she found her charge. And she was afraid of what the unknown future might bring. But she was also determined and filled with purpose.

"Poor child," Carlisle murmured. "Purgatory is no place for an innocent to be roaming around. Especially one such as yourself. Come, I will help you."

She eyed the handsome man in front of her, knowing in her gut that he was *not* her charge. Yet there was also a feeling of rightness when she looked at him. And so, when he offered her his hand, she smiled and took it, feeling no tug in her soul. There was no bond and no potential for one.

He's definitely not my charge, she thought. *He's just another tool, another pawn in the game.*

The thought was not bitter, merely an acknowledgement of how things had to be. Still, she hoped her charge presented themselves sooner rather than later. She was young, but she wasn't stupid. When a guardian was made and sent to one of the other realms, it meant someone important needed protecting. With no idea who that was or where they were, she had no choice but to trust her instincts until she found them. And she *would* find them, she promised.

Guardian angels never failed.

SIX YEARS LATER

She crept unseen through the dark corridors of the palace. Although she wore heavy boots, they made no sound on the stained wooden floors. She had learned the hard way how to be stealthy. And stealth was most certainly needed when one was breaking into the royal palace to off an old political figure who had pissed off the wrong person. She didn't know the details, and she didn't need to. At fourteen, it wasn't her first kill, and she knew it wouldn't be her last.

Ignoring the pang in her chest, she paused and listened to the sound of muffled voices. Her mark and five other politicians were in a meeting in the main conference room just three doors down from her current location. She could have simply broken down the door and killed him with one of her blades. It would undoubtedly be the most expedient option. But not the most subtle. Carlisle, who had turned out to be more of a lying arsehole than she had anticipated, had expressively told her to be subtle. So, she crept past the door, making her way to the visitor quarters instead.

It took all of three minutes to jimmy the lock, enter the room, set her boobytrap in the bathroom, and slip back into the hallway. The poor gryphon would get a nasty surprise when he went to take a piss later that evening. It would probably be too messy to be classed as subtle, but the guy would be dead with no witnesses. It would do.

She was about to run past an open doorway in the family quarters when an odd squeak caught her attention. Curiosity filled her, but she sternly told herself to get out of there. She was already being riskier than she had to be by entering the section reserved for the royal family members. But it had more secret passages than other parts of the palace and guaranteed an exit.

The noise sounded again, and something inside of her sparked to life. Something she couldn't name. Rubbing her chest, she tried shaking her head to dislodge the sensation. For the first time in years, since she had made an innocently ignorant promise to a psycho incubus, she felt her feathers ruffle. They were still trapped within her flesh, where they had likely already started to erode, but at that moment, they wanted out.

Tears pricked her eyes, and she ruthlessly scrubbed them away. Tears were for the losers and the weak. She was neither. But when the strangely happy sound of a gurgle met her ears again, she couldn't stop her feet from moving forward into the large room where a cot was set up, along with an endless supply of baby paraphernalia. She realised she must have stumbled upon the royal nursery, which meant the cot must hold the future king and his two brothers. Carlisle would have come in his pants to be in such a situation, she knew. When she informed him of this, she would be his favourite for quite some time. The thought cheered her and disgusted her in equal measures.

She loathed the man who had become her Master, but she also saw him almost in a paternal light. After being sent to Purgatory in a child's meatsuit, mentally and emotionally too young to comprehend the predicament she'd been thrust into, Carlisle had taken her in. He had fed her, clothed her, and housed her. Sure, he had also taught her how to kill, steal, lie, and cheat. But when you had nothing and no one, even the Master of an assassin den who tortured you to toughen you up, could be seen as *home*.

Shaking off her thoughts, she listened carefully. Once she was positive she was alone, she crept closer to the large cot. Curious, she looked over the wooden edge only to freeze, all of her muscles locking down when she spied the three babies. They were all swaddled next to each other in a row and looked like little baby tacos. She found herself smiling, positive that even the most hardened mercenary would get a little melty looking at the three dark-haired, chubby infants. Two were sleeping, but one was wide awake.

He must be the squeaker-gurgler, she thought. For a moment, his clear, green eyes lost the haziness of infancy and locked onto hers with the focus of a laser pointer. Without thinking, she stepped closer and reached over. She held her breath when her fingertip brushed through the dense, brown hair on his head. His eyes lit up, and he struggled a little, clearly trying to wiggle his way out of his baby straitjacket.

"Do you want to hold him?"

The voice startled her, taking years off her life. She couldn't believe she had been so enamoured by a brat that someone had snuck up on her without her knowing. She spun around, retrieving a dagger from her thigh holster, before pointing the lethal blade at the man. She blinked several times when she realised she was standing face to face with the King of Purgatory. "Fuck," she muttered.

King Maliq smiled, the lines around the corners of his eyes crinkling appealingly. "Very articulate. But perhaps you could refrain from using such language when you're around the children." He gestured towards the cot.

She looked around, not seeing anyone else. But she knew that wouldn't last long. The king, nor the triplets, wouldn't be left without guards for more than a few minutes. "Move back," she ordered the king. "And show me your hands."

Maliq slowly raised his empty hands, even going so far as to do a little spin. "No weapons," he promised. "And no guards riding to the rescue. It's just us. I have no intention of hurting you."

She snorted in derision. "Right. Like I haven't heard that before."

Maliq's dark eyes softened, and he made a pained sound in the back of his throat. "I'm sure that's true. I hate that for you."

"Whatever," she muttered, wondering what the hell was going on. The entire situation was bizarre.

"Isrephel, I've been expecting you," the king said, a genuine smile lighting his face once more.

Her dagger hand shook, and she took a step backwards. She hadn't heard her real name spoken since the time she had told Carlisle what it was. After that day, when she had signed a contract in her own blood, she had ceased to be Isrephel. Instead, she had become Sabre.

"How do you know that name?" she finally regained enough wits to demand.

"I know a lot about you, little angel," King Maliq replied.

He strolled further into the room, giving her a wide berth and dividing his attention between the babies and her still-raised dagger.

"I'm no angel," Sabre retorted. "Not anymore."

"Oh, sweetheart, you are the most angelic angel I have ever had the pleasure of meeting," Maliq assured her.

Sabre gritted her teeth, telling herself to stab the arrogant – and clearly crazy – king in the chest. "Fuck this shit. I'm outta here. If you try to stop me, I'll …" she looked around, wondering what she could use as leverage. When she spied the babies once more, she licked her lips, feeling nervous and sick. "I'll kill him," she hissed, motioning to the wide-awake baby.

Maliq's eyebrows shot up. "Really? You'll kill an innocent baby so that you can escape and run back to your assassin den?"

Sabre shook her head. She was confused as hell. Why was Maliq so calm? Why was she even still standing around having a conversation with the demon instead of gutting him and running away? And as for killing the baby, her stomach roiled just thinking about hurting the innocent, beautiful creature. In the early days of her 'apprenticeship' with Carlisle, many things had made her stomach roil. Not so much now. But it seemed that harming a baby was a line she didn't want to cross yet.

"No," she admitted. "I don't think I can do that."

"Excellent," Maliq said. "Now, you didn't answer my question," he pointed out.

"Huh?" Not very articulate, Sabre knew, but she was afraid she was tripping on something. She had come to the royal palace on a mission to kill, and here she was with the freaking king, chatting as if they were old friends. He even knew her angel name.

"The baby," he gestured to the crib. "Do you want to hold him?"

Sabre sneered, forcing herself not to look into the crib once again. "Why the fuck would I want to hold one of your spawns?"

Maliq smiled, the look was the epitome of indulgence, as if he didn't believe a word she was saying. It pissed her off. She may look like a kid, but she was far from innocent. The king took a step closer to the large cot, completely ignoring the huge blade in her hand. "I will fuck you up," she warned, brandishing her weapon.

Maliq had the audacity to roll his eyes as he reached into the cot, gently picked up a bundle of soft, pink fleshy baby and turned to her, carefully placing the child into her arms. Sabre didn't dare move. Hell, she could barely breathe. She just stared, wide-eyed, at the ruler of Purgatory as he handed her one of his precious triplet sons.

"Go on," Maliq urged. "Look at him." He then carefully removed the dagger from her hand, and for some reason, Sabre let him.

Sabre looked down automatically, finding the baby staring back at her with unflinching trust. His green eyes were the colour of apples, pale and just as sweet. A small hand worked its way free of the tight wrappings, and before she could process, the baby gripped her thumb in an iron hold. Sabre shivered from her head to her toes as the warm, pudgy hand claimed her possessively – and for all eternity.

She released a harsh breath and smiled, cooing inarticulately at the fat, adorable little lump. His eyes wrinkled at the corners – just like his father's – when he smiled a wide, toothy grin and Sabre vowed right then and there that nothing was ever going to hurt him. She was always going to be there to protect him, and she would obey his commands no matter what they may be. The baby cooed back, clearly well-pleased with what he was hearing, and Sabre grinned, bopping him on his perfect button nose.

"I will slaughter anyone who thinks to hurt you. Yes, I will," she said, her voice much higher than usual. "I will cut out their hearts and present them to you on a gold platter because that is what you deserve. Yes, it is." The baby giggled, and Sabre laughed right along with him. "You like the sound of that, huh? All the torn-out hearts will be yours," she vowed.

So caught up in the spell, the abrupt movement to her left startled her. She spun, protecting the baby, but giving the interloper her vulnerable back. She didn't care if she got stabbed in the back, she thought. As long her little guy was okay. Without thinking, she released her wings, wrapping them around the front of her body and encasing the baby in red feathers. When no hit or words came, she peeked over her shoulder. Maliq was still the only other person in the room. He had simply moved closer to place a cloth over her shoulder.

"It's a burp rag," the king offered an explanation. "Mikhail has terrible reflux."

"His name is Mikhail?" Sabre asked, moving her wings back from where they covered the infant entirely. At least, she tried to. It seemed Mikhail had other ideas. He had a firm grip on some of her feathers, and when she tugged them free, he successfully yanked one out. He waved the crimson feather like a flag, gurgling his happiness. "Ouch, dude. You think you're very clever, don't you?"

Maliq chuckled, watching his son's antics with affection. "Yes, his name is Mikhail. He is my firstborn son, the future king." He turned to Sabre, looking serious. "And your charge."

"My charge," Sabre murmured, looking at Mikhail in awe. Of course he was, she silently acknowledged. There could be no other explanation for what she was feeling. "Thank the gods. I was afraid I had failed, that I was losing my Grace. I never thought I would find my charge. I'm still a guardian," she stated.

"You are still a guardian," the king promised.

She was happy, joyous even. She was the guardian angel

of the future king. But her wonder was overshadowed by her circumstances. She was tied to the Blue Devil Den for another ninety-four years. Not only that, Carlisle and the rest of the lowlifes living there were a threat to Mikhail. Too big of a threat to be allowed to live.

"I have to kill them all," she told Maliq. "I'm not sure how I can best Carlisle, not with the no-injury clause in my contract. But I'll find a way. Will he be safe here until I can figure it out and return? I ..." she trailed off when she saw the pity on the king's face. Her delight, her relief, her soul, crumpled upon seeing that expression. "I'm not coming to live here. Am I?"

Maliq placed a large hand on her head, almost like a benediction. "I'm going to ask something of you, angel. Something nobody has a right to ask you. But I have no other choice. The future is sometimes shown to me. It's a curse, not a gift. But once shown it cannot be unseen."

Sabre looked down at Mikhail, swallowing noisily because he was just too darn precious. "The future is a giant pile of dragon turd, isn't it?" she guessed, looking back up.

Maliq was startled into a laugh. "It is. It most definitely is. And we have to let it unfold."

"We have to let ourselves get shit on?" Sabre questioned, bitterness rising to the surface. "I've already been shit on. Lots."

"I know. I'm sorry," was all he said.

Taking a deep breath, Sabre pressed a kiss to Mikhail's

forehead, whispering promises into his ear. She then placed him back into the cot with his brothers, noting another one was awake now as well. The yellow eyes were startling in such a young face, and he gazed at her seriously, much more so than his older brother. The frown on his face was rather adorable though.

"That is Abraxis, born second," Maliq said. "And Zagan is the youngest."

Sabre nodded, taking one last look at all three babies. She then turned around, tucking her wings away. She really hoped it wouldn't be the last time she saw them. "Tell me all about the shit," she commanded. "How long do I have to immerse myself in the filth before it really hits the fan?"

I

PRESENT DAY

"Wow," Brax said from his position beneath Sabre.

Sabre looked down, taking in the expanse of Brax's pretty chest. She was currently perched on top of him in their bed, straddling his waist as he lounged on his back with his hands behind his head. His hands were there because he couldn't be trusted to keep them to himself. Though to be fair, they were both naked, so it probably wasn't a reasonable request. Sabre was having a hard time keeping her hands from wandering over all of his toned, warm skin herself. But Brax had wanted to hear how she had been trapped by Carlisle and how she had first met Mikhail.

It wasn't a tale she had told a lot. In fact, she had only ever told one other person about how she had chosen to enter the Blue Devil Den but had also been tricked into it at the same time. As a mere child of no more than eight years old and having the memories of even fewer years than that, she hadn't exactly been equipped to make the best choices. And a promise given was a bond made. No matter the circumstances. She had left out a few details of her story, like her original name. The last time she had heard it aloud was from King Maliq the day she had met him. Her Heavenly derived name hardly seemed important or relevant now.

Refocusing on the demon between her thighs, Sabre responded to his comment. "I know, right? Crazy times."

Brax shook his head, his thick hair spreading over the pillow. It already needed another trim. "I didn't mean wow as in crazy. I meant wow as in, wow, Sabre you're a big softie."

"What?" she demanded, rearing back. "I am not soft!"

Brax smirked, unlocking his fingers from beneath his head and wrapping them around her waist. "Oh really? You should have seen your face when you were describing baby Mikhail. Plus, you baby-talked. Again."

Sabre scowled at her man, torn between wanting to hurt him and fuck him. He couldn't really be hurt, thanks to his genetic gift from his ancestor, but it was often cathartic to try. Fucking him was a no-brainer, and something she wanted to do almost constantly. And not just when he was spread out before her like an all you can eat sex buffet. It was strange, finally being horny after so many years of being sexless. But she was adapting well if their sexual marathons were anything to go by.

"What do you mean, *again?*" she demanded. "When have I ever talked like a baby before?"

"Um, how about every day when you see Styx," Brax volunteered.

Sabre opened and closed her mouth with a snap, not saying anything. She had no defence because the adorable hellhound had her wrapped around his cute, three-inch-long fangs.

"And then there's this ..." Brax continued on, his hands travelling from her waist to her breasts. He cupped them, squeezing them lightly. "More evidence of your softness," he practically purred.

Sabre arched into his palms, her breath catching. The way he touched her aroused her. But it also warmed her in other ways. Because that look he was sporting in his canary-yellow eyes was reserved solely for her. And it was real. She knew that. What's more, she trusted it.

He loved her.

Abraxis, current King of Purgatory and former General to the Demon Horde, loved her. A mere three months ago such a scenario would have had her laughing so hard she'd have ruptured her spleen. She also would have cut out the spleen of anyone who dared to suggest it. But now? Now she simply allowed the moan of ecstasy to escape her lips as she rocked her hips forward, grinding her sensitised clit against Brax's pelvis.

"*You* sure don't feel soft," she informed her guy, feeling his dick harden and return to its former glory from before their impromptu chat.

"Definitely not soft," Brax concurred. He pushed his hips up, his erection rubbing between the cheeks of Sabre's butt. "Think you can handle *hard?*"

She smirked down at him, confident in her abilities. She may not have slept with as many people as his slutty arse had, but she didn't need to. Not when she was able to bring a strong demon, descended from the mighty Cerberus himself, to his knees with a simple caress. "I can handle it," she promised him, leaning forward to plant a long, passionate kiss against his lips.

When she finally pulled back, they were breathing hard. Instead of rising up and taking in the hard flesh still prodding at her, she stared at Brax's gorgeous face for a moment. "I really do love you," she told him, stroking his whisker-roughened cheek.

The corner of Brax's eye crinkled as he smiled. "I love you, too. Very much."

Sabre sucked in a sharp breath, the words hitting her in the heart as powerfully and as surely as an arrow. "Thank you."

Brax's loved-up expression turned cheeky. "And so polite these days," he noted. "Careful, you don't want that badarse rep of yours to slip, my love."

Sabre felt a fizzle of unease spread throughout her system, the same as when he called her soft. She knew it was in jest. She also knew there was nothing wrong with being soft. Being soft or kind or sweet didn't make someone weak or incapable. But it just wasn't her. Growing up, she hadn't been allowed to be anything other than hard. Anything other than a killer. Just because she had herself a boyfriend now and some people who insisted on calling themselves her friends, didn't mean she could slip. In fact, more was at stake now, because she couldn't bear to lose any of them. She had to stay tough. Which is why, instead of seating herself on Brax's tempting cock and riding him like he was a wild bronco, she reached for a dagger instead.

Raising it high, she jammed it into her lover's gut. He didn't so much as flinch. His sexy eyes remained infused with humour, and dare she say *indulgence*. She watched as a hard exoskeleton rushed to the surface, the chrome armour overlapping itself much like fish scales. It stopped the wickedly sharp blade in its tracks, even going so far as to break off the tip. She smiled like she always did when Brax's defence mechanism kicked in. She thought it was the coolest thing on the planet.

"Feel better?" Brax asked.

Sabre shrugged, her fingers chasing the armour as it disappeared back into his skin until all that was left behind was tanned, hot flesh. Not even a blemish remained. "Kind of," she answered, and promised herself she wasn't pouting. But something in her tone or expression must have given her away because Brax placed his hand under her chin and lifted it until their eyes met.

"What's going on in that head of yours?" he asked, voice quiet but sincere.

She regarded him for a moment, wondering if she should tell him the truth or simply shrug off her contrary mood.

"The truth, Sabre," he said. He growled a little, the beastly rumble vibrating in his chest. "I want you to be honest with me. Always."

Sabre frowned now, not sure how she felt about someone being able to read her as well as Brax apparently could. She was known for her poker face. She could out-bluff and manipulate a veritas demon, even in the face of torture. But now it appeared that she couldn't even keep one tiny moment of insecurity to herself. Before she could respond, Brax moved quickly. He lifted her up by the waist as he scooted out from beneath her, his strength making her gasp. Propping himself against the headboard, he arranged her next to him on the rumpled sheets, ensuring they were both comfortable.

"Talk to me, Sabre. I'm listening," he urged.

"That's kind of the problem," Sabre admitted, twisting the sheets in her hands.

"You don't want me to listen to what you have to say? To care about your thoughts and emotions?" Brax asked, seeking clarification.

She looked up, finding his face open and honest. He wasn't irritated with her. And he wasn't pushing, not really. He was just a guy in a relationship who was being present for his woman. He was fucking amazing, and she was going to blow it. She just knew she was.

"It's not that I don't want to share with you, Brax. I want to. I want to give you all the things I've never given another. But it worries me too. I can't afford to drop the ball. If I'm soft, if I'm polite, if I'm easy to read, then I can't be an effective assassin. I can't be a good guardian. And I need to be, Brax. I *have* to be."

"Sabre ..." Brax murmured, reaching out and stroking her face with his palm. "I have never met a more skilled assassin. Or a more dedicated guardian angel. You are not losing your touch. That would be impossible. You're too good for that. Not to mention, it's who you are, Sabre. You'll always be *you*, and you'll always be true to yourself. You can't be any other way."

Sabre chewed on her lip. This talking crap and being emotionally vulnerable was hard. She didn't like it. "And that's okay? Me being who I am?"

"It's more than okay. Everything you are is perfect to me.

I promise you that. I was joking with you before. I wasn't implying you were weak or somehow diminished," he told her.

Sabre groaned and dropped her head into her hands. "I sound like a whiny little bitch, don't I? I don't know what's wrong with me."

"Could it be you're a little stressed? Perhaps overwhelmed by all the recent changes in your life?" Brax suggested, tugging her hands away from her face.

"What do I have to be stressed about?" she demanded.

"Geez, I don't know. Perhaps the recent severe torture you endured? Or maybe the revelation that you are in fact an agent of Heaven and have been undercover in the depths of depravity for a century? Or maybe it's falling in love for the first time or discovering you have more friends and family than you know what to do with? Not to mention the assassin den owner who wants you dead." Brax listed everything off one by one. "It's a lot, Sabre."

"Nothing I haven't dealt with before. Well, I haven't dealt with all of that specifically," she allowed. "I just mean in general. I'm used to this kind of stuff."

"I know you are. Because you're a strong, kickarse, ninja-angel who eats bad guys for breakfast," Brax praised.

Sabre smiled at him. She couldn't help it. "You are such a goofball." He really was, she thought to herself. And she loved that about him.

"I didn't mean to offend you," Brax then said.

Sabre sighed, running her fingers through her hair. "You didn't. Not really. More like scared me a little. I need to stay strong, Brax."

"You will. You are."

The simple words, spoken with so much conviction had her shoulders finally relaxing. She melted against his bare chest, her head resting over his heart. She listened to it beat for a moment before inquiring, "Did I ruin the mood? Or do you still want to sex me up?"

She found herself flat on her stomach with a mouthful of cotton sheet before she could even take another breath. Brax's heavy frame draped across her back, and he nudged her knees wide with his own. She felt her hands gripped one by one and pushed up above her head before he curled her fingers around the rails of the bed frame.

"Keep them there," Brax whispered in her ear.

Sabre shivered. She didn't know if the words were a demand or a suggestion. But either way, she was happy to obey. Brax's own hands then smoothed over her back from nape to arse, leaving the best kind of goosebumps in their wake. He massaged her butt cheeks for a moment before lifting her hips and spreading her wide, opening her up to his hungry gaze. When she felt a finger brush over her core, she shuddered and moaned.

"Mmm," Brax rumbled. "Already so wet for me. Does this feel good, Sabre? You like my hands on your body – *in* your body?"

Sabre's head whipped back and forth on the bed, her nose getting a bit squashed as she started to pant. Brax had pressed a thick digit inside of her and was stroking her from the inside, his actions mirroring his naughty words. He teased her a little at first, keeping the movements soft and slow.

She had come to realise that he was a little sexually sadistic, finding pleasure in withholding her own. He always delivered, but he liked to play first, ensuring her body was pushed to the brink of ecstasy time and time again before he finally allowed her to come. For someone as impatient as she was, it wasn't easy.

The past week-long sex marathon they'd had in Brax's royal suite, had shown her the benefits of Brax's dirty mind. Besides, it felt good to just let go. To not have to think for a while, to leave her body, her heart, and her pleasure in the capable hands of someone she could trust. Someone she knew would never abuse them. Brax was that person. And while that was all well and good, Sabre was starting to sweat from the fingers currently thrusting in and out of her. There was not enough friction happening to suit her.

"Damnit, Abraxis, get on with it!" she demanded, turning her head to look him in the eye.

His eyes practically glowed as they reflected the early morning light, revealing the DNA of the hellhounds housed in his blood. Sweat shone on his face and chest already, dampening the chest hairs there. He was rather hairy, Sabre acknowledged, eyeing the sexy snail trail from his belly button to his groin. The hair on his head was a little odd and grew insanely fast. It was thick and lush, giving her something to grip and she loved it. But the speed at which it grew was a little scary. Thankfully, his chest hair didn't grow at the same rate. It also wasn't as thick. It was just the right amount in Sabre's humble opinion.

From her position, she couldn't really see his dick in order to check on the hair there, but she conjured it up in her mind well enough. It too was dark and somewhat prolific. She had been amused to discover he trimmed there almost as frequently as the hair on his head.

She was glad. She didn't want to be reamed by bigfoot's cock.

The thought amused her, and she giggled. Brax's eyes narrowed and he removed his hand from between her thighs so he could smack her lightly on her left butt cheek, even as he kept her hips elevated with his other hand.

"What the hell? What are you laughing at?" he demanded. "I'm screwing you like a pro here," he pointed out.

"A pro, huh?" Sabre snorted. "I guess you would know," she said, alluding to his somewhat rich sexual history. She knew it was normal for people to have sex. Lots of sex. Most species didn't have the shitty sex drive angels did. But the thought of anyone being on the receiving end of Brax's dick the same way she was, made her feel very violent. Another slap to her butt, this one hard enough to sting, jolted her from her thoughts. She scowled at him. "I dare you to do that again."

An unholy light flared in his eyes and Sabre felt claws dig into her hips. Brax's lower fangs elongated, and a rumbling purr came from his throat. *Oh, yeah,* she thought. There was her demon coming out to play.

The thing with Brax was, he was an easy-going guy. When he wasn't being plagued by the systematic death of his entire family, he was happy by nature. But he was still an alpha demon from the royal line. He was still a beast at his core. And Sabre witnessed that side of him mainly during intimate moments like this. Where his rough hands and primal reactions demonstrated just how possessive he was. Just how much his need for her caused his patience to flee and his control to snap. It was arousing as hell, not to mention a big compliment. What woman didn't want to have the power to turn her man into a raging sex-beast?

The abrupt feeling of Brax pushing into her caused her to gasp. He was rigged to match the alpha beast in his soul. Long, wide, and impossibly hard, Brax's cock stretched her to her limits, ecstasy erupting everywhere he touched. Her hands spasmed where they still gripped the rails, and she lifted her hips as much as his clawed hands allowed. She desperately wanted to be on her knees so she could push back against his invading dick, but Brax pushed her flat, making enough room between her legs for his body as he stretched out on top of her. He was heavy, his six-foot-three frame heavily muscled. But she loved the feeling of being trapped beneath him, of being *impaled* by him.

"Now," Brax growled into her ear. "What was that about a dare?"

2

Brax knew Sabre was pushing his primal buttons deliberately. He didn't mind. Not in the slightest.

They had agreed to essentially take the last week off following the happenings and revelations at the Blue Devil Den. Not only had Sabre needed time to recover from her wounds, despite Draven healing her, but they had needed time together as a couple. Their relationship was still very new, and the time spent doing nothing but talking and fucking had been just what they needed to strengthen their bond. Brax could already see the proof of that in the way Sabre had opened up to him before. Communication was not her strong suit – unless it was sarcasm or threats. He was damn proud of her for willing to be vulnerable in front of him. Not to mention humbled.

He was sorry his comments had made her question

herself, even for a moment. It hadn't been his intention. Although he had been a morose, miserable bastard for the better part of a year since his brothers were murdered, he was naturally a fun guy. He joked, he bantered, he teased. Teasing Sabre was as fun as it was rewarding. Seeing her smile, seeing a blush spread across her cheeks, was priceless. She needed all the fun she could get, having missed out on it her entire life. But he knew she didn't see it that way. He would never deliberately do or say anything that would make her uncomfortable. He'd already fucked up in the worst possible way, not trusting her and sending her into the hands of a sociopath for literal torture. Sabre had told him there was nothing to forgive, but he was still working on forgiving himself.

Looking at her now, noting the devilish look in her plum-coloured eyes, it was hard to make out the vulnerable woman. But she was there, Brax knew. Just as he knew he was one of the only people in all the realms to get a glimpse of that woman. It humbled him. It also made him want to reward the feisty assassin. But before he got to that, he made a mental note to be more careful with his words in the future, even in jest. Sabre tended to take things rather literally.

The clenching of Sabre's internal muscles around his shaft, reminded him of the reward he wanted to bestow on her, as well as the dare she had issued. He loved the position they were in, with her flat out on the bed and him covering her from head to toe. Her legs were spread just enough to accommodate his between them, but he was more squashed than anything. The added tightness that the position afforded him damn near caused his eyes to roll back into his skull.

He raised up onto his hands to get some leverage and thrust into Sabre's heated depths a few times. Her moans of pleasure assured him she was as into it as he was. But Brax knew it wasn't sustainable, not when he wanted to pound her into the mattress. After one more sharp thrust of his hips, he rotated his pelvis in a circular motion, grinding down against her. She cursed and moved her head to the side, revealing her flushed cheeks and open, panting mouth.

"Damn, you're beautiful," he muttered, watching her eyelashes flutter. He pulled out, only to hike Sabre's hips up, before ramming back into her again. When she went to push herself up onto all fours, Brax placed his hand in the centre of her back, holding her down. "I thought I told you to hold onto the rails." The look Sabre tossed him over her shoulder was smouldering. He knew he would likely pay for his bossiness later, but he had no doubt it would be worth it.

Sabre gripped the bedhead once more, ensuring her shoulders remained pressed to the mattress with that pretty little arse of hers in the perfect position for him to spank. The crack resounded in the room, only to be followed quickly by Sabre's ragged moan. It was also accompanied by a curse and a low warning.

"Brax, you're walking on thin ice," Sabre informed him.

Brax smirked, feeling smug and more turned on than he probably had a right to. He knew Sabre wasn't into BDSM, nor was he, not in a serious way. But they'd had fun discovering what each other liked best. Over the past week, Sabre had pretty much given him carte blanche to try anything in the bedroom. So he had.

Sabre pretended to tolerate his playful spanks, but Brax knew it was a bit more than that. The tight grip of her body and the flash of warm wetness he felt when he smacked her other cheek was proof enough of that. He loved seeing the rosy mark his hand left behind. In fact, he loved seeing all kinds of marks covering her naked body whenever they made love. Hickeys, claw indents, scratches, they were all proof that she belonged to him. Not only that he had claimed her in the most intimate, primal way, but also that she had *allowed* him to.

"I am one lucky bastard," he murmured, rubbing his palms over her reddened arse.

"You sure are," Sabre agreed. "Lucky I don't flip you over and spank *your* arse like a bongo drum," she then murmured, all the while trying to get some leverage to impale herself more.

Brax choked on a laugh. He gave a thought to teasing her some more, perhaps prolonging their pleasure to the point where they both teetered on the edge of madness. But his patience was wearing thin, and his balls were beginning to hate him. So he took a surer grip on Sabre's hips and basically went to town. He pulled nearly all the way out, until just the flared head of his cock remained encased within her moist depths, before shoving back in. It felt so fucking good that he did it again, and again, and again. When his grip became too slippery with their mingled sweat, he told Sabre to get onto all fours. He planned to use his mouth to lock her into place for the finale.

Licking a long line up her neck, he adjusted his thrusts to be shorter but no less intense. Her skin was very pale, and the easy way Sabre tilted her head to the side, giving him more access to the tender and vulnerable skin of her neck, made his inner beast go nuts. He couldn't have stopped his fangs from piercing her flesh even if he wanted to. Which he didn't, he could admit, it was the whole point of the new position. Besides, why would he deny himself such pleasure? His lower canines elongated, their tips were sharp but he was able to control them to a certain degree. Kissing her one last time where her neck met her shoulder, he bit down.

He tasted blood and was careful not to bite further. He wanted to mate with his woman, not injure her. Though he and Sabre were not biological mates the same way werewolves or shifters would be, he was still able to bond with her. Repeated mating marks, as well as repeated *mating* were a sure-fire way to do it. He growled when Sabre's pleasure-filled moan met his ears, and he was more than happy to obey when she began shouting.

"Yes! Brax, more! Don't stop," she commanded him.

He remained locked into her, with teeth and dick, as he ruthlessly chased their mutual pleasure. When Sabre lifted a hand, reached between her own legs and began to press on her own clit, he lost what little control he had. Thrusting heavily a few more times, he fell over the edge of pleasure and into bliss, his orgasm barrelling through him. Sabre's shout assured him that she too was undergoing an out of body experience, even as her core milked his seed from him. He was undone. But he still had the presence of mind to pull out gently and lower Sabre's hips to the bed before he collapsed next to her. He was a breathless, overheated, and sweaty mess. But he was a satisfied mess.

Glancing to his right, he found Sabre still spread out like a starfish on her front. Her eyes were closed but her mouth was parted, her rapid breathing a perfect match for his own. Leaning over, he placed a kiss against her lips, gratified to feel the way she immediately kissed him back. "Are you okay?" he asked, brushing his fingers against the indents in her skin where his teeth had been. The small marks would heal in no time thanks to her angelic healing abilities. He tried not to be disappointed by that.

Sabre's eyes snapped open, and she scowled at him. "I'm better than fine. Which means your arse is saved from its own paddling. This time."

Brax laughed, rolling onto his back. "You did dare me," he pointed out. "You should never dare a demon."

Sabre grunted at him, rolling over and standing up slowly. She looked down at him for a moment before she said, "Daring a demon may be fraught with danger. But it doesn't hold a candle to daring an assassin. You just remember that."

It was the words, with their sexual undercurrent, as much as the view of Sabre's very fine derriere that had his cock trying valiantly to stand to attention again so soon. Jumping up, he joined her in the shower, wincing a little under the heat of the spray. Sabre loved to have her showers extra hot. "That sounded a little like a threat," he told her.

Sabre scrubbed her body and her hair in economical motions. She held his gaze with her own when she answered, "You should know by now that a *threat* and a *promise* are the same things to me."

She then washed off the soap and stepped out of the shower before he could make good on that – and the renewed erection he sported. He shook his head, smiling wide because he knew she meant it. His assassin never forgot a thing.

3

Twenty minutes later, he and Sabre were seated at the large table in the royal dining room. Seeing so many people crowded into the room was more than a little unusual. Not only had it been well over a year since Brax himself had sat at the solid, wooden table in the family quarters of the palace, but he was sure there had never been such an eclectic group of supernaturals there before.

His parents had not been snobs. Well, his father hadn't been, he quickly amended. His mother, on the other hand, had held certain standards, even though she had come from a lower socioeconomic family herself. Still, he didn't think there had ever been a mix quite like the one present today. Brax had invited his closest and most trusted friends, as well as asked Sabre to invite her friends and her allies. As much as he wanted nothing more than to screw Sabre senseless on every surface of his four-roomed suite for all eternity, it just wasn't practical. As the king, he had responsibilities. As a brother and a son, he had vengeance to attain. As a partner, he had havoc to reap on all those who had dared to harm his woman. And as for Sabre, she had her own complicated shit to deal with. A military-grade brainstorming session over a hearty breakfast had seemed like the best way to get things in motion.

He allowed his eyes to roam, cataloguing the inhabitants of the room. An angel assassin, a professional torturer, an organised crime boss that was for all intents and purposes a zombie, a teenage shapeshifter, a pixie, a guardian angel, and a handful of soldiers and royal guards who had been dead just months prior. He watched the laughter and the good-natured teasing, the cursing, and the banter as everyone vied for the best of the food, and he couldn't help but feel content. The only thing missing were his brothers.

Thinking of his triplet siblings brought a pang to his chest, but not the one he had become accustomed to over the past year or so. Now, it was bittersweet rather than brutal. Because now he knew one of his brothers was not actually dead. He found it miraculous that Mikhail was alive and well, but at the same time, he knew such a miracle wasn't going to happen for his baby brother, Zagan. Along with the relief, gratitude, and joy that Mikhail was still alive, also came a sharp flare of pain and resentment. Brax was pissed off with his big brother.

Shaking off such thoughts for now, he refocused on eating his breakfast. What was left of it, anyway. His guests had pretty much demolished all the platters of food. He whimpered a little when he looked at the empty plate in front of him where a huge pile of bacon had once been. He hadn't even managed a single bite of tasty piggy.

Jinx noticed his pathetic look and threw him a smile. "Hey, you snooze you lose, buddy." Brax mock growled back at her, flashing his fangs and Jinx simply laughed. Using a fork, she then picked up two pieces of bacon from her own plate and placed them on his. "Okay, okay. Down boy. No need to let the demon out of its cage. Here you go."

Brax looked at the bacon, knowing the gift was more than just some salty dead pig on a plate. Jinx was a white tiger shifter, which meant she loved meat. And he knew from experience that bacon was a particular favourite of hers. The way she had casually teased him, given him food from her own plate, and then turned back to her conversation with Gage, as if it had been no big deal, made Brax realise that he now had a whole new family. It wasn't one he would have ever had envisaged. But it was perfect, nonetheless.

"I agree."

The comment came from Draven, and Brax looked up to find his guardian angel smiling at him. Brax scowled at his friend from across the table, but it held no heat. He hated it when Draven used his angelic abilities to read him. But he wasn't really mad in this instance because he just felt too damn good overall.

"Are you going to eat that? Because if not, I will," Sabre informed him.

Brax put his hand out to cover the bacon on his plate and the fork that was intended for the bacon stabbed into his hand instead. Or it would have, had his legacy from his ancestor, Cerberus, not activated. His armour rushed to the surface, creating an impenetrable shield and stopping the fork from skewering him. And, more importantly, accessing his bacon. He looked up and met the eyes of his lover. "Nice try. This bacon is mine."

Sabre pouted a little and pointed out, "But you're just sitting there staring at it. It's going to get cold."

"Mine," Brax growled. Sabre's beautiful eyes darkened a little and he felt heat rush to his groin. He often said those exact same words when he screwed her into the mattress. He knew she was thinking the same thing as him when she licked her lips, her eyes smouldering as they mapped his features.

"Do I need to get the hose? Haven't you two had enough of that?" Draven's voice was filled with disgust. "Honestly, you're like a couple of cats in heat."

Brax shot Draven an irritated look, before scowling at the rest of the people seated around the table when they all laughed.

“Firstly, you’re just jealous,” Sabre responded, before turning to look at her besties, Gage and Jinx. “Secondly, do you think it's possible to die from listening to Draven?" Her tone was conversational as she continued to add salt to her eggs casually. “Because I think I could die from it," she informed them before they could answer.

Brax did his best to stifle his choked laughter even as Draven began to rise from his seat. He pointed a menacing finger toward the violent, antagonistic love of his life before Phaedra, the pixie seated next to him, grabbed his shirt and pulled him back into his seat. Much to Brax’s astonishment, Draven sat.

“Please don’t get into an angel death match at the table,” Phaedra pleaded. “It will ruin all this delicious food and I haven’t eaten this well in years.”

Draven looked at the pixie and cleared his throat. “Okay. Sorry.” He tossed Sabre a malicious look. “You’re a fuckwit.”

“Ooh, Draven said a bad word,” Sabre teased, smiling at Brax.

Once everyone had stopped laughing once more, Jinx spoke up. “I don't mean to be a party pooper or anything, but what now? Sabre is all healed up, which I'm very thankful for, and you two have surely boned each other enough to have Brax’s possessive demon arse satisfied that Sabre is all his. What’s our next play?”

“I think the first thing we should do is get in touch with

Mikhail," Hugo, the head of Brax's Royal Guard spoke up, flashing an apologetic look at Brax.

Brax took a careful breath in and released it slowly. It was still strange to hear his brother's name spoken in present tense instead of past tense. He smiled a little at his old friend and comrade in arms to show he wasn't annoyed. He agreed with Hugo. In fact, it had already been handled.

"He's already been notified and updated about everything," Sabre was the one to reply. "It was one of the first things I did after Draven healed me."

"You've spoken to Mikhail this past week?" Draven asked "How? You haven't left the palace."

Sabre shrugged as she buttered her toast. She was using an extremely sharp, shiny dagger instead of a butter knife. Brax shook his head as he watched, amused but more turned on than anything else. The violent side of Sabre really did it for him. Glancing at Draven and noting the frown on his face, Brax knew the same couldn't be said for his guardian. Even though Draven and Sabre were on better terms since her big reveal, they weren't ready to have slumber parties or start braiding each other's hair. Brax didn't give a shit. In fact, their continued bickering made him feel like all was right with the world. Besides, he knew Draven supported him and his choices one hundred percent, and that included his choice of Sabre.

"I dropped a message in our usual secret spy place, saying it was an emergency and I had urgent information.

Knowing Carlisle and his merry band of motherfuckers would be lying in wait to follow me, I sent Phaedra to talk to him instead.

Draven fumbled with his glass of water for a moment and looked at the short woman next to him. “You went and delivered such important information to the king?”

Phaedra looked at Draven with narrowed eyes. “I did,” she confirmed. “Do you have a problem with that?

Brax watched as Draven quickly shook his head, a slight pink tinge darkening his cheeks. He cocked his head and looked at his friend more closely. If he didn't know any better he would say Draven was embarrassed or something.

“No, no,” Draven said swiftly. “That's not what I meant. I'm sure you're very capable of keeping secrets and delivering important messages. I just meant that it was very dangerous.”

Phaedra relaxed, back into her seat, even smiling. “I can take care of myself,” she promised.

Draven nodded quickly. “I'm sure, yes. Yes, I'm sure.”

Brax felt his eyes widen, his gaze going back and forth between the pair. Draven’s flushed cheeks from before weren’t embarrassment, he realised. Draven *liked* the pixie. But that couldn't be right, could it? As far as he was aware Draven had never had any sort of relationship with anyone. Ever. The absent sex drive had a lot to do with it, but so did Draven’s deep sense of duty. His first responsibility was to

Brax. Not that Brax would have ever begrudged his friend a love life.

As if noticing he was the object of not just Brax's regard but everyone else's, Draven cleared his throat. "Moving on then," he stated. "Do we have a response?"

Sabre nodded. "Yes. And I told him to hang tight where he was and not to move until we know more. It's still too dangerous for him to be back yet even though the jig is up, so to speak."

Brax agreed wholeheartedly. He didn't want to get his brother back now just to lose him again because they prematurely revealed his location. He looked at Phaedra, unable to stop himself from asking, "How did he look?"

"Gorgeous," she promptly replied, smiling cheekily. "I've always liked a man with a bald head." She shook her head, looking a little bemused. "But then, that's not his real face, is it? I have to tell you if I didn't know he was using a fae glamour to hide his appearance, I would never have suspected it wasn't his real face."

"The magic comes from a very powerful fae," Sabre admitted.

"Well, I for one am very disappointed that Hound is really Mikhail." Jinx joined the conversation.

"What? Why?" Draven asked, turning to the teen.

"It's not like I can hump the guy like I was planning to now that I know he's royalty, can I?" she replied, her bottom lip poking out.

There was a collective groan from Gage and Sabre as Jinx continued to pout. For his part, Brax merely shrugged and said, "Why should that change your plans?" Everyone stopped what they were doing and stared at him. "What? It's not like Mikhail is a monk. And Jinx is an adult. Not to mention amazing. I can think of far worse partners for him than you," he assured the black and white-haired female next to him. The look Sabre sent him was filled with gratitude and heat. She seemed to be more than a little impressed with his show of support for her good friend.

Jinx's mouth dropped open before she closed it with a snap and quickly lowered her eyes. "Well, that is very nice of you to say. But I'm sure someone like Mikhail isn't going to want to be with someone like me."

Brax frowned, wanting to say more because her comment didn't sit well with him at all. There was nothing wrong with Jinx in any way. She was smart, funny, strong, and fiercely loyal. Not to mention very beautiful. Any man would be lucky to have her as a partner and a mate. Including his brother. But now probably wasn't the best time to press Jinx about her sense of self-worth. "Mikhail is aware of the situation and he's ramped up his security and staying put. We don't need to worry about him for the time being," he stated.

"There's absolutely no way Carlisle or the mystery elf – or whoever the fuck is running the show – can find where he is?" Draven pressed.

Sabre shook her head. “None. I guarantee it.”

Sabre’s word was enough for Brax, and also for Draven it seemed because he moved on. “That means the next step is locating your den Master and discovering what he knows.”

“I’d like to be in on that,” Mercy spoke for the first time. The pain demon looked very comfortable seated at the fancy dining table. As a torturer by trade, he shouldn’t have fit in so well. But somehow, he did. “When you capture him, bring him to me. I’ll have him singing like a canary in no time.”

Brax nodded at Mercy. “I like that plan. But the final kill is mine.” He didn’t bother trying to suppress the growl that rumbled in his chest. There was not much he wanted more than to tear Carlisle limb from limb for what he had subjected Sabre to over the years. The fact that the incubus was also in on the plot against the throne was just a bonus.

Having finished her toast now, Sabre used her dagger to spear a strawberry out of the large fruit bowl. Taking a bite, she said, “Okay. We find Carlisle, torture, maim, and rend. I like it. I have to head to the Blue Devil today anyway, so I’ll see what I can find out while I’m there.”

Brax turned to Sabre sharply. “What do you mean you're heading to the den?”

“Even though Carlisle isn't there anymore I'm still connected to it. As are the other assassins and mercenaries. None of us who have signed our names with our heart’s blood can ignore the pull for long. We will all have to go back every so often until the link is broken,” Sabre reminded him.

"Which can only be done with the death of Carlisle," Gage pointed out.

"Right," Sabre agreed.

"I don't like the thought of you going back there," Brax said.

Sabre flashed him a small smile. "I don't like the thought of going back there either, trust me. But it's one of those unavoidable realities. So we just have to deal." Sabre shrugged, "Besides, it gives me an opportunity to talk to some of the other assassins if they're around."

"It also gives the other assassins time to, gosh, I don't know, kill you dead," Brax retorted, glowering at Sabre. He knew Sabre was more than capable of defending herself, but he was feeling a little protective. He vividly recalled the way she looked battered, burned, broken, as little as a week ago. All thanks to the prick of an incubus.

Sabre shrugged negligently. "They can try."

He was about to open his mouth again when he felt a nudge against his knee. Looking up. he noticed it was Draven of all people. The angel shook his head minutely, telling him with his eyes to shut the fuck up. Brax knew he should because Sabre was the very definition of independent and he didn't want to stifle her. He didn't want to make her think he didn't believe she was capable. He also didn't want to change her in any way. He truly rejoiced in every part of her. But that didn't mean he could ignore his intense need to keep her safe and protected.

Looking at her now, he could see the stiff set to her shoulders and knew he was already coming dangerously close to stepping over the line and pissing her off. Especially when he factored in the teasing about her going soft earlier. So he sucked up his fears and objections for now. "Okay," he said. "Sounds like a plan."

The relieved look on Sabre's face was quickly followed by a look of warmth and gratitude, and Brax relaxed back in his seat, knowing he had done the right thing. *Relationships are hard,* he thought to himself. But then, nothing worth having was ever easy.

"I need to go back as well," Phaedra commented. "Even though I don't have the same sort of connection to the Den that Sabre does, I'm still technically bound to Carlisle's service until my debt is repaid. Which isn't for a few more decades. So I'll join you," she told Sabre. "Maybe see if there's anything left in my room that hasn't been looted."

Brax tossed Phaedra a look of gratitude. He felt better knowing Sabre had someone she trusted with her. "Hugo, I want you and some of the Horde to see what you can discover about that mysterious elf now that we know what he looks like."

Hugo nodded. "I'll get Shiloh on it. She's good at that kind of thing."

Sabre had been in the process of standing up but she abruptly sat back down, shooting Brax a filthy look. "Ah, Shiloh. Calling in your bimbo, I see."

Snickers and poorly concealed laughs followed Sabre's scathing comment. Brax kept his face blank by will alone. He was beyond amused and aroused. Sabre, he had learned, was particularly possessive as well as jealous of any mention of his past lovers. Shiloh, having just been found to be brought back from the dead, was one such past lover. Not that they had ever had anything other than one night of meaningless sex years ago. But still, Sabre continued to take exception to the dhampir lieutenant. "Shiloh is hardly a bimbo," he pointed out, stirring the pot.

"Is that right?" Sabre retorted, voice deceptively soft as she tossed her dagger in the air, making it spin and catching it by the hilt. She didn't even need to look at it because weapons were like an extension of her body. "You're very quick to defend her."

Brax huffed and rolled his eyes. "I see we're going to have to talk about what you're going to do every time you meet an old lover of mine. You can't go around shanking them all."

Sabre arched a brow, pointing her blade directly at his heart now. "How many lovers are we talking about? Because my kill rate is in the thousands. I have no issue adding McSluts to that number."

Brax choked on a laugh. Looking around, he found that everybody looked amused but that nobody was willing to help him out of his situation. *Cowards,* he thought silently. Instead of answering that his tally of sexual partners was well into the hundreds, he simply stood up and tilted Sabre's chair back with her still in it. He laid a passionate kiss against her lips until the need for oxygen forced him to pull back. He brought her chair back up and straightened. “Don't worry about my numbers. Numbers don't matter when you're the only one I see, when you're the *last* number I’m ever going to have.”

He walked out before she could catch her breath or respond. But he paused at the doorway to call back over his shoulder, “Keep that pretty little arse of yours safe when you're out there today. If you come back with so much as a scratch on you, there’ll be hell to pay.”

He thought he heard a muttered, “I happen to like hell,” but didn't look back. If he did, he knew he wouldn’t be able to let her go.

4

Sabre stared at the now, not so pristine, white mansion in the distance. She was eyeballing the Blue Devil Den from her hiding spot, thinking it prudent to do some recon before she approached the house.

Sure, some of the other assassins and mercenaries had joined with her to fight off Carlisle and his minions, but she was under no illusion that they were on her side. Most of them hated Carlisle with a ferocity that matched hers and they had been motivated by anger, opportunity, and self-preservation. Which meant there were going to be a lot of pissed off assassins coming and going to the mansion until Carlisle could be found and killed.

Looking around, she realised with a start that she was back where it all began. When she had first awakened from crossing the veil, it had been in this exact spot, though it looked different now. The trees were taller, and a lot of the landscape had changed, but she recognised it anyway. She shook her head, wondering if she was a masochist or perhaps a glutton for punishment because all she felt when she looked around was pain – and really fucking depressed.

"Which I have no right to be," she silently scolded herself. She had met her forever mate, her charge was alive and well, and her greatest enemy was on the run. All good things. So why couldn't she shake off her funk? Especially after talking with Brax that morning. She had been honest with him and had communicated the shit out of herself. She was practically a shining beacon for healthy relationships.

"You left without me."

Sabre dropped into a crouch, even as she spun around. She had a dagger in one hand and her Sig in the other. Phaedra stood in front of her, placid as can be. "Fuck," Sabre breathed. "I could have killed you."

Phaedra scoffed and rolled her eyes. "As if. Besides, *I* could have killed *you*. I should never have been able to get this close to you. What's going on? Are you still not well?"

"I'm fine," Sabre said, standing up. "I've had worse injuries than those and you know it."

"I do know that," Phaedra acknowledged. "But have you ever heard of the proverbial straw?"

"You mean the one that broke the camel's back?" Sabre questioned.

"That would be the one," the pixie confirmed.

Sabre paced around a little, feeling agitated and uncomfortable by the thought that she could be losing her edge. Finally, she paused and met Phaedra's eyes. "I can see your point. But don't worry, it would take a lot more straws to break me."

Phaedra nodded, not pressing further. She looked toward the Blue Devil. "Are we going in? It looks quiet and unoccupied."

Sabre grunted and continued to watch the house closely. She knew for a fact that outward appearances couldn't be trusted. Sure, it looked like a beautiful, expensive house on the outside. But inside, depraved minds lived and played, talked and laughed, fuelled by greed and their sick desires. Still, they couldn't stand there all day, so she finally replied, "Yes. We're going in."

"Good," Phaedra said. "I need to see if I've got anything left in my room. Do you think it's been trashed?"

"Oh, yeah. I'm absolutely positive it has," Sabre replied. "I'm sure mine is much worse though."

She then motioned to Phaedra and they set off. There wasn't really anywhere to hide as they picked their way carefully through the forested area before striding into the clearing. Carlisle had cleared the land in a large radius immediately surrounding the mansion so that nobody could sneak up on it. Sabre kept her weapons in her hands, and although Phaedra had no visible weapons, Sabre was positive she could take care of herself. She could use her magic in the blink of an eye, shrinking down to the size of a bumblebee. It made her an excellent spy.

Just as they were about to walk up the front steps, a whistling sound came from behind them. Sabre ducked and rolled, coming up with her arms outstretched and firing off two shots in quick succession. They missed, but then they were supposed to. She didn't know who the person was behind her, and just on the off chance that they weren't assholes in need of killing, she was going to give them the benefit of the doubt. Her opponent likewise rolled, his arms extended and holding two fully automatic machine guns from the human realm.

“Sabre,” Dendey greeted her. “You really fucked up this time.”

“Oh, I don't know,” she replied. “I think it's all probably a matter of perspective. From where I’m standing, things look rather peachy.”

Dendey shook his head. He didn’t lower his weapons, but he didn’t pull the trigger either. “You started a war, Sabre. A war between the biggest psychopaths in Purgatory. How exactly do you think this is going to end?”

She watched the dragon carefully as she recalled everything she knew about him. He had been bonded to the den for about twenty years and was strictly a mercenary, not an assassin. That's not to say he didn't kill fuckers here and there, because he did. But he was more of a bounty hunter and a finding of lost treasures kind of a guy rather than a homicidal maniac. He wasn't a friend or even a colleague. She had made sure not to socialise with anyone in the den, other than Phaedra and Mercy. But she'd never had any issues with the dragon. Taking a chance, she lowered her blade and holstered her gun. She then stood up slowly with her arms out wide showing she was unarmed. Beside her, Phaedra simply watched the proceedings carefully, showing no fear. Sabre had to hand it to her pixie friend. The woman had balls.

"I have no quarrel with you, Dendey, or any of the others. So long as they stay away from me and mine," she told him.

Dendey shook his head. "It doesn't work like that, Sabre. Do you have any idea how much the bounty on your head is worth? Bringing you in would be like finding Smaug's treasure horde."

Sabre felt her breath catch in her throat, the words ringing in her ears. She had a bounty on her head. She was a mark. She probably should have expected it, should have anticipated it. But the thought honestly hadn't entered her mind. She knew Carlisle wanted to get his hands on her just as much as she did him. But she had believed he would come for her personally. She should have known the spineless prick would choose the coward's way. It wasn't the danger to herself she was worried about. No, it was the threat to those she loved. If she had a bounty on her head, then everyone associated with her was at risk.

Thinking quickly, she offered, "What if I said I can make

a better deal than Carlisle?" Everyone had their price. She just had to figure out what that price was.

Dendey shook his head again as he stood up slowly, his reptilian eyes locked on hers. The safeties weren't on, but his guns were now pointed at the ground. "A better deal? Sabre, everyone's doing it for free."

Sabre groaned and swore. "Of course all of you fuckers are doing it for free. Come on, man. Don't you want to be free of this place? Free of Carlisle?"

"Not everyone is like you. Some of us *chose* to be a part of the Blue Devil Den. Some of us *wanted* this. We weren't stolen as children. Our choices weren't taken from us. We weren't conditioned. And those people are out for blood. Especially when you add on the fact that you've been lying for years and are a traitor. I mean, really, Sabre, a *righteous angel?!*" Dendey exclaimed, looking pained. "All those golden feathers in those wings of yours! Bleh!"

Sabre scowled at him, not liking his tone. The way he said *righteous angel* let her know that it was synonymous with *yuck.* "You have wings too," she pointed out.

Dendey snorted, "Yeah, but mine aren't feathery. Look, I'm not your friend, Sabre. I'm not on your side. This is the only time when you get to walk away. If I see you again, I'll kill you myself." And with those final words, he shifted into an outrageously beautiful dragon, his weapons and a backpack clutched between his talons as he took flight.

"Fuckity fuck!" she swore as soon as the dragon was out

of view. She yanked on her hair, releasing a thin scream before turning to Phaedra. “Come on, let's move.” They needed to get in and out quickly before anybody else showed up.

They carefully made their way to Phaedra’s room first. Stopping at the threshold, Sabre pushed the open door wider. As suspected, the place had been completely destroyed. Clothes and the few personal items Phaedra owned like books and some cosmetics were strewn all about. The sight made Sabre feel like shit. “I'm sorry.”

Phaedra looked at Sabre in surprise. “What are you sorry for? You don’t need to be sorry. This place,” she gestured to the room, “it's not my home. I was a prisoner here just as much as you. These broken things here? They don’t hurt me. Don’t take on guilt that isn’t yours, Sabre.”

Sabre blew out a breath, nodding thanks to her much shorter friend. They quickly picked up what was salvageable, putting it in a backpack before making their way swiftly to Sabre’s room. The door was completely broken down, as well as half of the wall to the right. It looked like someone had been thrown through the wall. She still did her due diligence to make sure there were no incendiary devices or boobytraps set up. In the end, they decided not to venture into the room, anyway. The smell alone was enough to have them abort, and they looked through the hole in the wall instead. The place reeked. The bunch of filthy fuckers had defecated in there, and everything was beat to shit. The walls, the curtains, the bed, and even the floor were ripped apart. Everything was filthy and covered in shit, piss, or blood. There were crude messages and warnings written on the wall above her bed in blood, and a severed hand lay on her pillow like some kind of macabre gift.

Sabre took a few steps back so she could breathe. "Let's go. I need nothing from here."

They made their way back out silently. There was nothing to say. But as they reached the bottom step, they came face to face with not one, but three assassins. The three men smiled but there was nothing friendly about the expressions. Rather, they looked demonic, like all of their sicko dreams were about to come true. Sabre's smile started out small but quickly grew wide. Familiar endorphins started to ping through her system, her pulse pounding wildly with the prospect of a fight. The men in front of her were her enemies. They always had been. Who better than to beat out some of her frustrations on than a bunch of Carlisle groupies?

"Hello, boys," she drawled to Christoff, Madden, and Buck.

"I'm going to gut you like a fish," Madden growled.

Sabre grinned. "I was hoping you would say that."

5

“You got this?” Phaedra asked from where she was partially protected by Sabre’s taller frame in front of her.

“I got this,” Sabre promised, wanting to bust some skulls and cause a little bloodshed. Her emotions were all kinds of fucked up. She needed some violence to soothe herself.

“Cool,” the pixie chirped. She then shrank down until she reached Sabre’s ankle, giving her a salute and darting behind a rock.

Sabre faced the three assassins in front of her once again. Madden snarled at her, his sharp teeth resembling those of a shark. He was a cannibal, and not in the fun way Gage was. Buck and Christoff had always been Madden’s lackeys, as well as giant arse-kissers to Carlisle. She’d had to fight off their advances on more than one occasion in the past. She had always won. "Well ...?" Sabre taunted when no one made a move.

"Don't try to negotiate," Buck warned her. "We won't listen."

Sabre laughed, watching as all three men recoiled. "Who said anything about negotiating?" She rolled her shoulders a little and felt her wings extend from her back. She raised them high seeing the way their gazes locked onto the crimson and gold feathers with rapt fascination. It felt damn good to be able to have her wings out whenever she pleased now. All guardian angels were essentially battle angels and fighting with their wings out was a matter of pride. It was just one more aspect of her heritage she'd been forced to sacrifice over the years. And these idiots in front of her wanted to align themselves with the douche who had taken that, plus so much more, away from her? Oh, she was going to fuck them up, she thought.

"Before things get messy, I'm going to give you a chance. Tell me where Carlisle of the tiny penis is hiding, and I'll kill you quickly."

Christoff scoffed, "Not a chance. You'll never find him. Not before he finds you and everyone you love. He –"

Christoff died with a gurgle, the knife she had thrown landing directly in the centre of his throat. Madden and Buck watched their colleague fall to the ground, their mouths falling open in shock. Sabre shrugged, explaining, "I didn't like his answer. Care to try your luck, Buck? Hey, that rhymes!"

"You fucking cow!" Buck roared, flames beginning to manifest around him.

She didn't want to risk the ifrit tapping into his powers fully, so she raised her gun and shot him in the forehead. He continued to smoulder a little, even as dark blood oozed from the large hole in his head. "Moo," she said, tossing the gun aside.

She could have dispatched Madden as easily and as quickly as his boys, but she wanted to have a little fun. Madden's face turned red with rage and he let out a bellow. Sabre flapped her wings and shot into the air. She then descended on the remaining assassin from above, landing heavily on his shoulders and forcing him to the ground. But he was a strong bastard, and the weight of her downward motion didn't faze him much at all. He flipped her off him immediately. She regained her balance quickly, but not quite fast enough to dodge the sharp claws aimed at her head.

Sabre felt the burning scratch on her neck and saw some blood drip onto the dirt at her feet. "You made me bleed my own blood," she said.

Madden grinned, looking smug. "I'm going to do much more than that." He inhaled deeply, closing his eyes for a brief second and moaning. "Damn, that angelic blood of yours smells delicious. I can't wait to take a bite out of your flesh. I think I'll start with your tits," he informed her, leering at her breasts.

Sabre looked down at the small mounds trapped securely behind her leather bustier. She scrunched up her nose as she replied, "Not much of a meal. They're kind of small."

Madden charged again, going for brute strength. Sabre sidestepped and punched him in the kidney causing him to roar in pain. He went down on one knee and swung his fist, catching a glancing blow to her stomach. Thankfully, it wasn't enough to knock the wind out of her, but she was sure she would end up with a bruise. Recalling what Brax had said about remaining unscathed *or else*, Sabre was tempted to let Madden get a few more hits in. Especially when he started mouthing off again.

"I can't wait to take your pretty, angelic cunt back to Carlisle. Daddy's very unhappy with you," Madden goaded.

The thought of Carlisle as her *daddy* had Sabre gagging. "Ugh! I just vomited in my mouth a little." Madden glared at her and Sabre held up her hand. "No, truly. There's a chunk and everything."

Madden sneered at her. "Typical Sabre, so cocky. You always did think you were hilarious. You were his golden child. But look at you now, the most wanted supernatural in all of Purgatory. Rather ironic, don't you think?"

"Ironic? Wow, don't hurt yourself with all the big words there," Sabre fired back. But his words hit home. Others were coming for her, it was inevitable. And when they couldn't get to her, they would try for Jinx, or Gage, Or Brax, or numerous other people she knew and liked.

As she continued to trade blows with Madden, she did so with only half her focus. She was too busy calculating just how many immediate threats were out there to give the werecreature the thrashing he deserved. She had seen about half of the assassins and mercs teleport out with Carlisle, thanks to that stupid sphinx, Bevin. But at least two of them had looked like they were mortally wounded. Another five had been killed on the day of the big fight. Perhaps five or six had actively aided her in the fight and potentially could be convinced to at least allow her to talk first, instead of simply going for her throat. After she dealt with Madden and his two friends, that would leave maybe five Blue Devil Den members who actively wanted to kill her. She could take those out with no problem. But it was the other assassin dens and guilds that were the problem. Anyone could take up the contract, not just Carlisle's lemmings.

But maybe she could get them to rethink that, she thought as she and Madden circled each other. Maybe all she needed to do was leave a clear message – a warning for others as to what would happen to them if they came after her or those she loved.

Suddenly sick of playing around, Sabre addressed the last thing Madden had said. "I was never his. Come on, come closer and take a look," she urged as she reached into her pocket. "See if you can figure out who I really belong to.

There are some nifty teeth marks that you can probably still make out."

When the dipshit squinted at her neck, she launched forward, brandishing her spiked knuckle duster. She aimed straight for Madden's eye. He obviously wasn't expecting the move. He had not noticed she'd been working the brutal weapon onto her hand the whole time she had been talking. His eyeball literally popped under the impact and viscous eye fluid sprayed onto her hand. She made sure to keep her mouth tightly closed. Past experience had taught her how awful eyes tasted when they got in your mouth. The sound Madden made was unholy. It was an animalistic screech of pain and fury. Sabre pulled her punch and blood immediately spewed from the ruined eye socket. She brought up a titanium tipped arrow from where it had been secured against her thigh and positioned it at the back of Madden's neck.

"I never liked you," she informed him. "And I may be an angel, but this right here," she pressed the arrowhead into his skin a little, "is still a pleasure for me." Then she rammed the arrow into his brainstem. Madden's heavy body crumpled to the ground immediately.

"Wow ..."

Phaedra's voice came from behind her, and Sabre turned to find that the pixie was full-size once more.

"Do you think maybe you have some pent-up tension

there, girl?" Phaedra inquired, surveying the gruesome scene with a practised eye.

Sabre snorted, appreciating her friend's attempt to lighten the mood. Overall, it had been a rather shitty trip. "Maybe a little," she admitted. "I know I shouldn't. Especially after the pounding Brax gave me this morning. You'd think he would have pounded all the stress right out of me."

Phaedra giggled, the tinkling sound echoing in the bloody driveway. "One would think. But sex stress isn't the same as killing stress." She walked closer and looked at the bodies splayed on the ground. "You're still *you*, Sabre," she said quietly, correctly interpreting the source of Sabre's tension. "You don't need to prove yourself to anyone. You've done enough."

Sabre didn't answer because it would never be enough. Her work would never be done. She was a guardian angel, and her fate was not her own. It never had been.

She took a deep breath and folded her wings away, taking satisfaction from the dead bodies around her. Then she went about making her statement for any other dipshits that dared to show up at the Blue Devil Den.

6

Brax sat at the king's desk in the royal office, staring at papers he had read multiple times and still had no clue what they were about. He sighed, tossing his pen down as he leaned back in the chair. He was trying to step up and fulfil his royal obligations. His family weren't just empty figureheads, they worked *for* the people and *with* the people. It had always been the way. But he couldn't deny how much he hated his current role.

"This isn't me," he said aloud. And now he knew why. Because the rightful king was still out there. Mikhail was the one who should have his arse glued to the chair, sifting through political documents. Brax wanted nothing more than to be reunited with his battalion. He wanted to train and spar and go out into Purgatory to bust some criminal balls. He knew the timing wasn't right and was doing his best to respect that. But it was damn hard. Especially when his woman was out there, kicking arse and taking names. "And here I am, trying to figure out if an interest rate hike would ruin the economy," he murmured.

A clicking sound caught his attention and he turned his head to find Styx making his way over. The giant Hell dog with the dark eyes, blue tongue and dopey personality placed his heavy, boxy, head on Brax's knee. "You get it, don't you? You'd rather be outside chasing bunnies and rolling in dead birds. I feel you," he commiserated, rubbing Styx between the ears. The pair of them sat in silence for a while, watching each other gravely, until they were blessedly interrupted by a knock on the door.

"Come in!" Brax practically shouted. Anything was better than what he was currently doing.

Draven walked in with a questioning look on his face. He looked around the room, noting nothing amiss. "Where's the fire?"

"There is no fire. That's the problem," Brax told his friend.

Draven pursed his lips in disapproval. "Really, Brax? After the chaos of the last year and a half, not to mention the stress and craziness of the last couple of months, you'd think a little paperwork would be just what the doctor ordered."

"Not my doctor," Brax retorted.

Draven shook his head, amusement finally lighting up his blue eyes. "No, I guess not. It's a good thing your chosen partner is an unscrupulous assassin. You suit each other in some ways at least."

"She has scruples," Brax was quick to defend Sabre. "They're just not the same as most peoples. And, wow, that was almost a compliment you just made about us."

"Yes, well, in times of war and familial genocide, a hired thug is sure to come in handy," Draven allowed, looking around the office as if he hadn't seen it a million times before.

Brax watched him closely. Other than Sabre, who he was still learning the intricacies of, Draven was the person he knew the most. In fact, he could read his guardian like a book. And right now, Draven was decidedly uncomfortable about something. "What's going on?" he demanded.

"Something's happened," Draven said, looking serious.

Brax burst out of the chair, causing Styx to yip and bound around the room, searching for a hidden threat. "Is it Sabre? Is she hurt? Is it Mikhail?" he questioned erratically, his stomach swooping.

Draven winced, looking apologetic. "Nothing is wrong with them – with anyone. I apologise. I didn't mean to alarm you."

"Fuck, Draven. You scared the shit out of me," Brax scolded. For the last few years, whenever Draven told him something had happened in that depressive tone of his, it was usually because one of his family members had been murdered.

"I'm sorry. I'm just ... flustered, I guess. I woke up this morning to something unusual," Draven admitted.

Brax paused his agitated movements and stared at his guardian. He did look a little flushed, Brax acknowledged. And then a thought hit him, and he grinned. "Is this about a certain pixie? Because if you woke up feeling, uh, *uncomfortable*, perhaps even *sticky*, that's totally normal."

"What?" Draven gaped at Brax. "You think I'm talking about nocturnal emissions?"

Brax felt his eyes widen before he burst into laughter. He laughed so hard that his gut hurt. "Nocturnal emissions? I can't breathe," he gasped, shoving Draven good-naturedly. "I also can't wait until I tell Sabre you said that. They're called wet dreams, my man. Say it with me now."

"Quit it," Draven hissed. "I most certainly will *not* say that. And if you tell that wretched woman anything of the sort, I'll swap all your shampoo for *Nair*."

That shut Brax up quick. His hands flew to his thick hair, doing his best to protect it from an uncertain future. "And you say Sabre is evil."

Draven huffed. "Yes, you definitely deserve each other. You're both so dramatic."

Brax grinned, unable to deny he was having a good time. He had almost forgotten how much he enjoyed Draven's company, as more than just an advisor or babysitter, or even worse, a duty. Yes, Draven was stuffy and overbearing, but he was also quick-witted, his humour drier than a desert, and more loyal than a Labrador. Brax realised with a start that he had missed his best friend, even though they spent every day together. Somehow, along the way when Brax had lost himself, he had also lost pieces of his relationship with Draven. The revelation floored him and he had to clear his throat a few times before he could speak.

"I'm sorry," he eventually said.

Draven frowned at him, concern causing wrinkles on his otherwise perfect face. "Sorry? For what? Brax, what's wrong?"

"I've just been ... so far from myself. I didn't realise how far until Sabre came into my life. I know you think I haven't been a shitty king, but I have. And I've been an even shittier friend. I apologise," he said, meaning every word.

Draven pulled Brax in for a hard hug, murmuring, "You owe me no apologies. I am your guardian. You are my responsibility. I am sorry I couldn't find a way to help you. But," he said, pulling back, "I don't suppose I am sorry it was Sabre who did. Especially after this morning," he added.

"What do you mean?" Much to Brax's confusion, Draven stepped back and started to unbutton his shirt. "Whoa, this is getting a little weird. I've missed our bromance but this isn't exactly what I had in mind."

Draven shot Brax a scathing look. "Pull your head in, Abraxis." He spun around, showing Brax his bareback. "Look," he demanded.

Brax watched as Draven's brilliant white wings unfolded

from beneath his skin near his shoulder blades. It was a strange phenomenon to witness. It wasn't like shapeshifting, and it wasn't magic either. The wings were as much of a part of an angel as their arms and legs. They were always there. And yet, they weren't. Brax took a step back because Draven's wingspan was massive, bigger even than Sabre's. He was about to ask what Draven was talking about when he spotted it. "Holy fuck," he exclaimed. "When did that happen?"

Draven turned back around, tucking his wings behind him. He reached back and pulled some of his primary feathers over his shoulder. Fanning them out, he stroked a finger reverently over one in particular. "I noticed it this morning. It's gold. I have a gold feather," he breathed, looking overwhelmed.

Brax couldn't blame him. Angels who performed righteous tasks, who fulfilled their duties and their fates, were divinely recognised with silver or gold changes to their wings. There weren't many angels around who could boast the metallic plumage. Because there simply weren't that many epic destinies these days. Sabre's truly otherworldly feathers of crimson and gold were unheard of in any history book. It's why all of Purgatory knew, without a shadow of a doubt, that Sabre was on a righteous path. That she had been performing Heaven's work faithfully, despite all the blood and death she directly caused.

"Wow," Brax said. "Draven, this is amazing. Congratulations."

"Thank you," Draven responded with less enthusiasm than Brax would have expected under the circumstances.

Brax stepped forward, reaching out to feel the golden feather. Draven stood still, allowing the intimate touch. Although it shined with a vibrancy reminiscent of the precious metal, it felt as soft as any other feather. It was truly beautiful, not to mention very cool.

He had yet to touch Sabre's wings, but he desperately wanted to. Not only were they magnificent to see and a testament to her strength – and her heart – but they were also sexy as hell. He wanted to see her naked, with her wings outstretched, as she shouted his name in ecstasy. Although he trusted that they were both serious about their relationship, and he knew she was his chosen mate, it was still rather new, and her wings were a sensitive topic. Especially given she had been forced to hide them for a century, all the while allowing people to believe they were rotting, eroding, and broken.

One day ... he promised himself, he would ask Sabre to fulfil his fantasy. But in the meantime, he refocused on the angel in front of him. "You don't seem happy," he commented.

"I am," Draven was quick to reassure him. "I most definitely am. It's something all angels strive for. It's not the feather itself. It's the *why* of it that has me a little stumped."

Brax stepped back, shrugging as he crossed his arms over

his chest. "Clearly you've done something to please the powers that be upstairs."

"Yes. And that's always a good thing," Draven acknowledged. "I just don't think it has anything to do with me directly, or my duty to you, rather," he quickly amended. "And that's what has me fighting my feelings of annoyance. My chagrin is overwhelming my pride."

"I have no idea what you're alluding to," Brax admitted, feeling confused as hell. "What do you mean?"

Draven exhaled heavily and paced around a little. "It has nothing to do with me. I have been fulfilling my duties faithfully since the day we met. I have saved your life more times than I can count. I have given sage counsel, wiped your nose when you had a cold, held back your hair when you've been blind drunk and vomiting up your poor decisions. I've taught you how to fight, and how to be diplomatic. I've stood side by side with you on the battlefield, helped you cut down your enemies and watched your back." Draven paused, jamming his hands on his hips as he scowled at Brax. "I mean, I've even watched you fall in love and allowed you to claim the antithesis of my kind."

"Wooow," Brax said slowly, whistling through his teeth. "You are fucking amazeballs. I mean, I don't know how I would have managed to stay alive without you there to hold my hand this whole time."

In typical Draven fashion, he brushed off Brax's dry, sarcastic words. "Please, without me, we both know you wouldn't have survived that time the fairy tried to bite through your foreskin. So let us not pretend, shall we?"

Brax felt his face flush with heat and he quickly looked around the room, worried someone might have magically popped in and heard that little peach of a secret. "Draven! What the fuck?! I thought we agreed never to speak of that again, that it was wiped from our *mutual* memory banks."

Despite his best effort, he had never been able to forget the day he had been swimming naked in the pond at the back of the palace. A family of fairies, *royal* fairies, had lived on the palace grounds for hundreds of years. His father had always warned them to leave the small beings alone, that the lovely pond surrounded by the picturesque garden in the northern corner of the grounds was solely for the fairies. He had been a cocky, self-assured, thirty-something-year-old demon when he had accepted the dare put forth by Mikhail and Zagan. And that had been to skinny-dip in fairy territory. He had learned a few very valuable lessons that day.

The first one was that although his defensive armour was quick to action, self-determining of what constituted danger, and impenetrable to almost anything in the universe, it wasn't as fast as fairy teeth. The second one was that if something managed, by some miracle to be faster than his armour, when his shield finally did kick in, it would lock the aggressor in place. And third, and perhaps the most traumatic of all, he owed his foreskin to Draven.

Draven smirked at him, blue eyes twinkling with mirth

now. "My dear boy, there isn't enough magic in the universe, not even in the finger of God himself, to make me forget that."

Styx chuffed from his spot in the corner and Brax pointed a finger at him. "Don't you start," he warned. "I also still recall how unhelpful you were that day." Draven let loose enough to actually chuckle, and Brax glared at him. "I think we're getting off track."

Draven cleared his throat. "Right. I was making a point ..."

Brax widened his eyes in mock surprise, saying, "You have a point? More than just tooting your own horn, that is."

"Yes, you little demon, I have a point. An important point," Draven hissed at him, scowling once more.

"And what is it?" Brax asked, amused – and *bemused* – with the whole conversation.

"Despite all of that, I've never received a silver feather, let alone a golden one. I think this," he touched his new feathery addition, "is because of Sabre."

"What?" Brax asked. That was not what he had been expecting to hear.

"I think it's because I aided Sabre. Whether it be because I healed her injuries, or because I saved her from a more serious injury, perhaps even death, from that spear Carlisle threw at her. I'm not sure. It could even be because I've accepted her as your mate. But no matter which scenario it is, I believe it has to do with her," Draven revealed.

Brax thought about it for a moment. He wasn't a fan of coincidences and the timing fit. It did make sense, he supposed, given the enormity of Sabre's task and all she had gone through to achieve it. However, he didn't understand why Draven was still looking so worried. "Does it really matter how it came about? It's not a bad thing, no matter the circumstances," Brax pointed out.

"No," Draven agreed. "Not a bad thing at all. I'm just concerned. Because if Sabre's task is that important, if indeed *she* is that important, in the grand scheme of things, it makes me wonder just what in the realms is going on. If toppling the line of Cerberus will result in repercussions so significant that the Gods have a personal stake in it, what does it mean? And do we assume that the person responsible for killing your family is privy to this information? Is this why they are doing it?"

"That ..." Brax said slowly, "is very disconcerting."

"Indeed," Draven concurred. "I think this feather – and Sabre's multiple ones – proves that whatever it is, it's big, Brax. Bigger than some kind of personal hatred for the royal line. We're talking Heavenly big, fate of the whole world, kind of thing."

Brax's knees went a little loose, and he sat down in the visitor chair with a thump. "Well fuck," was all he could think to say.

Draven nodded his head, eyes serious. "My thoughts exactly."

7

Sabre nodded her head to the guards as she walked past, returning the greetings with her own. She had known many of them by name before, thanks to her service to Mikhail. In fact, she had even killed some of them, she thought, grimacing a little when those ones avoided eye contact.

My bad, she thought silently. She was doing her best to get to know them on a more personal level. Not only were they responsible for keeping Brax safe, but they were also Brax's old army buddies. She particularly liked the man Brax had chosen as the head of his personal Royal Guard, Hugo. He was a deceptively unassuming guy with bright red hair, deep brown eyes, and a lean body. He was quiet and respectful but also warm and welcoming. He gave bullshit as much as he took it and had been Brax's friend for a long time.

But then, when you were a phoenix, you had a long time to give, she mused.

"Is he in there?" she asked the phoenix, gesturing with her chin to the office door.

Hugo grinned at her. "He sure is."

Sabre smiled back and said, "Thank you." Just as she was about to turn the door handle though, Hugo stopped her with his next words.

"Draven is in there too."

She stopped and glared at Hugo. "Did I say thank you? I meant fuck you. *Fuck you*, Hugo." Hugo laughed even as Sabre continued to scowl. Hugo seemed to derive some kind of sick pleasure from her hate-hate relationship with Draven. "You know, there's something very wrong with you," she informed the redhead, before finally opening the office door.

"Have fun," Hugo snickered one last time.

Sabre shut the door behind her with more force than was strictly necessary. Turning, she froze where she was. Draven was pulling on his shirt. His abs were corrugated into a defined six-pack and his pectoral muscles flexed as he hastily buttoned the shirt from the bottom up. She wondered if there was such a thing as brain bleach. Though she had no issue checking out a good-looking body, she had a major issue when that body was attached to the arse-monkey, Draven. She closed her eyes, shuddering when the image remained.

"You can open your eyes now," Draven's dry voice reached Sabre's ears after a moment.

"Is it safe?" she muttered, opening one eye at a time. "Am I interrupting something?" she asked, a little terrified of the answer.

"No!" they shouted at the same time.

Sabre felt her eyebrows raise. She looked from one stoic face to the other, noting the slightly flushed cheeks and the guilty eyes. "Yeah," she said, "I don't believe you. What's going on?"

"Nothing," Draven insisted, at the same time as Brax replied.

"Draven got a gold feather," Brax practically yelled, pointing at Draven.

Draven turned disbelieving eyes to his charge. "Really, Abraxis? Didn't we both just agree we were going to keep this between us for now?"

"I'm sorry," Brax apologised, looking sheepish. "She voodoo'd me."

"Voodoo'd you?" Draven repeated incredulously. "She's nowhere near you. She barely even looked at you. She asked you one question, Brax. One."

Brax nodded his head vigorously, yellow eyes wide. "Her powers are mighty."

Sabre laughed, appreciating her man's humour – and his dorkiness. "And don't you forget it," she said, making her way closer to him.

Brax smiled at her and placed a chaste kiss against her lips, which she readily returned. She loved the simple press of his lips against hers just as much as his tongue down her throat. She then turned to Draven. “Wow, Draven, a golden feather, huh? You’re a big boy now. Angel puberty has finally hit.”

Draven looked disgusted. “Please never refer to it like that again.”

Sabre snickered and prepared herself to snipe at him again when Brax touched the side of her neck. The scratch from Madden hadn't yet healed.

“What's this?” Brax demanded roughly.

“It’s nothing,” she told him.

“Sabre ...” he then said, his voice dangerously low.

She couldn't suppress her shiver of desire. That voice of his, when it rumbled deep in his chest and she could feel the vibrations of it throughout her entire body, was one of her favourite things.

“I'm leaving,” Draven announced.

“Draven ...” Brax called, perhaps wanting Draven to stay and explain about the feather more. But the angel didn’t pause his steps.

“Nope. I know what that look means. It means if I don’t leave in the next ten seconds I’m about to be traumatised,” Draven murmured, opening the door quickly.

“Draven, wait,” Sabre said, just before he shut the door. “Congratulations.”

She watched his blue eyes flare with surprise for a moment before he dipped his head in acknowledgement and closed the door with a soft click. She turned to Brax, “Did you see that? I can be mature. I don’t have to insult Draven with every breath I take.” Too bad her man wasn’t interested in celebrating her restraint with her.

Brax tilted Sabre’s head to the side, running a gentle finger over the mark on her throat. “What happened?” he asked again.

She knew she wouldn’t get out of the upcoming conversation with a mere excuse, so she explained what she and Phaedra had discovered on their trip to the den, ending with, “I can't take the risk of any of them coming after you. Or Jinx. Or Gage. Or even that one-pubic feathered idiot, Draven.”

Brax grunted, crossing his arms over his chest. “So you plan to go out and kill every remaining member of the Blue Devil? What about the other assassin dens? Or the other criminals for hire?”

“Of course not,” Sabre assured him. “That wouldn’t be practical.”

Brax took a deep breath as if striving for patience. “And just what do you deem as a *practical* solution, then?”

“I left a warning, a message if you will,” she told him. “I don't know if it's going to work. But I guess we'll soon see.”

Brax nodded his head, having listened attentively to every word she’d said, as he always did. He tried to lift up the leather bustier she wore, no doubt to view the injury she had mentioned on her ribs, but it was too tight. She slapped his hands away. "I'm fine. Honestly. He hardly touched me at all. I completely dominated that fight, I assure you."

Brax looked at her drolly. "I'm pretty sure your version of fine and my version differ greatly."

"Based on what?" Sabre demanded.

"Based on the last time you said you were fine, for one," came Brax's immediate response. "You had multiple broken bones, contusions, and burns. Not to mention a concussion."

"And I was still fine," she pointed out, even though she could admit it had hurt like hell.

He sighed, gripping the bridge of his nose between his forefinger and his thumb. "Okay, you're fine," he conceded. "Tell me more about this warning you left. You said you wrote a message?"

This was the part of her tale that Sabre was afraid to tell. Yes, she was an angel. Yes, she was righteous and in possession of her Grace. But she wasn't necessarily a *good* angel. Or even a good *person*. In fact, she was pretty confident that what she had just done only an hour before, let alone what she had done over the last one hundred years of her life, constituted *bad*.

Very bad.

Stalling a little, she hedged, "It was more of a visual aid. Although, I did leave a written note as well."

"And it said ...?"

Pursing her lips, her shoulders slumped a little in resignation as she gave him a rundown of the mess she had left behind. "Well, with Buck, I decided to butterfly him. I sliced him from sternum to groin, pulled out his ribcage, and flared it open. He looked like a macabre, broken, red and white butterfly.

"Christoff, I decapitated, considering the job was already started. What with my dagger being embedded in his neck and all. I then put his head on a stick and shoved it into the ground in front of the den's door. I set his body on fire and left his ashes smouldering in front of his lifeless eyes.

"As for Madden, he was the biggest and broadest, so it made sense to carve my message directly into the skin of his back. Which I did, with my trusty ice pick."

Brax didn't flinch during her tale of post-mortem mutilation. Instead, he

merely asked, "What did you write?"

Sabre licked her lips, forcing herself to keep her eyes level with his. "Fuck off or you'll be next."

Brax nodded once. "Concise, clear, to the point."

Sabre nodded her head because her throat was too dry to speak. She was terrified.

Neither of them spoke for a moment, but eventually, Brax sighed and placed his hands on her shoulders. He smoothed them down the length of her arms before he caught her hands up in his own. "Sabre. What exactly do you think I'm going to do? You're holding yourself so stiffly, as if you expect me to punish you or something."

"I'm not afraid of you hitting me," Sabre said quickly.

"No, I wouldn't expect so," he murmured, eyes wandering over her features. "It's not my fists you're worried about. It's my words. What do you think I'm going to *say* to you?" he then clarified.

Sabre shrugged, feeling the distance between them when all she wanted to do was be as close as humanly possible to him.

"I will tell you every day until it gets through that thick head of yours. There is nothing you can do and nothing you can say that will shock me enough to stop wanting you. Nothing that will shock me enough to stop *loving* you." Brax's voice was strident as he continued, "Sabre, filleting a guy, cutting a guy's head off and shoving it on a pike. Carving messages into a dead man's flesh ... it doesn't bother me. *You* don't bother me."

Sabre ruminated on that for a moment, letting the truth of his words sink past her emotional walls. The relief she felt left her feeling weak at the knees. But she drummed up a smile for him. "Well now, if that's the case, I think that says a little bit more about your issues than mine."

Brax chuckled, drawing her into his arms and Sabre went willingly. They both stayed that way for a long moment before Brax said, "Now, come on. Top off. Let me check out the rest of you."

Sabre pulled back and made a face. "You just want to see me naked," she accused.

“Of course. Every minute of every day.” he readily agreed but didn't budge.

She rolled her eyes but finally undid her top letting it fall to the ground. She had to give him credit, he didn't so much as glance at her tits, which were only encased in a strip of white elastic, before he put his hands gently over the forming bruise on her lower ribs. “See,” she said, giving it a prod. “It’s just a bruise. It will be gone by morning.”

Brax hummed, grudgingly agreeing with her assessment. This time when his eyes met hers, they were filled with heat. A heat that Sabre was more than willing to help extinguish. She kissed him, trying to convey her gratitude for everything he meant to her. A man who didn't flinch when she told him she liked to play with dead things was definitely a keeper.

Brax yanked her sports bra off, gaze feasting on her naked breasts. Reaching up, he pulled on each nipple simultaneously, eliciting a keening cry from her lips. Brax kept rubbing them, tweaking them, and essentially working them over, watching her reaction the entire time. She clenched her thighs together, wondering if she could come from his touch on her nips alone when he pushed his hand inside of her pants. He pressed down hard on her clit, rubbing in circles. She came without much further encouragement, his mouth on her nipple and his finger at her core. She shuddered and moaned her way through her orgasm, Brax’s strength more than enough to keep them both upright.

When she caught her breath, she looked up at his

gorgeous face, finding herself still encased in his arms – and Brax still encased in all of his clothes. She looked down at the prominent bulge in his pants, confessing, "I think I maybe forgot a little something ..."

Brax drew back, eyeing her. "Little?"

Sabre laughed, feeling fantastic. "Okay, maybe not so little."

He planted a kiss on her lips one last time before raising his hand and licking the evidence of her pleasure off his fingers. Sabre found it erotic as fuck. After that though, instead of pushing her down on her knees or unzipping his pants and jacking off onto her chest – as he loved to do – he tried to help her back into her sports bra. She took it out of his hands, confused.

"This one was for you," was all he said when she shot him a questioning look.

Sabre wasn't sure she understood what was going on. Even though they were committed, they were still getting to know each other. And she was a complete novice when it came to relationships on top of that. But she'd always thought there was some kind of rule about orgasms being mutual.

Brax chuckled, smoothing the lines on her forehead. "You look so confused."

"I am," she admitted.

"Not everything has to be equal all the time," Brax explained patiently. "Yes, our relationship will always be about give and take. But right now, I feel the need to *give* and *not* take. I feel the need to look after you, to make sure you're okay. And when I know I've succeeded in doing that, whether it be the best orgasm of your life or making you feel secure with my words, then I'm happy. I'm satisfied."

"Your dick doesn't look satisfied," she informed him. His words warmed yet another darkened corner of her heart.

Brax chuckled and agreed, "He's not. But he has a little brain. He can't be trusted."

This time, when he went to help her redress, she let him, savouring the feeling of being nurtured for a change. *I could get used to this,* she thought. *But not too used it,* the other half of her brain cautioned, reminding her of the dangers in Purgatory. She needed to stay strong and focused. She wondered if she would ever achieve the balance she felt she so desperately needed. Until she figured it out, she knew she would be stuck on either end of an emotional seesaw.

As Brax was putting her sports bra back on her, he brushed his thumb over her still hard nipple. "You know, when you're aroused and I've been playing with these, they become all red and purple and pouty. They match your eyes."

Sabre snorted, rolling her eyes. "Oh, come on."

"I'm serious," Brax vowed. "They darken like the skin of a ripe plum." He bent his head and gave her right nipple a lick. "Delicious."

Sabre shivered. "You, sir, are dangerous," she informed him.

Brax smirked and went to reach for her again when there was a knock on the door. He made a sound of frustration, before calling out, "Just a minute." Then he helped her swiftly pull on her clothes. Once they were both presentable and leaning against the royal desk, Brax told the visitor to enter.

Sabre's mood crashed when she saw who it was. Shiloh. "What do you want?" she demanded, the moment the other woman stepped inside.

Shiloh stopped at the threshold, leaving the door open. "I have an update for Brax."

"For *whom?*" Sabre asked, the casual way that Shiloh addressed Brax made her teeth grind together.

Shiloh watched Sabre carefully as she cleared her throat. "Uh, for King Abraxis. I have an update for King Abraxis."

"Better," Sabre murmured, still glowering in the pretty woman's direction.

"Sabre," Brax warned her, but his tone was amused. "Come in, Shiloh. Anything new about the elf?"

"Yes, actually," Shiloh replied, drawing the laser focus of both Brax and Sabre. "An elf matching the description has been seen every so often at Inferno."

"Inferno," Brax spat the word out.

Sabre placed a comforting hand on his arm, knowing Inferno was the name of the nightclub where his younger brother, Zagan, had been killed. "You're sure?"

Shiloh nodded. "Positive. I took the photo I pulled from

the palace security cameras and showed it to the staff there. It's him."

"Did they have any information about him?" Brax questioned, standing up.

"Not really," Shiloh said, looking apologetic. "Only that he has been going there for a couple of years now. Perhaps once every few months. And that he hangs out with," she paused, glancing at Sabre, "Carlisle."

Sabre swore along with Brax. It definitely sounded like their guy. She didn't know much about Carlisle's habits outside of the den. Other than the fact that he liked to get laid. A lot. As an incubus, that was par for the course. One of the avenues Brax had his soldiers pursuing were all the sex clubs. Sabre planned to check some out herself soon, as well as the brothels. "Does Inferno have a basement for sex? Or maybe rooms?" she asked.

"Yep. Private rooms," Shiloh confirmed.

"Makes sense then," Sabre stated. She turned to Brax. "What do you think?'

"I think we're going clubbing," Brax declared, looking mad and in desperate need to kill something. He turned to Shiloh, dismissing her quickly but with sincere thanks for her hard work.

Shiloh opened the door and walked out, and Sabre turned her head to the side, getting a gander at the lieutenant's arse. It was decidedly perky. Unable to help herself, she chased after her. "Hey, Shiloh," she called out. The dhampir stopped and turned. "You may have bigger tits than me, and that butt of yours is to die for, but when I'm aroused my nipples match my eyes."

Shiloh looked unsure and completely baffled as her eyes sought out aid from those around her, namely the equally as baffled soldiers in the hallway as well as an impatient looking Draven. Sabre could have told her not to bother. Nobody could save the other female.

"I'm ... happy for you?" Shiloh's response sounded more like a question than a statement.

"You should be," Sabre confirmed. "And do you know who told me my nipples match my eyes? My boyfriend did." Sabre stood up a little taller when she said *boyfriend* because it made her feel just so fucking proud. Abraxis was hers, and not only did she want the whole world to know it, but she also intended to keep it that way. Shiloh looked over Sabre's shoulder, clearly seeking out Brax. Sabre wasn't sure what her man said or did, but Shiloh finally responded.

"I'm happy for you?" This time, the words were half-question, half-statement.

"You should be," Sabre repeated. "I'm fucking happy for myself too. Which is why I will slice off your head and wear it as a hat if I discover you trying to fornicate with Brax again. That's right," Sabre growled when she saw Shiloh's eyes widen in awareness. "I know all about the previous fucking you two did."

Shiloh held up her hands in apparent surrender. "I have

no interest in, err, *fornicating* with your boyfriend. I happen to bat for the other team now."

Sabre stilled, cocking her head to the side. "You like vaginas now?" Sabre heard Brax make a sound between a gasp and a gargle but decided to ignore him in favour of listening to Shiloh. The female guard's answer could be the difference between her life and death, after all.

Shiloh's eyes lit up with mirth and she bit her lip, barely containing her amusement. "I do like vaginas now. Very much. I happened to meet a lovely fae princess after that time you murdered me, resurrected me, and forced me into hiding."

Sabre chose to ignore the heavy sarcasm in Shiloh's voice. Instead, she nodded her head, feeling well pleased. "That's excellent news. I won't have to get stabby with you for a second time." She spun and smiled up at Brax, feeling positively cheerful. "Did you hear that? Your penis is off the menu."

Brax was shaking his head, shoulders moving with laughter, the anger and pain of just moments before forgotten for now. "Thank you, Sabre. It's good to know my penis is no longer going to be on Shiloh's breakfast order."

Sabre saw his amusement easily enough, and though she was happy she could make him feel better, she still wanted him to know she was serious. Which was why, when she patted him on his cheek, she did it with more force than was strictly necessary. She knew she probably sounded like a crazy, possessive shrew. But she had never been in love. Hell, she hadn't known she was *capable* of it. So what if she wanted to mark her territory and make sure every female and male in Purgatory knew she would get trigger happy if they so much as looked in Brax's direction? Her beastie-boy was looking just a little too smug with the proceedings, however, so Sabre decided to bring him back down to reality.

Gently of course.

"Don't worry, sweetheart. Just because sex with you was so bad it made one woman seek out different reproductive organs to fulfil all her orgasm needs, I'm still willing to stick around," she promised him.

Brax's face went from cheery to scowling within the blink of an eye. "Hey! That is not what Shiloh said. It wasn't bad sex, right?"

Sabre felt her opinion of the other woman rise when she simply shrugged and turned away, completely ignoring the current king's continued shouting of, "Right?! Shiloh, it wasn't my penis's fault. Right?"

8

It took almost a week before Brax was able to get his ducks in a row and head to Inferno. By the time his newly appointed Royal Guard and Draven were satisfied with the security situation, they had met with the nightclub's management and head of security four times.

There had been meetings, new cameras installed, and additional security measures put into place before they had finally agreed to allow Brax to go to the club. It pissed him off. Being royalty was always a bit of a pain in the neck. He couldn't just walk around like any other regular demon in Purgatory. But being a General, he'd had more freedoms than he'd realised. He was treated more like one of the people than the prince he had always been. Because he had proven himself in battle and was thankfully just one of the boys when it came to soldiering.

Mikhail had never had that luxury though, and Brax felt a pang of guilt that he'd never thought to ask his brother if he was okay with that. Did he care? Was he happy being the king, with all the responsibilities, and the burdens, and the drama? Brax promised himself he would ask Mikhail in the future. Because, thanks to the woman by his side, he would get a future with his brother. A second chance.

He looked at Sabre as she walked by his side, her eyes alert. She had been another reason for the delay. She had insisted on wandering around Purgatory, alone, in the hopes Carlisle or one of his assassins would show up. Brax hadn't liked it one bit. Only one assassin had been stupid enough to make a move after her little message-on-a-man the other day. She had incapacitated the scorpion shifter before taking him back to Mercy where the pain demon had worked the poor schmuck over. In the end, the shifter had had no clue where the den master was holed up, nor anything to do with the conspiracy. Brax sighed, feeling impatient and dejected. He needed action. He was getting itchy.

"You okay?" Sabre asked, reaching out and grabbing Brax's hand.

Brax smiled, thrilled Sabre was okay with public displays of affection. He knew how hard all of this was on her. It was a big transition, going from a feared assassin working in secret, to the mate of the king and exposed as an agent of the heavens. "I'm okay," he assured her. "I just want answers. I want progress."

"Me too," Sabre told him. "And are you okay being here?"

Brax swallowed hard, looking around. "I'm doing okay. It's a means to an end."

He, and many others, had come to the nightclub after Zagan was murdered, but all their efforts to find witnesses or the culprit had been in vain. There were no leads to be found. No evidence to help. He hadn't given any thought to the club since then and certainly hadn't visited. He would have much preferred to stay well clear of the place where his little brother had been burned alive.

"We'll figure this out," Sabre promised him, squeezing his hand.

They wandered around for a bit, observing. Their little group was attracting a lot of attention, which was inevitable when your entourage consisted of a king, an angel assassin, a weretiger, a zombie-man, a pixie, and a guardian angel. Not to mention all of the Horde soldiers scattered about. They weren't exactly being subtle. But Brax was sick to death of subtle. And the last time Sabre had used more *direct* methods, it had produced results. Like, discovering the true cause of his father's death.

But it wasn't like Brax was expecting the elf to show up or anything. That wasn't the point. It was to talk to the patrons, to see if anyone knew anything about the guy. Like his fucking name or where his family was from. They had already interrogated all of the staff and come up with nothing during the intervening week. Brax looked at Sabre, his eyes travelling from her head to her toes and felt his pants constrict. They were all wearing clubbing clothes. Although they weren't there to party, they had thought it best to blend in with the scene more.

"Have I told you how fucking amazing you look in those clothes?" he asked.

She was still in leather pants, but she had forgone her usual matching corset and was wearing a tank top instead. It was nothing overly fancy, but it was white, tight, and had a racerback that did wonderful things for her shoulders. It also dipped low in the front, revealing the swells of her breasts. And that was the other thing, Sabre was actually wearing a bra.

Typically, she wore wireless sports bras. Not that Brax minded. He would take her breasts any way they were wrapped up. But seeing her put on the black, push-up bra is what had led them to be an hour late to the club. She looked edible. And she was all his. He, on the other hand, was wearing dark jeans and a t-shirt. That was it. But, the shirt was tight and strategically ripped, along with his jeans.

"I'm glad you approve," she replied.

"I pretty much approve of everything you do," Brax told her.

Sabre rubbed her chest, right over her heart. "Wow, I felt that right here ..." she told him. There was no hint of sarcasm in her voice.

"Aww, look at you, being all romantic and shit," Jinx teased Sabre from next to them.

Sabre glowered at her young friend. "I can and will hurt you, you little rodent."

Jinx rolled her eyes and grabbed an amused Gage's hand. "Right. Like anyone believes that. Come on, Gage. Let's go undercover. Dance with me." Then she dragged a willing and grinning Gage onto the outer edges of the dancefloor.

"This place is like an orgy, except with music," Draven pointed out, judgement in his tone and on his face as he watched the writhing bodies move to the heavy beat of the music.

"Like you would know what an orgy is," Sabre retorted. "And please, do us all a favour and never say that word again. Besides, everyone has clothes on." She tilted her head to the side, studying a particularly raunchy couple of satyrs. "Except them."

"Why don't you try it? You know, blend in," Phaedra offered.

Draven frowned at the pixie. "Try what? And I don't *blend*. I'm not *supposed* to blend."

Phaedra grinned at Draven, her cheekiness shining through her eyes and her dimples flashing. "Try dancing, of course." She leaned in close to Draven. Even standing on the tips of her toes, she didn't come up to his chin. "And you could blend with me if you wanted. I could show you."

Brax held his snicker back when Sabre gagged from

beside him. Draven looked uncertain and uncomfortable, but there was a look in his eye that Brax had never seen before. Want. Longing. So, Brax did what any good wingman would do, he shoved Draven. Hard. Luckily the short pixie was stronger than she looked and she caught Draven, stumbling only a little. Draven's arms automatically clutched at her, holding her close to prevent a fall. Then he just stood there with his hands on her waist and his wide eyes on her face.

"This is the part where you move," Brax whispered to Draven. Well, it was more of a yell with how loud the music was.

Draven's head whipped around and glared at Brax. "I'm going to kill you."

Brax widened his eyes, aiming for innocent. "Kill me? Your charge? I don't think so. Now, go." He gave Draven another nudge. Phaedra threw him a wink as she tugged Draven a little further onto the dancefloor. Not too far, but just enough where Brax could no longer hear what she said. Brax did see the blush that rose to Draven's cheeks though.

"Aww, why did you have to go and do that?" Sabre whined. "I thought we agreed this wasn't something we were going to encourage because it induces my gag reflex."

Brax snorted, hauling her in close against his side. "I didn't agree to anything. You're the one who has been whining, rather persistently I might add, about their obvious attraction all week."

"It's just plain wrong," Sabre insisted.

"I think they look cute together," Brax said. And they did. Phaedra's much darker skin tone made a beautiful contrast to Draven's lighter one. As did her short, dark bouncy curls, and short, curvy body. Draven's blond hair and hard, muscled body towered over hers. He looked stiff at first but Brax was surprised to find Draven could actually keep a rhythm. "Will you look at that. Draven can dance."

"If you call that dancing," Sabre said, her lips curling in distaste. "I've seen my victims move like that in their death throes."

Brax laughed and shook his head. "You have such a way with words." Looking around, he watched Jinx and Gage laughing and dancing next to each other, and Phaedra working her wiles on Draven. Despite the circumstances and the history of the club, he was enjoying himself.

"You're enjoying this, aren't you?" Sabre asked, studying his face.

Brax shrugged, admitting, "I am. It's been a long time since I was social like this."

"It's been a lifetime since *I* was social like this," Sabre followed up, her eyes tracking the motions of Draven. "This is so disturbing to me," she muttered, a look of horror on her face as she watched Draven dip the pixie. "But I can't seem to make myself look away."

"Maybe I can help you with that. Dance with me," Brax said, nuzzling the back of Sabre's ear. He felt her sharply indrawn breath and smiled, knowing he was going to win this particular battle.

"I don't dance," came Sabre's flat response.

"Come on," he crooned, "just one little dance."

Sabre shook her head. "Fuck, no. I love you, Brax, but not enough to dance. There are limits to my love."

"Limits?" Brax tsked, his hand travelling from her stomach to the underside of her breast. He then started to rock his hips from side to side, staying flush with her back. His other hand guided her hips. "That doesn't feel like true love to me."

Sabre licked her lips, her head falling back to rest on his shoulder. "Yeah, well, take it or leave it, buddy. I'm not dancing with you."

"Hmm," he murmured, teasing the shell of her ear with his lips as he kept up the rhythm of his body. "You already are," he whispered to her.

Sabre stiffened for a moment before she relaxed back against him once more. She reached down and grabbed the hand holding her hip. "Sneaky, sneaky demon."

Brax chuckled. He spun her around so she was facing him and she immediately threaded her arms over his neck, her body as tight against his as possible. The semi he sported almost perpetually these days became a full hard-on and he pushed his hips against hers. "Want to do it in one of the private rooms?"

Sabre sputtered a laugh, her eyes alight with mirth. "You want me to fuck you in a public place?"

Brax shrugged, his hands wandering to cup her delicious butt. "Not public. Private room."

"Those are called semantics, my king," Sabre pointed out.

He was just about to answer when he felt someone bump into him. Looking over his shoulder he came face to face with a dragon. Not in dragon form of course, but the man's facial features were a dead giveaway. He stiffened and Sabre acted before his brain caught up with his eyes. She grabbed the man by the arm and pressed a switchblade to his neck within seconds. Draven was likewise already on the man, gripping his hair from behind.

"I come in peace," the dragon said blandly.

Brax didn't appreciate the way he was looking at Sabre at all. Like he knew her. And he certainly didn't like the way Sabre was glaring at the dragon. "My woman here doesn't look like she believes you," he pointed out.

"I don't," Sabre stated, blade remaining steady. "Last time I saw you, Dendey, you told me you would kill me."

"You said what, motherfucker?" Brax snarled, gripping the man's shirt and hauling him in close.

"Must we be so dramatic?" Dendey inquired, looking bored with the whole situation. "I have information. Perhaps we can go somewhere more private?"

Brax flicked his eyes over Dendey's shoulders, receiving a

nod from Draven, before dragging the man into a private room. "Talk," Brax commanded, all but tossing the guy away from him.

Dendey caught his balance easily enough, adjusting his clothes and eyeing the large number of people crowding into the small room. His gaze paused on Gage and he cocked his head. "I know you."

Brax looked at the akuji to find his black eyes focused on the dragon in return. "Gage?"

Gage nodded his head, acknowledging, "He's fought at the warehouse a few times. Always brings in a crowd. A dragon is always good for business. There's not many of them around anymore."

"You're right about that, about *all* of that," Dendey said. "Which is why I'm here."

"I thought we weren't friends. I thought you *chose* to work with Carlisle," Sabre pointed out. She was very still, all loose-limbed and focused, ready to eviscerate at any moment.

"I did choose to work with Carlisle. His den has the best reputation in Purgatory. Which means the best *treasures* in Purgatory are on offer," Dendey explained.

"And it's all about the money with your kind," Draven sneered.

Dendey shrugged, appearing calm and collected. He pointed his thumb at his chest, saying simply, "Dragon."

"You said you had information," Brax prompted. He had no desire to trade insults with the guy all night.

"Right. Carlisle and his elf friend are holed up in a strip club on the outskirts of the city. At least, they were until about an hour ago. They most likely aren't now," Dendey revealed. When nobody moved an inch, the dragon looked around once more. "Huh, I was expecting a little more enthusiasm. Perhaps a thank you."

"Nobody is going to thank you," Brax informed the man.

"Unless it's with acid to your face," Sabre added.

Dendey shook his head, a smile quirking his lips. "Good to see you haven't changed, Sabre. I got your message, by the way. The one you left carved into Madden's back. I made sure to repeat it back to Carlisle."

"And this would be at the strip club?" Brax inquired. His body vibrated with the need to act. It took everything in him to remain cool and aloof. He didn't trust Dendey and he wasn't about to go running off to an unsecured location just on the man's word alone. None of them were. He was impatient, not stupid.

"Right. Peddlers," Dendey named the location. Brax waved a hand and Hugo strode out of the room, his radio already at his ear. Dendey watched the guard leave, his eyelids moving vertically across his eyes when he blinked. "Like I said, I doubt you'll still find them there," he repeated.

"And why is that?" Draven asked from his position beside Brax.

"Because I set it on fire before I left," Dendey replied.

"And why would you do that?" Brax questioned, watching the man closely.

Dendey's jaw clenched in the first show of true emotion since he'd walked into the room. "I overheard Carlisle and the elf talking about their little endeavour. It's not just the royal line they've been killing. They've taken an interest in other supernaturals as well." He paused, smoke literally curling out of his nose. "Including dragons."

Brax reared back, more than a little shocked. That wasn't what he had been expecting to hear at all. He looked at Draven and Sabre, asking, "Is this news to both of you?"

Draven nodded, looking thoughtful as well as concerned. "Yes. Though, to be completely honest, I have been very focused on what directly affects you. It's kind of my job," he added, arching a blond brow in Brax's direction.

Brax exhaled, annoyed. "Right. Sabre?"

Sabre was frowning as she answered, "I hear about all kinds of deaths all the time. I haven't noticed an upswing of murders in any one species though, other than the demons linked to Cerberus."

"I'm not lying," Dendey assured them. "As your flesh-eating friend pointed out before, there aren't many dragons left in Purgatory. When more than one goes missing or is killed within a decade, it's noticeable. There have been three. Overhearing Carlisle laughing about their last successful kill of a female dragon just last week, had me question my alliances."

"So, you were happy to work for a man who killed indiscriminately as long as you were well paid. But when you find out he's offing your own kind, you turn on him? Yeah, some great morals you have there," Jinx spoke up from her place near the door.

Dendey gazed at her, face carefully blank. "We dragons value few things; fortune, treasure, and our young. The female killed last week was a child."

"Carlisle killed a kid?" Sabre asked, looking puzzled. "That's not his typical style. Don't get me wrong, he'll kill anything for the right amount. But kids are usually off limits to him, both sexually and as marks."

Dendey shrugged. "I don't imagine he did it himself. The man is a coward. I'm simply telling you what I heard. That is the extent of it, I'm afraid. But hearing that was enough to make me, shall we say, touchy." Dendey looked down and flexed his hands, watching as they became long-clawed talons instead of fingers.

Brax didn't like the dragon, not one bit. But he did believe him. Making eye contact with Sabre, he saw her nod and he knew she believed Dendey too. Before he could ask more questions, Hugo walked back in and confirmed that Peddlers, a brothel posing as a strip club, had been burnt to ashes that night. "Some evidence would have been nice," he gritted out, facing the dragon once more. Dragon fire was hot as hell and burned everything it touched. Brax had no doubt that nothing remained of the building, let alone anything inside of it.

"Not my concern," Dendey stated.

Brax's temper flared and he grabbed the man by his neck, squeezing with enough strength to cut off his air. "I'm jonesing for a fight. And you are mighty convenient," he growled. "Your attitude sucks."

"It does suck," Sabre agreed, watching the show. "He told me he wasn't my friend. It hurt my feelings," she said, bottom lip trembling.

Brax looked at his lover, appreciating the way she attempted to calm him down. He was sure it wouldn't look that way to normal people, but her wit and her easy support of strangulation were enough for him to ease back. Still, he gave the neck he was holding one last squeeze before he released a breath, pushing Dendey away. The dragon wasn't his real target. Nor, it would seem, his enemy. He said as much, adding, "But that will change if you threaten Sabre again or piss me off."

Dendey bent over at the waist, breathing heavily. When he straightened, he grimaced and touched his neck. "That's a hell of a grip you have there ..." he paused before seeming to arrive at a decision, "Your Majesty."

Brax inhaled, appreciating the shift in attitude and the small display of respect. "I appreciate the information. I still don't like you. Now, fuck off," he told Dendey. The dragon dipped his head ever so subtly before making his way from the room. As soon as he was gone, he turned to his friends. "What the fuck?"

"That was unexpected," Draven acknowledged.

Sabre snorted rudely. "Says the king of understatements."

Draven glowered at Sabre. "You are so annoying."

"So's your face," Sabre shot back.

The old insult caused Brax to laugh, along with everyone else. When the hilarity finally died down, he said, "But, seriously, what the fuck? We have them going after dragons now? What the hell is going on?"

"I don't know," Draven said, shaking his head. "But we had better look into it. We've been guilty of tunnel vision for a long time, I think."

"You mean *I've* been guilty of tunnel vision," Brax corrected. "Because I've been focused on finding the person responsible for killing my family, and *my* family only. I haven't given a shit about anything else. I'm out of touch with what is happening in the kingdom. This kind of thing would never have slipped past Mikhail."

"Hey," Sabre said softly, drawing his attention. "What Mikhail would and would not have done is irrelevant. He's not here. He hasn't been here. You have. And you've been doing the best you can with the hand you've been dealt. We've talked about this before, remember?"

Brax smiled, but it didn't reach his eyes. "I remember. I still feel like shit though."

"If it makes you feel any better Mikhail feels like shit too. He doesn't think he has been super successful as a secret rebel spy," Sabre shared.

Brax huffed because he could well believe it. Mikhail wasn't exactly one to rough it. Shaking off his unhelpful emotions, he went about giving orders to Hugo; follow up at the strip club, chase down any and all leads, gather any evidence or remains, talk to witnesses, and report back in the morning. He would make a trip there himself tomorrow. They then left when nothing further was gleaned from the patrons or the staff at the club.

As they were walking out, the night air cool and fresh, Sabre leaned against Brax. "You know, you sounded very kingly in there, giving orders."

He thought about it for a moment before shaking his head. "Nah, I sounded like a General, barking orders to my soldiers. Not like a king leading his people."

"You miss it, don't you?" Sabre asked. "The army stuff?"

"I do," he admitted. "I really do."

"You'll get back there. I promise," Sabre declared.

Brax smiled and stopped walking. He tucked a stray hair behind Sabre's ear. "You know, I believe that. Because *you* said it. And you always keep your word to me."

"Damn straight," she agreed, pressing her lips against his in a searing kiss.

Brax pulled back, suddenly in a much better mood. "Come on," he urged, dragging Sabre along, studiously ignoring Draven and the rest of their entourage. But just as they rounded the bend on the street, Brax noticed something that had him seeing red. Growling low, his figurative hackles rising and his literal claws unsheathing, he darted forward. "Hey, you!" he yelled, just barely catching the young male vampire by the back of his shirt as he attempted to make a hasty exit.

The kid swore, wriggled, and kicked, demanding, "Let me go!"

Brax snorted, just about had it with arseholes for the night. "I don't think so. Do you know whose car this is?"

He looked at the one physical possession Sabre actually took pride in other than her weapons. Ever since his inner beast had claimed Sabre, Brax had been a wee bit territorial when it came to her. That possessiveness also included her things. Which was why seeing the vamp trying to jimmy open Sabre's car door with a pick had him ready to rip out the kid's heart. Before the Neanderthal part of his brain could act, however, Sabre and the rest of their group caught up to him.

"Hey, babe. What have you got here?" Sabre asked her plum eyes laughing into his.

Brax smiled at her, his bottom fangs still protruding more than normal. "This kid was trying to steal your car."

"I'm not a kid!" The *kid* hastily denied, kicking Brax in the shin.

Brax swore colourfully, shaking the vampire like a ragdoll. "Don't do that again," he warned.

Sabre laughed even as she stepped in close, her face going somewhat cold and blank. "That's strike two, fang-head. First, you try to jack my car. Now you kick my man. Apologise." It wasn't a suggestion.

The young man swallowed noisily. "Sorry," he mumbled.

"Hmm," Sabre mused, walking around the kid in a tight circle.

Brax told his dick to keep it down, no matter how arousing he found his mate to be when she was in badass mode. Draven, Jinx, Gage, and Phaedra were watching the whole scene silently, and the last thing Brax needed was Draven commenting on his lack of control yet again.

Presently, Sabre bent and picked up a thin silver object from the ground. She tsked. "Seriously? What the fuck were you thinking?" She grabbed the front of the kid's shirt aggressively. Brax let him go and stepped back, happily ceding the offender into her capable hands.

"I, I ..." was all the poor guy could get out before Sabre dragged him closer to her shiny car.

"Do you really think this is acceptable behaviour?" she yelled and pointed her finger at him. "Shame on you. Shame, shame, shame."

The young vampire looked like he was about to piss his

pants as he stuttered out another apology. But Sabre just shook her head, disappointment in every line of her body. She held up the thief's tool once more. "This is a hook pick. What you need for this type of lock is a *double ball* pick." Thrusting her hand in Jinx's direction, she wiggled her fingers. "Jinx, where's the pick set I gave you for your last birthday?"

Jinx grinned and reached into her back pocket, pulling out a slim, soft leather case. "Here ya go," she said merrily, handing it over.

Sabre opened it up, deftly pulling out a fine, golden pick. "Here. Try it with this."

The vampire looked at the pick, looked at Sabre, looked at the pick again, before turning to Brax. "What is happening?" he whispered.

"What indeed," Draven answered, shaking his head, voice full of sarcasm.

Brax simply grinned, his beast now happy and more than a little amused with how the situation was playing out. The night may not have gone how he had been hoping, or even how he anticipated, but it sure was entertaining, nonetheless.

"I'm serious," Sabre said.

"I think I made a mistake," the kid murmured, eyes downcast. "I'll just be going."

Brax watched calculation enter Sabre's eyes, as well as pity. He could understand the latter. The vampire looked to be around Jinx's age, perhaps even younger, and was wearing tattered, thin clothes. He was also skinny as hell, looking half-starved. Clearly, he wasn't a very good thief.

"Do you live around here?" Sabre asked. The kid shrugged and Sabre sighed, poking him in the chest. "Words, kid. Use your words."

He whipped his head up, anger flashing across his face. "I'm not a kid! And I live everywhere ... and nowhere ..."

He was homeless. Brax felt kind of bad for shaking him now.

"I bet you see a lot of things," Sabre suggested.

Brax's ears perked up and he gave the skinny street rat more of his attention. They had questioned the staff and the patrons of Inferno, but he hadn't considered anyone on the streets. No wonder his woman was such an accomplished badarse, she factored in everything. "What's your name?"

The kid clenched his jaw stubbornly for a moment before he looked around and saw how he was caged in between a bunch of different supernatural beings. He wouldn't be getting away until they were satisfied. "Eric," he finally answered.

"Eric, have you ever seen a blond incubus entering or leaving Inferno?" Sabre questioned him.

Eric tilted his head to the side, pocketing Jinx's pick. "You mean Carlisle?"

All of them took a collective step closer. "You know him?" Brax pressed.

"Not really ..." Eric mumbled, eyes darting around for an escape route.

"Well, unluckily for you, Eric, *not really* is enough to get you kidnapped," Sabre told him, cheerfully. "You're coming with us."

9

The next morning, Sabre watched as Eric wolfed down his breakfast, practically inhaling the food. The vampire was far too thin and had clearly been on the streets for a long time. Given how young he looked, she wondered at what age he had found himself alone and without a home.

"How old are you?" she asked him, watching the spoon full of cereal hover mid-air for a moment before he shoved it in his mouth.

"Eighteen," he answered around a mouthful of *Puffies*.

Not technically a kid then, Sabre acknowledged, *but not an adult either*. Eric had put up a token fight when she'd informed him she was going to kidnap him. He'd ceased his struggles though when Jinx had stepped up and smiled at him, promising him that it would be the best kidnapping of his life. He had looked gobsmacked, and not by Jinx's words, Sabre was sure. No, it was because Jinx was a stunner. Eric had then meekly allowed Hugo to take him back to the palace, where he had been given a nice guest suite for the remainder of the night.

Sabre continued to observe him as he ploughed his way through the cereal, the toast, the bacon, and finally the fruit spread out before him. He was in clean, fresh clothes and he smelled much better than the previous night. Brax was likewise watching their new guest and Sabre could see the pity in his eyes. But also the wariness. She approved. Eric may look like a lost urchin, but he could just as well be a trojan. "How long have you been on the streets?"

Eric leaned back in his chair and rested his hands on his stomach. "I don't know, a while."

"How long is a while?" Brax's voice was stern as he questioned the young man.

Sabre understood. She wanted to discover as much information as possible as well. No rock would remain unturned. The new information from the night before was startling and frustrating because she had no idea why it was relevant. What did royalty and dragons have in common? Brax already had a bunch of his people looking into it, including Draven, who had left early to check out the site of the burned-out strip joint personally. He hadn't wanted to leave Brax alone with their new guest in residence, but Sabre had pointed out that she could kill Eric with her pinky finger if she needed to. She'd made sure to say so in front of Eric too. He had gulped and promised not to cause trouble. Brax had chimed in reminding his guardian that he was a big boy who had been wiping his own arse for years. Sabre snickered remembering Draven's response.

"I blame you for this crass attitude," Draven had hissed.

Sabre had preened under the compliment, practically glowing. She was impatient to get her boots on the ground as well and conduct her own investigations in her own way. Her own way equalled getting a little dirty.

"A few years. Four maybe," Eric finally answered Brax.

"Why?" Brax then asked.

Eric sneered his way, showing some pluck. "Because mummy and daddy didn't love me and I didn't have a palace to go to."

Brax's lips twitched. "Fair enough."

The mild response seemed to deflate Eric a bit. "What do you want from me?"

"Information," Sabre replied, getting down to business. "Last night you mentioned Carlisle by name."

Eric shrugged, looking around. It was just Sabre, Brax, Jinx, and Gage present but he still looked uncomfortable. "Yeah."

Sabre rolled her eyes. She was used to dealing with a teenaged female weretiger, but it appeared teenaged male vampires were just as eloquent. "How do you know him?"

"I don't *know* him," Eric insisted. "I've just seen him

around. He goes to Inferno every so often. Usually on the themed nights."

"If you know his name, then you must know him more than just from across the street," Sabre pointed out. Eric glanced at Jinx once more, his cheeks pinking a little. Sabre realised he was embarrassed to talk in front of the pretty girl. Jinx noticed his regard and spoke up.

"Hey, I know Sabre seems like a hardened bitch, but she isn't as scary as she looks," Jinx teased, winking at Eric. "Honest. We're the good guys. You can trust us, can tell us anything. The royal line of Cerberus needs you. Will you help us?"

Sabre wanted to throw her glass of orange juice at Jinx for the bitch comment but the clever way she appealed to Eric was having the intended effect. The young man sat up straighter and nodded his head. Sabre shot Jinx a grateful look.

"I honestly don't know him. Only his, uh, *pheromones*," Eric finally admitted.

Sabre frowned, not liking the implications of that at all. Jinx stiffened in her seat, along with Brax and Gage. *Yeah,* Sabre thought, *nobody is on board with Carlisle possibly using his incubus powers on Eric.* "Carlisle isn't into kids," Sabre pointed out. She didn't mention the fact that Eric was male because Carlisle had no bias toward biological sex. He had no bias toward species either. The sex demon fucked anything and everything. But not children. She knew that personally.

Eric sighed. "I thought we just covered this. I'm not a kid. I'm eighteen. I'm legal."

"Fucking hell," Brax grumbled, looking mad enough to spit nails.

Sabre understood. It was just one more thing to kill her den Master for. "He used his incubus pheromones to put the whammy on you?" she questioned.

Incubus powers were insidious by nature. They made people horny beyond belief and then the demon would feed off the sexual energy produced. It didn't have to involve intercourse, but it most often did. Most people believed they were into it or didn't see anything wrong with getting their rocks off with a handsome man who was an expert in the sack. But consent was dubious at best when someone's will was impeded by heady pheromones.

"He didn't whammy me," Eric stated firmly. "I approached him. Sure, I could feel his pheromones from across the street, but they weren't enough for me to beg him to suck my cock or anything."

"Language," Gage cautioned, speaking for the first time. Gage was a quiet man by nature, but when he spoke, people listened. "You're at the breakfast table."

Sabre shook her head, because Gage was always trying to get her and Jinx to be polite, have better manners, and be less crass. It was a losing battle, but Gage never gave up.

"Brax literally just said *fuck off*," Sabre pointed out, drawing attention away from Eric for a moment. She knew he was uncomfortable, that's what the crudeness was all about. It was a defence mechanism. She would know.

Gage frowned at her. "I know. I was just about to rap the king across the knuckles."

"I'd like to see you try," Brax taunted lightly.

Sabre was happy to see the way Eric brightened and to hear his amused snicker. She winked at Gage, beyond grateful to have such great friends. "So he didn't whammy you ...?" she prompted, turning back to Eric.

"No. I approached him. Offered him a trade. His blood for, well, you know ..." Eric revealed, biting his lip. "Incubus blood is really powerful. It can sustain me for weeks. It was a no brainer. No biggie."

But he looked ashamed and Sabre knew it was a big deal. Nobody should have to trade their body for food, no matter what type of food it was, blood included. She looked at Jinx, making sure she was doing okay. Talk of such things would no doubt bring up memories and Sabre was concerned old wounds would be reopened. Jinx's bi-coloured eyes met hers and Sabre knew Jinx had just decided to make Eric her new best friend. *Which means I've just adopted a vampire*, Sabre thought to herself.

"Do you need blood now?" Brax asked, his amber eyes kind but his fists clenched. He was pissed.

"I wouldn't say no," Eric answered with a shrug and a small cheeky grin.

Sabre sucked in a breath because he was really very handsome. Once he got some meat on his bones, he was going to be a stunner.

"I'll grab some," Gage offered, already standing up. "There's a bunch of blood in the fridge next to my organs."

Brax leaned in close to Sabre, his breath tickling her ear as he murmured, "You know, just a few short months ago, a comment like that would have sounded strange. Now? Not so much."

Sabre grinned, turning her head. They were so close their noses touched. "Aren't you just a lucky boy?"

"I am," Brax confirmed, seriously.

Sabre felt her breath catch and her gooey heart took a tumble.

"Wow, so it really is true," Eric commented, breaking up the lovefest. "You've gone soft."

Sabre reared back. "I beg your pardon!"

"Uh-oh," Jinx breathed, wincing.

Brax sighed in disappointment, leaning back in his chair. "And here I thought we were getting a new recruit. That's too bad, kid. I was just beginning to like you."

"I'm not soft," Sabre warned. "I am a vicious, lethal, killing machine. I've killed more people than the entire Demon Horde combined. And I've liked it."

Eric's grey eyes widened, and he looked around for help.

None was forthcoming. "I'm sorry. I didn't mean to offend you. You are for sure a badarse. I'm absolutely terrified, practically pissing my pants," he promised.

Sabre glared at Eric some more, slightly mollified because she could in fact see the wildly beating artery in his neck. "Do I have to pull out a few fingernails to prove my point?"

"No!" Eric practically shouted. "Point proven. I believe you."

Gage came back in, carrying a large cup and placed it in front of Eric. "Drink up. I warmed it. I probably should have checked with you first, sorry. I know I like my body parts warmed up whenever possible, but I shouldn't have assumed."

Eric took the glass, tentatively looking into it. His rumbling stomach could be heard by all in the room. "You eat flesh? Do you drink blood too?"

Gage sat down next to Eric instead of at the other end of the table where he had been seated before. He nodded, urging Eric to drink up. "Go ahead. Nobody here will care that you're drinking blood in front of them or judge you for it. Yes, I drink blood too. But it's more incidental than anything. I'm an akuji – a type of zombie – so I need organs and flesh to sustain me."

Eric listened raptly as Gage explained what he was and how he ate, all the while chugging down his blood. "Wow, that is so cool."

"Oh, yeah. Sure. It was really cool being killed and then Sabre bringing me back to life. *But,* into a body that had already started to decompose," he added sardonically. But the smile he tossed Sabre was genuine, showing he was okay with how his fate had worked out.

"Now that you've eaten, drank, insulted Sabre, and learned the mystery that is Gage, perhaps you're ready to answer some more questions?" Brax asked before Eric's curiosity got the better of him and he questioned Gage more. It was obvious he was intrigued.

"What else do you want to know?" Eric wondered, looking more alert. His eyes were the colour of smoke now, darker than they had been before he drank the blood.

"Have you ever noticed an elf with Carlisle?" Brax followed up his question with a description of the wanted man.

Eric nodded. "Sure. His name is X."

Sabre sat forward on high alert. "What?" She didn't mean to snap, but Eric's flinch told her she had.

"Uh..." Eric eyed them all. They were all looking at him intensely now. "I overheard Carlisle call him that. X."

"Anything else? Where he's from? Where he lives? What his master plan is for the universe?" Sabre peppered him with questions.

"Ah, no. Sorry. Just X," Eric chuckled nervously.

"X is clearly a pseudonym," Brax grunted, looking annoyed.

“And not a very imaginative one at that,” Jinx added, scrunching up her nose.

“Still, it gives me something else to work off, I guess,” Sabre allowed. She could ask around for a guy called X at the very least. “Thank you.”

“I should be thanking *you*,” Eric replied softly. “It’s been a while since I felt this full. Or this clean. Or this warm.”

“Well, you can add *this welcomed* to the list,” Brax informed him. “You’re welcome to stay here.”

Eric looked shocked and more than a little flustered. “What? Uh, thanks but that isn’t going to happen. No way can I stay here.”

Brax frowned, looking displeased from being told no. “And why is that?”

“Because I’m me,” Eric responded as if it should have been obvious. “I’m a homeless vampire who steals and bargains for blood and food. You’re the king. This is the royal palace.” He pointed at Brax and then gestured around wildly to his surroundings. “That is Sabre, the infamous assassin, turned unlikely hero,” he waved a hand at Sabre. “I’m ... nobody.”

“Yeah, well, not anymore,” Brax said gruffly. “Now you’re one of us.”

Sabre had never loved her man more. “Good luck,” she quipped to a shellshocked Eric. “You’re gonna need it.”

10

A week had flown by, and although Sabre had been out doing her assassin shit every day and every night, she had very little to show for it.

She *had* succeeded in disembowelling another one of the Blue Devil's assassins, which brought Carlisle's cronies down to less than a handful. It had cheered her for a short time, especially when she had walked into the palace with blood and meaty things still on her boots. Draven had just about popped a blood vessel.

The killing of one's enemies was a good thing, and in the past, never failed to make her feel satisfied. So why was she sitting in the garden where Brax had first detailed her job to her, feeling dejected and useless? She blew out a breath, knowing she was most pissed about X, the elf. He didn't exist anywhere. Not in any records, not in any family tree, and not even in the underground rumour mill. The only evidence he existed were the accounts from the staff at Inferno, Brax, Draven, and Sabre seeing him that one time. And, of course, Eric's testimony.

Looking over the courtyard, Sabre saw Draven talking with Phaedra. He actually looked relaxed and happy. A smile lit up his face and she swore the fellow angel damn near glowed. Despite what she acknowledged out loud, Draven was sickeningly handsome. She could also admit he was a darn fine guardian to Brax and also a good friend. It made her feel a little less murdery towards him. He chose that moment to look up, and assuming he saw a look that wasn't unadulterated scorn on her face, he gave a little head nod. Finding herself off balance for so many reasons, none the least her continued concern that love was making her lose her edge, Sabre did the only thing that would restore order to her world.

She decided to cause fuckery.

And because Draven was looking so happy – as well as cosying up to her pixie friend – she chose him as her victim. "Hey, Draven," Sabre called out, garnering the attention of everyone on the palace grounds. There were at least a dozen guards scattered about, not to mention some cousins.

Draven turned to look at her, his perfect, golden eyebrows raised in silent query. His blue eyes were, for now, earnest with genuine curiosity and welcome. Sabre felt a bubble of evil euphoria rising within her as she mentally scrolled through her insults. She had more stored away than even *she* could use in multiple lifetimes. Deciding simplicity was a classic for reason, she took a deep breath, really working to expand her lungs, before yelling, "Why don't you go shit yourself?"

Draven's beautiful face instantly morphed into a fierce scowl, and he pulled out a sword seemingly from thin air. His white wings sprouted from his back as he stalked over to her, yelling all the while, "Sabre, you crazy bitch! I'm going to gut you!"

Sabre grinned and palmed a dagger. She was feeling better already. Just before Draven made it to her, a white tiger jumped in between them. One blue eye and one green eye peered at her out of a feline face that clearly portrayed, *don't even think about it.* "Jinx," Sabre whined. "What are you, the fun police?"

Male laughter drew her attention, and she looked to her right. Eric covered his mouth with both hands as he laughed. He fit in with their group well. But was it possible to fit in *too well?* Sabre wondered. Eric and Jinx had become fast friends, practically attached at the hip. Sabre didn't begrudge Jinx for making new friends, nor did she make a habit out of dictating who she could and could not talk to. She only hoped Eric wasn't going to break Jinx's heart. Because Sabre would then break his, and she didn't mean emotionally.

"Jinx, please step aside. It's time I taught Sabre some

manners," Draven said, glaring at Sabre over Jinx's black and white furry back.

Sabre scoffed, spinning her dagger in her hand. "As if you'd get the chance before I rearranged your face."

"You are vile," Draven informed her, pointing his sword at her head.

"So's your face," she instantly shot back.

Draven launched himself into the air briefly, landing lightly in front of Sabre, Jinx now behind him. "Drop dead," he all but commanded her.

She smirked, retorting, "You first."

"It's kind of like watching school kids bully each other," Eric said to Jinx, who was now sitting placidly at his side. "I mean if school kids were endlessly powerful, psychotic, and immature."

Sabre glared at Eric now. "You know I can hear you, right?"

Eric shrugged, looking sheepish, but not apologetic. He was proving to have a quick tongue and a nimble mind. Not to mention being cheeky and a bit of a prankster. With his sun-kissed blond hair, grey eyes, and strong jawline, he was pretty much the whole package. At least, he would be, when he put on a bit more weight. He was still too thin to be considered healthy, but there was a wholesome glow in his cheeks now.

Turning back to Draven, she let another insult fly. "Your hair is thin and lifeless. It lacks shine and I can see dandruff."

Draven gasped, literally falling back a pace. He touched his perfect hair and fired back, "You're a marshmallow."

Sabre slammed her mouth shut and narrowed her eyes. "As in tasty?" she questioned, her voice like silk.

Draven's eyes widened and he looked at Jinx, who was already making her way back over to his side. She sat her big butt directly in front of the other angel as if he needed genuine protection now.

And he just might, Sabre said to herself, *depending on what his answer is.*

"Sure, as in tasty," Draven hastily replied.

That's when she knew she must have looked like a crazy, murderous assassin. There was no way Draven would typically use the word *tasty* and definitely not in relation to her. She took a deep breath, reminding the sicko within herself that her lover would not appreciate it if she cut off his guardian angel's wings and shoved them up his arse. "I'm not soft."

It was a statement.

It was a warning.

Draven shook his head, his face taking on a look of empathy and understanding. "Sabre ..." he began.

But she was done with their banter. She'd started it, but Draven had hit a nerve. A nerve that was exposed to the air and aching like a bitch. "I'm off to the mansion. It's that time again. Tell Brax I'll see him later."

She moved swiftly, ignoring the voice of one angel, one vampire, and a tiger's roar.

Sabre sat on the ground, watching the den with the attention of an eagle, waiting for a mouse to scurry into her line of sight so she could pounce and squeeze the life out of it.

She had entered the property already, crossing the threshold for a brief few seconds before making her hasty exit. It was enough to satisfy her end of the deal as far as the contract went, and it gave her more time to sit and brood and pray for an enemy to appear so she could kill them. "I'm not a marshmallow," she said out loud.

"Are you so sure about that?"

The sudden appearance of Carlisle in front of her caused Sabre to react instinctively, as well as answer her heart's desire. She palmed her gun, aimed it at his head, and fired over and over until the 9mm semi-automatic ran out of rounds in the magazine and started clicking over and over again. She gritted her teeth and lowered her pistol when she saw Carlisle standing directly in front of her smoking a cigar. The fucker didn't even have the decency to duck. He knew that she couldn't harm him, no matter what.

Looking over his shoulder, she saw the bullet holes in the tree behind him. Her aim had been as perfect as Robin Hood himself, but the bullets had still missed their target. She tried with her other handgun anyway. She raised her arm – as steady as a rock – and fired directly at his forehead. Her aim had been true, but the deadly, speeding projectile missed his head completely.

Standing up, she reached for her bow and took out an arrow, aiming for the centre of Carlisle's chest this time. She let the arrow fly, only to watch it land harmlessly with a thunk into the ground right in front of his feet. Carlisle had the audacity to blow her a kiss, so Sabre pulled out a grenade from her back pocket, yanked the pin, and threw it directly at his smug face. The grenade went well wide, landing several metres away. She and Carlisle watched as it rolled down the nearby embankment before a massive explosion rent the air. Dust and debris kicked up into the sky, and several rocks rained down on Sabre. But not onto Carlisle. It was like he was protected by an invisible forcefield.

Pure stubbornness had her pulling out a short sword from her boot. She gripped it in her right hand and was about to charge when Carlisle whistled shrilly.

"Are you really going to keep going on endlessly with these weapons of yours?" he asked incredulously. "You know you can't hurt me, no matter what you do."

"Yes," Sabre hissed. "I am going to keep trying forever. Because maybe the shitty, soul-deep contract you have protecting you from my wrath, will fail. Maybe if I keep trying, one of these weapons will eventually hit their target."

Carlisle looked bored, his eyes scanning her from head to

toe. "Will you at least tell me how many weapons you have, then? Should I sit down for this? How long is it going to take for you to exhaust your stockpile? Or better yet, exhaust yourself?"

Sabre's grip tightened on the pommel of her sword to the point of pain. She loathed to admit it, but the incubus had a point. "I hate you," she told him flatly.

"Do you really?" Carlisle's beautiful voice questioned. "Are you sure you really want to hurt me? There are more pleasurable ways we could be spending our time." And then he released his powers.

The pheromones wafted to her and she barely twitched, easily shaking off the sudden spark of horniness she felt as a result of the sex fumes. No matter how potent his spunk pheromones were, he had never been able to tempt her to his side. A part of that was due to the desireless nature of angels. But a larger part was because of her history with him – because the man had trapped her and then tortured her for years. She had told him the truth when she had battled him almost one month ago; he hadn't broken her. Not her mind at least, and that was the one place that mattered.

And even if her brain had been malleable enough to forget the torture, the pain, and the degradation of being one of Carlisle's assassins, Sabre was now deeply in love. He could throw his skanky sex demon powers at her all day. She wouldn't be sucking his cock any time soon.

"Really?" she sniped back at him. "Are you really going to

keep throwing your pheromones at me? They never worked before. And now, thanks to Brax, they never will."

Carlisle's handsome face turned calculating. "Ah, yes, you're in love now, aren't you? And to the king no less. But wait, he isn't really the king, is he? Not the rightful one. That would be your charge, Mikhail. Tell me, Sabre, just how did you manage to get yourself caught up with all these famous people?"

"Just lucky I guess," she responded dryly, trying to think of a way to at least capture the incubus.

"Luck had nothing to do with it," Carlisle told her.

She told herself not to engage with him, not to ask, but she couldn't help herself. "What are you talking about?"

"Well, you're a created angel, aren't you? The powers that be could have placed you anywhere in Purgatory when they sent you through the veil. But they put you *here,*" he said, pointing to the grass beneath his feet. "Right here. Right in my path. Did you never wonder why?"

"You were a means to an end," she told him. But the seeds he was planting were starting to take root.

"Is that so? A means to *what* end, do you suppose?" Carlisle questioned archly. He took one last drag of the cigar before dropping and crushing it with his shiny, black shoe.

"A messy one, I promise you," Sabre replied, meaning every word. She wanted to hurt him so badly she could taste it.

Carlisle looked at her with something akin to pity in his

brown eyes. "Sabre, Sabre, Sabre," he tsked. "You're not some saviour. You're not a hero in an epic odyssey. You are expendable. That's why they tossed you down to me when you were nothing but a child – a *created* child. You weren't even born. It's pathetic, really. *You're* pathetic. You were made to be used, created to be hurt. And I for one have been more than happy to make good on that all these years."

"No," Sabre declared. "I am more than what you think of me. I am more than what they made me – more than what *you* made me." She continued, telling herself Carlisle was the one she was trying to convince. "I was playing you the whole time, including the first time we met. I knew there was something up with you, you made my skin crawl. But I *chose* to follow your path anyway. I trust the process."

"The process of a lifetime of murder," he clucked his tongue. "How charming," Carlisle smirked at her.

"There is a design," Sabre conceded. "A method to this madness. But it isn't yours."

"My dear, you keep telling yourself that if it makes you feel better. But I have been playing this game longer than you've been alive. The wheels were set in motion years ago."

"If that's true, then you are just as much of a pawn as I am," she pointed out.

"Perhaps I am," Carlisle mused. "But I won't always be. You're in check, my little assassin. Just a few more moves now until it's checkmate."

Before she could close the gap between them, Carlisle

held up two fingers, his sign for being done. A portal swirled to life behind him and he stepped through. Sabre threw her short sword for the hell of it. Unfortunately, all she was met with was a cackling Carlisle in an ever-decreasing rip in the fabric of reality. When the portal was gone, so was her nemesis. And her blade was lying broken on the ground.

11

Brax grunted, the breath leaving his lungs in a painful rush as he fell heavily to the ground. His magical skin shield didn't do much to soften a hard landing. Several snickers and poorly concealed laughter met his ears and he glared up at the people surrounding him.

"Is anyone going to give me a hand up?" he demanded of his Demon Horde.

"Pfft," Hugo scoffed at him. "You're the one out of shape, my lord. Get your own flabby arse up."

"My arse is not flabby!" he yelled at his insolent lieutenant. He then kicked out with his right foot, nailing Hugo in the knee.

The phoenix swore, toppling to the ground. But he made a mad grab for his comrades in his desperation and ended up dragging them all down like a stack of dominoes. Brax dragged himself up and dusted off his clothes, smiling with satisfaction when he saw Hugo at the very bottom of a supernatural puppy pile.

Finally growing impatient with himself and sick to death of his own company, he had abandoned his duties in the royal office and decided to get a workout in. Draven hadn't said a word about quitting for the day but had simply followed along behind. It had been a long time since he had trained properly. Sure, he kept himself in shape – in more ways than one these days, thanks to Sabre – but he hadn't dedicated himself to training in too long to remember. When he'd first entered the training facility on the palace grounds, everyone had stopped and stared. Where once he had been a part of the army, a part of the team, now he was an outsider. Nothing but a pencil pusher. The thought had pissed him off and he had challenged the first soldier he had seen. Unfortunately, it had been a cyclops.

Uno was huge, over seven feet tall and built like a tank. He also loved throwing his opponents around like they were a frisbee. Even Brax, at six-five, could soar through the air when tossed over the shoulder of a cyclops.

The bunch of ingrates on the ground began to untangle themselves and Brax had to admit he felt better than he had in a long time. Sabre had the right idea; a good fight was very cathartic. *Almost as cathartic as good sex,* he thought, already planning to put his pinging endorphins to good use the moment Sabre returned.

Draven had told him all about the incident with Sabre, including their juvenile repertoire. But it wasn't the name-calling that bothered him. It was Sabre's continued concern over being weak or soft. He had thought their little chat weeks ago had resolved the issue for her. But it was clear that wasn't the case. Perhaps he had been naive to believe some open communication, followed by some mind-blowing sex, would be enough to cure her of her insecurities. Or perhaps he had just *hoped* it would be.

"Are you ready for more, General?"

Brax whipped his head around, finding a dozen of his soldiers from Purgatory's army standing at attention in front of him. He wasn't the least bit ashamed to admit he felt his eyes sting a little. It had been a long time since anyone had called him *General* instead of *King*. He cleared his throat, "Ready to give you all a sound thrashing, do you mean? You bet your arses, I am."

Thirty minutes later he was sweating and panting, his muscles aching. But he felt exhilarated. He also felt like he was more equipped to handle Carlisle or any other fucker that decided to test their dick size and make a move on them. It didn't sit well with him that Sabre was the one out on the frontlines doing all the slaughtering. He knew she was a guardian and her very reason for existing was to protect others. But she wasn't *his* guardian. She was his *woman* and his mate. He wanted to do a little maiming in her honour.

Maybe lay some torn out hearts at her feet or something to prove his alpha status.

Glancing at the clock, he noted the time and frowned when he realised how late it was. Sabre should have been back by now. "Draven ..." he called, only to stop what he was about to say when he saw Sabre leaning against the far wall.

She was as beautiful as always, her black hair shining under the lights, and her unique eyes locked on his. Her cheekbones were sharp, her chin a little pointy, and she exuded authority with every breath she took. Ignoring the ribbing he was receiving from his soldiers about being entranced by his woman, Brax made his way over to her. He lowered his head to give her a kiss but she pulled her head out of reach. His gut clenched.

"Sabre? What's going on?" he asked, already borderline frantic. He checked her visually for injuries but couldn't see any.

"It's nothing, I'm fine," Sabre told him, catching his hands in hers and giving them a familiar squeeze. "I'm sorry. Truly, I'm fine."

He backed her up, placed his palms flat against the wall on either side of her head and went practically nose to nose with her. "Truth?"

Sabre opened her mouth then closed it again. She blew out a frustrated breath. "Truth. Right. Sorry," she said again.

"I don't want your apology, Sabre. I just want to make sure you're okay. What's going on?" He was relieved when she reached up and gripped him on the forearms where he was still boxing her in.

"I had a little run-in with Carlisle," she confessed.

"You what?!" he bellowed, spinning around. "Horde! Fall in!" he commanded, feeling his fangs pierce his lip.

"Whoa, there, General. There's no need to call up your army." Sabre jumped in front of him and held her arms out to ward him off. "He's gone. He got away. He never touched me. And I never touched him. More's the pity ..." she added, grumbling under her breath.

"He didn't touch you?" Brax needed to hear it again.

Sabre shook her head. "Not at all. I swear."

Brax felt his shoulders slump, the adrenaline leaving his body as suddenly as it had arrived. "Okay. Good. That's good. Stand down," he told his soldiers. They saluted him and began to disperse a little but didn't go far.

"But did you hear the other part I said? He got away. I couldn't catch him or hurt him," Sabre said, head downcast like she had failed him or something.

"I heard you," he assured her, frowning. "I just don't care as long as you're okay. I mean, sure I want to rip out his spine and then beat him with it. But I wouldn't expect you to be able to capture him on your own. There's only so much you can do when you literally cannot hurt the guy."

"I guess. But it makes me feel incompetent," she revealed in a rush. "What's the point of being a tool if I can't hammer the guy?"

Brax took a moment to study her. She was chewing on her thumbnail, something very unusual for her. It was a nervous gesture. Sabre didn't get nervous or suffer from anxiety. The wretched incubus had clearly said something to shake her confidence. Brax vowed to get to the bottom of it when they had more privacy, but in the meantime, he wanted to see her smile.

"Carlisle is a wanker and he'll get what's coming to him. I promise you. I want to hear all about it, but first things first ..." he flashed her a grin, watching her perk up a bit as she eyed him suspiciously. "I know what will make you feel better," he said. "I'm going to hulk-out."

Draven's pained groan could be heard clear across the room. "Don't do it!" he pleaded, shouting their way.

"You're not the boss of me, Draven!" Brax shouted right back, resisting the urge to poke his tongue out like a child. Looking at Sabre from the corner of his eye, he saw her lips twitching and the beautiful sparkle returning to her mauve eyes. Typically, such a look was reserved for dancing on the graves of her enemies, but he would take it.

"I'm doing it," he stated decisively. "I'm hulking-out."

"Abraxis, I swear if you hulk-out ..." Draven's threat trailed off.

Brax disregarded the angel completely, as did everyone else still in the training centre. They all knew his threats were baseless. Turning to Sabre, he crooked a finger at her. "Come one, pretty angel, care to strike the first blow?"

Sabre licked her lips, eyes darting to the soldiers around her. "How much street cred am I going to lose for doing this?"

"Lose?" Shiloh, of all people, said as she stepped up in front of Brax. "Honey, this will *gain* you street cred." Then she wiggled her eyebrows at Brax and turned on the flamethrower.

Brax swore, throwing his arms up in front of his face instinctively. The fire wouldn't harm him at all, but the heat was intense. Not to mention, it was burning his fucking clothes off. He swore like a sailor, dodging out of the way of the flames. "I didn't say fire was okay! Since when has fire *ever* been okay?!"

Shiloh dialled back the fiery weapon, adopting an innocent expression. "There are no rules when it comes to the hulk."

Then Shiloh shared a devilish look with Sabre, and he knew he was well and truly fucked. The last thing he'd intended was for the two women to bond. He spent the next fifteen minutes running around, dodging weapons of various kinds that were thrown with various alacrity. His exoskeleton remained firmly in place the entire time, and he revelled in the pings and clangs of the weapons as they bounced harmlessly off him.

The whole time, he roared and grunted like the Incredible Hulk, playing his part of the indestructible, rampaging giant. Hulking-out had become a thing a long time ago between him and his brothers. He had shared the game with his army friends, and then, of course with Sabre. Especially given how much she loved to bring his armour to life.

Halting directly in front of Sabre, he struck a pose to rival even the buffest bodybuilder. He raised his arms level with his shoulders and bent his elbows. His bicep muscles bulged. “Have you seen my beach ball?” he asked her. He shifted his arms to make a big circle in front of him, fisting his hands, and causing his muscles to pop in his arms, shoulders, and chest. “It’s this big. Last seen ...” He moved once more, turning to the side and pointing with one hand straight out from his shoulder and the other bent at the elbow just below, but parallel to it. This flexed his triceps. “... over there,” he finished the lame joke.

Sabre covered her mouth with her hands, her eyes sparkling with mirth, even as a giggle escaped. “Really? The old ‘have you seen my beach ball’ chestnut?’ Shame,” she tsked, wagging her forefinger at him. “Shame, shame, shame.”

Brax dropped the pose, giving a negligent shrug, before grinning and hauling her in with his arms. She placed her hands onto his bare shoulders and he ran his own hands through her dark hair. “I’d do anything to see that smile. You know that right?” he whispered into her ear, nuzzling her neck and fighting the urge to purr like a kitten.

Sabre sighed, her weight falling against Brax’s. “You’re too good for me. *You* know *that* right?”

"Nope," he replied, giving her a squeeze. A hard one. "I'd say we'd rather evenly matched. An assassin who can't be beaten and a king who can't be hurt." He pulled back and gestured to his unblemished skin, of which, there was a lot on display thanks to the flamethrower.

Sabre ran her hands over Brax's chest, a thoughtful look on her face. "More like a reluctant assassin and a reluctant king."

Brax eyed her, wanting to smooth the frown lines on her forehead away. "Well, we all know *I'm* not a fan of this gig. The crown doesn't fit my head the same way a sword fits my hand. But are you really unhappy with your kill-kill life? I thought you enjoyed it."

Sabre's frown increased as she muttered, "I *do* enjoy kill-kill."

"What's the problem then?" he asked, noting they were relatively alone in the vast space of the training centre. Most of the Horde had dispersed and packed everything away. Draven was still over against the wall, looking comfortable and chilled as if he wasn't bored out of his skull and had nowhere else to be. And it was true, Brax knew, Draven was content to just *be*. Wherever Brax was, wherever Brax needed him, Draven would just *be*.

"Carlisle said I was created basically just to be a fuck-toy. Not literally, more like figuratively," Sabre admitted, pulling out of Brax's arms and ramming her hands onto her hips.

"He said I was expendable and created just to be fucked with, nothing more than a weapon."

"Did he just ..." Brax murmured, his hands clenching. When he finally got his hands on Carlisle, he was going to enjoy squeezing the life from the incubus's body.

"Yeah. And, well, it makes me want to rebel against the system, you know? Like, if the powers that be deliberately put me in the path of Carlisle to become some weapon, I want to say *fuck you and the horse you rode in on*. You know?" Sabre explained, pacing back and forth in front of him.

"I can understand that," Brax replied. "I even *feel* that. Being born royal comes with a set of pre-planned rules and expectations. Luckily for me, I was born second, and I've been able to meet those expectations with little angst for most of my life. I haven't had much reason to rebel against the system. That was until Mikhail kicked the bucket and I had to step up. Those are some big shoes to fill."

Sabre stopped her frenetic movement and looked down at Brax's feet. "Your feet are plenty big enough. Trust me."

Brax shrugged. "A means to an end." He knew he could say that and mean it without feeling suffocated because Mikhail was still alive. But had his brother not been ultimately going to take the crown back? Brax knew he would be feeling a whole lot differently.

"That's what I told Carlisle. That he was just a means to an end," Sabre said, biting her lip.

"And so he is. A means to facilitate your becoming the

best assassin in all of Purgatory. You *are* a weapon, Sabre. You are a *tool.* You were created with a purpose, just like all of us were. But that purpose was *not* to be Carlisle's. It was a to be a guardian. But not just any guardian – a guardian angel amidst a conspiracy to eradicate the royal line. You are a guardian born into a time of war, Sabre. That is why your path has been different. This is who you needed to be."

"You really believe that," Sabre stated, looking into Brax's eyes.

"I really do," he promised her. "I think you're perfect. Perfect for your job. Perfect for Mikhail. And more importantly, perfect for me."

Sabre looked at him, nodding her head. "You're right, that is more important."

"Damn straight," he told her firmly. Then he looped her arm through his as he began to walk out. "Besides, can you imagine being placed in the path of a bratty, teenage, demon prince and being forced to follow him around like a puppy as he struggled to learn how to hold a sword and which soup spoon to use at a banquet?"

Sabre barked out a laugh, shaking her head. "No. I really can't. I think I would have used the spoon to gauge out my own eyes from boredom."

"It was tempting," Draven spoke up, overhearing their conversation. He pushed himself away from the wall and joined them as they made their way out of the training centre. "Especially when Brax kept using the soupspoon to stir his tea."

Brax grunted and scowled. "Those teaspoons are so tiny. A soupspoon is a much more size appropriate for my hands. I'm a *demon*, Draven. Not a sprite."

Draven sighed and shook his head, disappointment in every line of his body. "This is what I've had to work with."

Sabre grimaced at Brax. "Yeah, you're right. I'm glad I only had to worry about which weapon was the pointiest and sleeping with one eye open so I didn't get garrotted in my bed. Dealing with spoons would have crushed my spirit for sure."

Brax loved the small nudge Sabre gave his shoulder before she walked off in front of him and Draven, calling out to Shiloh and asking her where she kept her weapons stash. "She really means that."

"She does," Draven agreed. "You're doing very well."

Brax looked at Draven. "Well? What do you mean?"

"Navigating a relationship. You've never had a relationship before, let alone one under such complicated circumstances. You're handling it well," Draven said.

Brax ran his hand through his hair, deciding he was going to need to trim it again already. "I hope so. It feels like I am most of the time. But then, Sabre gets this look ..." he trailed off, watching her as she spoke animatedly with Shiloh.

"She loves you. Perhaps even more than you love her," Draven pointed out.

"I believe that. I really do," Brax said quietly, but unable to shake the small, tense feeling in his gut. "I just hope it will be enough."

12

Two days of travelling had not put Sabre in good spirits. Despite joyriding in her car and speeding past every Demon Horde officer she could see, she did not arrive at the location of Lucifer's direct veil happy. Which meant the poor wendigo guarding the magical doorway copped her foul mood.

"Alba!" she shouted, finding the icky male lounging on a beach chair next to a rock in the middle of nowhere. "Call Lucifer right now and get him to open the veil."

Alba jolted, the beverage he was drinking spilling all over his shirt. It was the colour of blood but the consistency of a thickshake and Sabre really didn't want to know what was in the ghastly smoothie.

They were about two hours from the closest bumfuck

town in either direction, on a lonely stretch of road a few minutes off the main highway. A large rock in the shape of a koala was the only marker to indicate where the sole veil that opened directly onto the King of Hell's doorstep was. It was a good two-day drive from the main city that housed the palace and the den. Sabre could have accessed other magical doorways but none of them opened as close to Lucifer's house as the one guarded by the wendigo. And that would have meant a longer, more winding trip through Hell's many circles. Not to mention how time was sometimes whacky in Hell.

A couple of days after her interaction with Carlisle, her inner circle had called a council of war. Much to her chagrin, the circle seemed to be expanding and it now included an eighteen-year-old vampire, a dhampir who had once sexed up her man, a phoenix guard, and a douche angel with one gold feather. They had decided Lucifer was a good next step but Sabre had been unable to contact the other angel.

Communication between realms was not easy unless one had a magical device or could create portals. Such devices were reserved for witches and the like, and the beings who create portals were few and far between. Lucifer was one, Mikhail another. Unfortunately, Lucifer hadn't attempted to make contact for over two weeks and there was no handy dandy witch to give him a buzz so Sabre had been forced to drive out to Koala Rock and knock on Luca's door herself.

"Sabre!" Alba exclaimed, standing shakily from his chair. He almost knocked over the large, matching beach umbrella in his haste to rise. "Ah, long time no see."

"Not long enough," she assured him. She disliked the wendigo intensely. "Call Lucifer. Now." Alba was in possession of a magicked phone that could call Lucifer.

"Umm ..." Alba said, looking around the barren landscape.

Sabre pinched the bridge of her nose, digging deep for patience when what she really wanted was to be digging deep into Alba's intestines. "Alba, I'm going to be honest with you here. I'm in a bad mood. You see, I left the royal palace on a high. Me and my demon lover had just boinked against the wall in his office. We'd totally aced the whole simultaneous orgasm thing and had even communicated the shit out of our feelings. It was fab. But then, you see, I had two days of nothing but my own thoughts for company and now I'm feeling all needy and insecure. I have doubts and emotions and confusion. It's left me more than a little tetchy. So I suggest you do as I say."

"Oh, that's ... unfun," Alba responded.

"Unfun is exactly what it is!" Sabre agreed, pointing a finger at Alba's chest. "And just when did my life become unfun? You'd think multiple orgasms from a girthy dick would ensure life was decidedly *fun*fun. That's double the fun, in case you missed it," she informed Alba because he was a little slow on the uptake. "But no, turns out the girthy dick also comes with girthy problems that require higher reasoning. I've tried to cut out the feelings, but they just grow back."

Alba's eyes were wide, and he nodded his head very fast. "Uh-huh. Feelings aren't like limbs; they do tend to regenerate."

"They do," Sabre grumbled, kicking at the ground. "It sucks. But it only sucks when I'm not around Abraxis. When I'm close to him everything is clear. But when I have time in my own headspace my brain fucks it all up. Why is that?"

"It sounds like a trust issue to me," Alba offered.

"Trust? I trust Brax. The guy's one of the most trustworthy, genuine guys on the planet," Sabre was quick to reply.

Alba nodded. "I've heard that. Nice demon. I, uh, was talking about you. Not trusting *yourself*."

Sabre narrowed her eyes and tapped a cliff point blade against her temple. "I trust myself. I've had no one but myself to rely on for years. I've *had* to trust myself."

"Sure. Of course," Alba readily agreed, eyeing the blade warily. "What do I know? I know nothing."

"Hmm," Sabre grunted at him. "The last time an arsehole gave me advice I didn't want to hear I killed him before ripping out his trachea for my friend to eat."

"Ha!" Alba laughed, but it sounded strained. No doubt because he knew she wasn't lying or exaggerating. "Maybe, uh, stop asking random arseholes for guidance?"

Sabre snapped her knife closed, the sound echoing

between them and making Alba jump. "Now, *that* is excellent advice. So ... Lucifer?" she prompted, pushing all doubts and feelings from her mind.

Alba held up the ancient-looking phone. "It's ringing."

Five minutes later, Sabre found herself in front of Lucifer's door. But it wasn't the fallen angel who greeted her, it was his second in command, Alexis. Alexis was the demon lord of the innermost circle of Hell. She was curvy, busty, and as sweet as sugar ... until she wasn't. The demon was the granddaughter of Medusa and could turn a soul to stone whether they were corporeal or not. "Alexis, hi," Sabre greeted her.

"Hi, Sabre. It's good to see you," Alexis said, smiling widely. "I'm sorry you wasted a trip, but Luca isn't here."

The smile on Sabre's face slipped off. "Where is he? I really need to speak with him."

Alexis shook her head, the dark green strands of her hair flying in all directions. "I actually don't know. He up and disappeared about a week ago. He didn't even tell me where he was going. Just left a note saying he was fine and that he'd be back when he was back."

Sabre frowned, thinking it over, before deciding, "That's not like him."

Alexis's brow wrinkled. "I know. But things are heating up, getting weird. And considering we're in Hell, that's saying something."

"What do you mean?" Sabre asked. She was worried

about her old friend but also knew Lucifer could take care of himself. Now that she wasn't going to be able to talk with him, she felt more urgency to return to Brax. To where she felt steadier.

"There are more souls heading this way," Alexis admitted. "More than usual. From both Purgatory and Earth."

"More evil douches dying doesn't seem like a bad thing to me," Sabre said.

"That's just it, not all of them belong here. Some should have a first-class ticket to Heaven, but they're falling to Hell instead," Alexis explained, her hair giving a subtle hiss.

"I didn't think that was possible," Sabre said, confused.

Alexis shrugged. "It shouldn't be. There is a failsafe in place to prevent it. Multiple, actually. But I had to help a delightful little old human lady out of a vat of lava just yesterday. Fortunately, Esme had a sense of humour about the whole thing. But many don't."

"No, I don't suppose they would find being embroiled in lava amusing," Sabre allowed. The look she shared with Alexis said they couldn't personally understand it, because both women found a good broiling very entertaining. "Do you think it's related to the whole Cerberus killing spree thing?"

Alexis leaned her shoulder against the doorjamb of Lucifer's very picturesque house. "I think it's likely. I mean, only idiots believe in coincidences, right?"

"Right," Sabre agreed. "So we have dragons being killed

and now souls going to the wrong eternal resting place ..." Sabre shook her head, unable to piece together the puzzle into anything resembling order. "I don't get it."

"Neither do I," Alexis admitted. "But I'm working on it. I promise. I'm on your side, Sabre. Hopefully, when Luca gets back, he'll have some new insights."

"Maybe he will," Sabre permitted. "And thank you. I know I can always count on you and Lucifer. I won't waste any more of your time. Sounds like you're busy, especially with the boss going AWOL."

Alexis's pretty smile was strained now, and her golden eyes looked worried. "Very busy. I'll get Luca to call you or pop in as soon as he gets back."

"Thanks." Sabre fist-bumped the demon lord. "Later."

She was thinking too hard and muttering too loudly to herself when she first stepped through the veil to notice the huge, red stain on the flat rock face. It wasn't until she almost tripped over something on the ground that she looked up and saw what was an arterial spray pattern across the koala's broad tummy. Looking down, she found the glassy eyes of a very dead wendigo. "Fucking hell, now what?" she wondered, crouching and pulling out several weapons.

"Are you Sabre?" The light, lilting voice preceded the elf as he stepped out from behind the bloodied rock.

Sabre remained where she was, her only movement the

flicking of her gaze over the apparently unarmed male. “X, I assume?”

The elf smiled at her before giving a small bow. “At your service.”

13

Sabre watched the slender elf closely. He stopped moving far enough away from her that she couldn't simply grab him or kick him with her legs. A quick roll and a slash with one of her many blades, however, and she could take out his Achilles tendon in seconds. She did neither of those things. Yet.

He didn't look like much from the outside, she speculated. He was three inches shorter than her own six-foot-nothing, with brown hair, and brown eyes, wearing clean but non-flashy clothes. He was not outrageously handsome, but not ugly either. Overall, he screamed normal.

And that's the whole point, isn't it? she thought to herself. *You don't want to stand out in a crowd, you want to blend in.* Which was the complete opposite of his apparent business partner, Carlisle.

Studying the man in front of her with the muddy brown irises and the innocent expression, she looked deeper, not blinking, and barely even breathing. Micro-expressions were hard to read on some people, and her opponent was one of them. He was good at staring, she'd give him that. But she had all damn day. It took more than a few minutes to get the answers she was looking for but get them she did. And they chilled her blood. Because she may have no idea who X was, or why he was doing the things he was doing. But she knew *what* he was.

And that was one sick fuck.

She could see the calculation and intelligence in his eyes, and the charm to match them. It was a dangerous combination. It meant he was good at manipulation; he was good at getting what he wanted. She could also see the hubris, the smugness. He was confident because he'd already won – many times over. And he most definitely intended to keep on winning. He also had zero regrets. And the way he was standing there, a small smile tugging the corners of his mouth as if he knew exactly what she was doing, and that he loved her discoveries, caused her belly to jitter a little. Because she knew, she just knew, he was feeding her all of the above.

"Fuck," Sabre spat out. "You're an Ace."

And then, much to her horror, the man clapped his hands and laughed as if wholly delighted with her, proving her statement beyond a shadow of a doubt.

In the assassin game in Purgatory, an Ace was someone at the pinnacle of the profession. They were a savant, a virtuoso, a maestro. They were capable of destabilising an entire nation with nothing more than the words on their lips and the weapons on their body. They could infiltrate, manipulate, and assassinate as easy as walking down the street. And no one would ever know. Sabre was good. In fact, she was fucking incredible at what she did. But she wasn't an Ace. Why? Because she had a conscience and a moral code, despite what others might think. But the most significant difference?

I have a soul, she told herself. Something that was distinctly lacking in an Ace.

Sabre cursed as inventively inside her own skull as she could. She'd thought they had been dealing with a regular villain. Maybe some bored supernatural who was a child of divorce and didn't get enough hugs as a child. A guy who used his spare time to masturbate furiously to thoughts of mass destruction and images of broken crowns or some shit. But they were dealing with a guy who not only wanted to cause excruciating chaos but who was more than capable of it.

The one silver lining when dealing with an Ace? They had rather high opinions of themselves. She could use that. Where there was cockiness, there was an ego, and where there was an ego, there was a little boy that could be made to cry.

Rising slowly to her feet, she kept her weapons in plain view but didn't bother using them. They would likely do no good. And as much as it pained her, she was now on an information finding mission, rather than a capture or kill mission. Not that she wouldn't give it her best shot, of course. If an opportunity to maim the guy presented itself, she would run with it. But she was already getting annoyed with herself over the impending failure.

"Why X?" was the first question she asked, more to get him talking than anything else.

He shrugged minutely, keeping his face and voice bland. "Because Z was already taken."

"Cute," she acknowledged. She tried very hard to not think about how hurt Brax would be to hear his murdered baby brother spoken of so flippantly. "Why are you conspiring against the line of Cerberus?"

"Maybe I just think the line of Cerberus is outdated and could use some fresh blood?" It was a question, rather than a statement.

She listened intently and watched his expressions and his gestures. The man didn't so much as twitch or blink now. He was good. She had to give him that. "I don't think that's it at all."

"No?" he inquired, a hint of curiosity peeking through.

"No," she repeated. "You're being too patient for that. You're playing a long game. You're not in it for instant gratification."

"Oh, I assure you, the gratification from my kills has been very instantaneous," X murmured, looking a little dreamy.

"But not your ultimate goal," Sabre prompted before adding, "and not your *only* goal. So, how about you try that one again? I mean, new blood? It's like you're not even trying," Sabre goaded, smirking a little.

The elf stared at her with dead eyes for several seconds before he burst out laughing, clapping himself on the thigh. "Okay, okay, you win. That was a rather boring fake motive, wasn't it? But I figured I'd give it a shot. It worked well on your Master, after all."

Sabre rolled her eyes, snorting rudely. "Carlisle isn't exactly the sharpest tool in the shed."

"On that, we are in agreement," X allowed as he started to walk around her in a slow circle.

Sabre turned with him, not wanting to expose her back to the deadly, and she could quietly admit, *freaky* evildoer. She was not confident that she could take him. The knowledge burned her arse and was a hit to her own ego. It was also very bad timing, given how her inner cry baby was extra sensitive to being seen as a loser lately. But she wouldn't let her insecurities get her killed. There was something more to him than just an elf with a psychotic agenda. Something was definitely not quite right with him. She needed to figure out what it was.

"Tell me," X invited, "what do you know about the Founding Fathers?"

"The Founding Fathers?" Sabre asked, confused by the abrupt and random shift in the conversation. Not that she was willing to let it show of course. "Do you mean like the Founding Fathers of American history in the human realm?"

X waved an elegant hand, dismissing the notion. "No, no, no. Nothing as mundane as that. I'm referring to the Founding Fathers of the supernatural world, the *Forebearers* if you will. That is probably a more accurate title, and far less misogynistic, as I'm sure they weren't all male."

"The Forebearers ..." Sabre murmured. "The precursor to the seven major supernatural species of Purgatory?"

"Bingo," X declared, making pistol fingers at her. "It's true what they say about you; you're more than just a pretty face."

Sabre ignored *why* X was talking about the original supernatural beings for a moment. Instead, she focused on what she knew of her history of Purgatory, as well as the other planes. Her knowledge was probably better than most, she admitted. She wasn't just some uneducated assassin for hire. She was a guardian. And not just any guardian, but a guardian of the royal line. As such, it was her responsibility to not only know a *little* about a lot of things but a *lot* about a lot of things. King Maliq had ensured she'd had access to the royal library as well as a multitude of other resources. He wasn't taking any chances with the safety of his son. Or his sons' futures.

She knew there were reportedly six main species of

supernatural beings, or seven if humans were included. Which, she figured, they had to be given humans were able to wield magic as well. She knew each lineage could be traced back to the one progenitor of their individual gene pool, despite the many thousands of years of evolution. That one person was the Forebearer. "Demons, angels, humans, shifters, vampires, dragons, and fae," she listed them all off.

"Look at you with the history lesson," X smiled at her like a proud papa. "And you even included humans. Not many people do that."

Sabre sighed, doing her best to sound exasperated and impatient. It wasn't hard. "What about them?"

He paused his slow circling, tilting his head to the side. "Do you really expect me to give you more than that? If you think this is the part where I monologue about all my evil plans, hence giving you a chance to capture me or kill me, you can think again."

"Then what *is* going on now? What's your point?" Sabre demanded, carefully palming one of her perdu blades. The very pointy weapons were essentially invisible to the naked eye but they could pierce almost anything. They couldn't get through Brax's legacy from Cerberus – she had tried one sex-filled sunset – but anything other than that, they had a good chance of harming. Hopefully even Aces.

"I need to have a point?" X gasped, hand flattening against his chest.

"Oh, I dare say there is a point to everything you do,"

Sabre told him. "You wouldn't waste time or energy on something that wasn't important. So, why did you give me the information?" She had no idea what the Founding Fathers or the Forebearers had to do with anything, but she had little doubt that it was relevant to the grand plan.

X eyed Sabre for a moment before he revealed, "I'm bored."

Sabre blinked a few times before seeking clarification. "I'm sorry, you're what?"

"Bored," the guy enunciated the word carefully. "You were correct when you said I was playing the long game. In fact, I've been at this game for years and years." He began to circle her again, much like a shark circling its prey. "I was getting bored out of my skull if I'm being honest with you. If you hadn't shaken things up, my dear little assassin in disguise, *I* would have. You did me a favour. This is my way of thanking you."

"You are intent on wiping out an entire ancient line of royal supernatural beings, but it's boring for you," Sabre said humorously. "Wow, and I thought I was a little touched in the head."

X laughed, the sound light and happy. "It wasn't in the beginning. But it was definitely heading in that direction." A look of cruel calculation flashed in his eyes as he continued, "I mean, watching dear Abraxis lose that sparkle in his eye and that bounce in his step ... Well, that was gold. Braxy-boy turns Emo-boy. It was very entertaining."

Sabre's hands fisted reflexively when she heard her man being belittled in such a way. The fact that this fucker got off on Brax's emotional pain and trauma made her want to throw the perdu knife immediately. But there was still information to be gleaned, and an advantage to win. "I happen to think Brax looks good in black," was her only, level reply.

"Oh, he does. That is true. He withstood being the last remaining direct heir better than I thought he would, I admit. I knew I needed a little something extra to push him over the edge. I was about to kill that annoying angel of his when you came along and mixed things up entirely," X confessed.

Sabre perked up. "Draven? You were going to murder Draven? Don't let me stop a truly great plan."

The elf laughed, slapping his thigh again. Sabre tracked the motion with her eyes. It was the second time he had done that, meaning it was likely habitual rather than an act. She filed it away, along with any and all other tells and clues like the way he had said *Braxy-boy*. It was demeaning but also teasing, and Sabre knew that whatever this guy's motive was, at least a portion of it was personal.

"You see, this is why I like you," X told her. "Because you really mean that. You're just as deranged as me. And you make me laugh."

"I'm happy to be of assistance," she responded dryly, refusing to be drawn into a debate over his comments. She wasn't anything like him. And she didn't want to admit he was right about Draven, so she simply closed her mouth. *Besides, he's probably only half right about Draven these days,* she told herself.

"Good. And like I said, I'm in your debt. So ... get to work. Go play Sherlock. What could the Forebearers have to do with my dastardly plan?" X rubbed his hands together. "I'm sure we'll be seeing each other again soon."

"Wait!" she shouted as he made to move away. She was itching to throw her invisible blade at his hairline and see if she could scalp him, but they had been chatting for a while now and Alba's lack of scheduled check-ins might be noticed soon. She could find herself with back-up if she played her cards right.

"I'm afraid I really must be going," X said regretfully. "I'd hate for you to try something stupid and have to kill you. As I've said, you're good entertainment value."

"What about Carlisle?" Sabre said swiftly.

X paused, facing her fully once more. "Carlisle?"

Sabre thought fast, doing her best to keep X occupied. "Yes, where does he come into this?"

"Ah, the handsome incubus. Why don't you ask him?" he suggested.

"I'm trying to," Sabre admitted. "If I can only find him. Wanna help a girl out? Maybe tell me where the slug is hiding so I can pull his colon out of his arsehole?" She wasn't really good at coy or flirty, but she did her best. She kept her fingers crossed the whole time so it didn't count.

X laughed again, shaking his head. "You really are a delight. I can see why Abraxis likes you so much. Are you sure you don't want to switch sides? I can give you something Braxy-boy can't."

"I highly doubt it," she was quick to reply.

"Tsk, tsk, tsk," he tutted, wagging his finger at her. "So much blind faith in your man. He'll fail you. Just like he failed his brothers."

"Brax hasn't failed anyone," Sabre retorted.

X looked at her with something akin to pity in his eyes. "He has. First, he failed his big bro, finding him bleeding out on the floor like that. And then there was baby bro. Going up in flames in that nightclub? And Brax was helpless to do anything about it. What good is having an entire demon army at your disposal if you can't even save your own brothers?"

Sabre knew the same thoughts haunted Brax every waking hour. And in his sleep. He often muttered the names of his siblings when he was sleeping, trapped in a nightmare that was only too real when he awoke. She lost her logical head for a moment and took an aggressive step toward her adversary. "*You* did that to him. He didn't fail himself or his brothers. You set him up to fail."

"Perhaps you're right," X allowed. "But I'm not convinced it worked fully. After all, Miki isn't really dead, is he?"

Sabre's smile was savage now as she looked disdainfully

at the elf. “No. He’s not. But that’s not Brax’s fault, either. Is it? It's mine.”

Nobody had made a formal announcement declaring that Mikhail was still alive. They also hadn’t told anyone outside of their inner circle that she was indeed Mikhail’s guardian angel. But it hadn’t taken long for word of her resurrection powers to spread. It was a little hard to deny it when a bunch of people came back from the dead and were indebted to her. And there had been that showy thing she had done with her wings when she had been verbally sticking it to Carlisle. The rumour mill had done its job, putting two and two together, and Sabre was not so subtly talked about as being Mikhail’s saviour and guard.

The amused expression bled from X’s face the longer he stared at her. “You know I have to say, that was an epic surprise. Sabre the irredeemable angel. The antithesis of the divine blood pumping through her very veins. Sabre, thought by one and all to have had no Grace left in her sterile, broken wings. But then, *boom!* Plot twist. Not only is she still an angel filled with Heavenly Grace, but she's super fucking *righteous*. I mean, come on. All those gold feathers. You must have performed so many honourable acts to be gifted those beauties.”

Sabre didn't say anything, refusing to be drawn into the conversation. Because although the gold tips of her wings were in fact proof of her righteousness, they were also a reminder of the cost of doing her duty. It was a duty she conducted to the best of her ability. She didn't resent it. She wasn't even hurt by it anymore. But the *why* of it all had been plaguing her, thanks to Carlisle's words. Not to mention, the stress of the fine balancing act she was doing. It was easy to ignore the fact that she was Mikhail's before she was Brax's. That she had a bond and a responsibility to Mikhail that superseded her heart turning to goo. But she knew she was going to have to face it. And soon.

X continued when Sabre remained quiet, slowly walking around her once more. "And then there was the bomb you dropped; not only a righteous angel made from the hands of Heaven itself, but the guardian to the rightful king. The rightful king that, *gasp*," his hand flew to his mouth, "was murdered. You can't make this shit up. It's pure gold. I did not see that coming at all."

"You're welcome," Sabre spat out between clenched teeth, tracking him with her eyes and mirroring him step for step.

He smiled, no longer looking so ordinary, but more insane. "But be honest now, how does it feel to be a resurrection angel? That must be one hell of a burden. Your kind has been unseen and unheard of since the time of the original King of Purgatory – Cerberus himself – the Forebearer of all demons. Don't you think you're far too important to take on a lover? And perhaps more importantly, don't you think Mikhail is going to insist that your duties far outweigh falling in love?"

Sabre was so focused on the last two sentences that she didn't piece together the new kernel of information for a moment. She blamed it on the direct blow from X. Her fears and worries over being in love and over her shift in priorities, kept getting thrown in her face. If it wasn't her enemies reminding her of her predicament, it was Draven or even Brax – with his continued desire for open communication. When she finally did recognise that X had slipped up once more, the delay was just one more thing to blame for going 'soft' on.

Cerberus was the original demon. He was a Founding Father, she practically shouted to herself. Her hairs rose on the back of her arms, and she just knew this was the crux of the whole conspiracy. She was suddenly itching to talk to Mikhail about it, as well as Brax and all the others of course. But wanting to talk with Lucifer again was fast becoming more urgent. Because she knew for a fact that he was one of the first archangels to be created and he might have vital knowledge in his gorgeous head.

Feeling impatient now and knowing she had likely garnered as much information as she could, she threw her perdu blade without further thought. She aimed the small, invisible blade at X's stomach. She wanted to incapacitate, not kill. But the spry elf executed a flip and a roll, landing unscathed a few metres away.

He shook his finger at her again. "Now, now, Sabre. That was very naughty. I thought we were having a conversation here. And this whole time you were plotting my demise."

"I aimed for your gut, not your head. You wouldn't have died," Sabre informed X, more than a little annoyed that he had dodged her as effortlessly as Carlisle had.

"You called me an Ace," X reminded her. "Do you really think an Ace wouldn't be able to see a perdu knife? You've been holding it in your hand almost the entire time."

"So you have good eyesight. You're also very nimble," Sabre said, giving credit where credit was due.

X shrugged. "Elves are known for being nimble."

The twinkle in his eyes and the smirk on his face had her itching to slap him. Plus, there was just something about the way he'd said *elves,* a slight inflection that had her instincts screaming at her. She was missing something else important. She just knew it.

"You're looking a little flustered there, Sabre. You're not losing your edge, are you? Going weak?" he taunted.

She clenched her jaw, warning herself to let the words flow over her – and not *into* her – which was his intention. Sizing him up once more, she pulled a gun from her thigh holster. The safety was already off, which was very dangerous. She wouldn't recommend making a habit of that to anyone. Gun safety was very important. But she was in no danger of shooting her kneecap off. Not since she had learned that lesson the hard way at the hands of Carlisle when she had been a mere twelve years old. She pulled out a small vial from her pocket with her other hand and tipped the contents directly into the gun's barrel. It was saxitoxin, a paralytic agent. One Drop would be enough to render her prey immobile for hours.

X watched her movements with amusement and no fear at all in his eyes. "Enough playtime," he decided. "In fact, I think that's enough talk time, Sabre. The rapport we spent all this time building is crumbling as I watch you try to shoot me with a neurotoxin. I have one last word of warning for you. I'm coming for friends. I'm coming for your family. I am going to hurt them in ways even you can't possibly imagine. And I'm going to make you watch. If you thought being in love was brutal, wait until I rip out your lover's heart while he's still alive and place it at your feet."

Sabre was ashamed to see her hand shake and the gun wobble.

X smiled one last time at her. "Oh, yes. So very entertaining this will be."

"Like hell," she cursed. "I'm going to hurt you a little so that my friends – my *family* – can hurt you a lot."

He looked her dead in the eye and said, "Good luck," before literally disappearing into thin air.

"What the fuck?!" Sabre yelled, beyond furious. Elves had their own magic, it was true. But their magic wasn't an unlimited stream like their Fae relatives. They could not simply disappear like that. She stalked over to the place where X had been standing just seconds before, searching carefully but finding nothing. He was just gone, leaving no trace.

"Fuck!" she spat out, yanking on her hair hard enough to pull several strands from her scalp. She revelled in the sharp sting – it was far less than she deserved. Still, she carefully moved her gun away from her temple. The final nail in her coffin of shame would be if she accidentally paralysed herself only to be found next to a decaying Alba.

The opportunity to take out the Big Evil had been right there, but instead of shanking the motherfucker immediately, she had talked with him instead. *Talked!* "You're more than losing your edge, Sabre," she told herself, staring unseeingly at the bloody, koala-shaped rock. "You've already fucking lost it."

And she knew just who to blame.

14

Brax was pissed off and worried. It had been five days. Five. That was one day more than Sabre's little trip into Hell should have taken.

He paced back and forth along the tree line of the garden on the palace grounds where he now knew a secret tunnel was located. It was one of the ones Sabre had used to gain access to the palace – and to Mikhail – over the years. It was also the one she had used when she had met with him the first time. It held a somewhat sentimental value to him now. And to Sabre, he figured, because she used it when coming and going most of the time. Even though she could simply walk out the front gate.

"She's fine," Draven said from behind Brax where he was sitting on the ground with Styx's head on his lap.

Brax stopped his pacing and glared at his friend. "You don't know that."

Draven arched a single eyebrow, his demeanour unflappable in the face of Brax's tension. "Nothing short of an atomic bomb could stop that woman. And even then, I have a feeling it wouldn't be enough. Much like a cockroach."

"This isn't a joke, Draven," Brax snapped back. Styx's head lifted and he whined, ears flattening back against his skull. Brax sighed, feeling like shit. "Come here, boy." Styx got up and walked swiftly to Brax's side, leaning his substantial weight against his legs. "I'm just worried about Sabre," he told the hellhound.

"I wasn't being flippant," Draven said. He stood as well and dusted off his pants, even though there was no need. It was as if the pristine angel deflected the dirt and the leaves just by breathing. "She is capable."

"I know that. But she's not indestructible. I should have gone with her," Brax declared. He would have but the logistics just plain didn't work. He had all manner of kingly crap to do, but what's more, there was no way Sabre and Draven could have survived a road trip together. Even thinking about the prospect had been enough for Sabre to break out in hives.

"It's not your task," Draven informed Brax, responding to his previous statement.

Unfortunately, it was the wrong thing to say. Brax

rounded on his angel. "Not my task? To be there for my partner? To support her? To make sure she's safe?"

"Your paths can run parallel and not intersect all the time. That doesn't mean you're not meant to be together. That doesn't mean you can't be successful with life ... with love," Draven said, voice mild.

Brax shook his head, thumping Styx on the side in the kind of rough pat that he loved. Getting through the leathery hide of a hellhound was tough. "I'm not so sure. We don't have any problems when we ... *intersect*. But it seems like Sabre has a crisis of faith every time she's away from me. That can't be healthy."

Draven's blue eyes narrowed on Brax's face. "Are you sure it's Sabre's faith that is wavering?"

"What's that supposed to mean?" Brax demanded, getting more pissed by the second.

Draven shrugged, looking carefree and relaxed. "It seems to me that whenever Sabre is away, it is *your* doubts that creep in. You're worried she's going to be confronted with something, or someone, who will mess with the status quo."

"Because she inevitably does!" Brax shouted. "That is exactly what always happens. And I'm left trying to play catch up and clean up when she gets back."

Draven shook his head, looking disappointed. "You're not giving her enough credit."

Brax stared at Draven, agog. "Hold up. Are you on *Sabre's* side?"

"And here I thought you had been doing well," Draven mumbled. He walked to Brax and placed a hand on his arm. "I am on *your* side. As I have always been. As I *will* always be. I'm just saying don't borrow trouble. We have enough of it as it is."

Brax swallowed, feeling sick and nervous. "I know. That's part of the problem. We have all this trouble on our doorstep and none of it is getting resolved. Sabre doesn't do well with being ineffectual."

"She's not the only one," Draven told him. "How do you think Sabre feels when she goes off to fulfil her duties and returns to a worried and nervous partner?"

Brax opened and closed his mouth, at a loss for words because he was suddenly annoyed with himself. He looked at Styx. "How would you feel if I ran up to you and asked you how your trip into the forbidden forest every day was?" he asked the hound. Styx looked at him like he was a moron, quite literally rolling his eyes and lifting his upper lip in a snarl.

Styx took an almost daily sojourn into the forest that backed onto the palace grounds. It wasn't exactly forbidden as the name suggested, but most citizens chose to hike in other forests in Purgatory given all the weird noises and even weirder happenings amongst the trees. Styx loved the dark, dank trees even though his species was more suited to arid environments. Brax didn't know what he got up to in there, but he always came back happy. And smelling of dead things. And often with dead things still stuck in his teeth. Brax had worried about him when he was a pup but had since gotten over his concern. Because Styx was a big boy and more than capable of looking after himself.

Was Draven correct? Was he doing the same thing with Sabre, worrying unnecessarily and heightening tension?

"I can't *not* worry about her," Brax said in the end, looking at Draven.

"Of course not. You're in love," Draven stated. "But you could try not questioning her the moment you set eyes on her."

"I don't do that ... do I?" He winced even as he asked the question. Because yeah, he did do that. It seemed he was really good at talking the talk – telling Sabre how much he believed in her and accepted her just as she was. But he wasn't so good at walking the walk. "That must be really annoying."

"I'm sure it is," Draven confirmed. "Of course, it's hard not to ask questions when she comes back looking dejected and all unsure."

Brax shot Draven an annoyed look. "What the hell, man? Will you make up your mind? I'm either in the wrong or she is. Which is it?"

"Neither. And both." Draven shook his head, sharing a

commiserating look with the hellhound. "He's still not getting it."

"What aren't I getting?" Brax asked, trying to push back his frustration. It was hard. He kind of wanted to punch Draven in the face.

"You're acting like there's a fault, like one or both of you are lacking," Draven noted.

"Something *is* lacking," Brax exclaimed. "I figured I would be enough. That we would be enough *together*. I didn't think there would be constant insecurities to battle every time we weren't in eyeshot of each other."

"You *are* enough. And together, you are decidedly *more* than enough. These are mere teething issues. It's not as if you have been together all that long, despite the depth of your feelings for each other," Draven reminded Brax. "And keep in mind, you haven't really been tested yet. You've yet to meet up with Mikhail and come to terms with that betrayal, let alone navigate your relationship with Sabre when she takes on full-time guardian angel responsibilities with him once more."

Brax's rammed his hands on his hips, shooting Draven a sharp look. "You are just a ray of fucking sunshine. Here, how about I turn around so you can have easier access to my back. You know, to drive that knife of yours in a little deeper."

"Good Lord," Draven grumbled. "You are so dramatic."

"I'll show you dramatic," Brax vowed, rolling up his

sleeves. Draven was saved from a serious mauling by a rustling sound from behind him.

"There, she's back," Draven soothed unhelpfully. "Perhaps try saying hello without demanding to know every tiny detail of what happened and looking for scratches or cracks that are irrelevant."

Brax didn't bother to answer Draven, he spun and sighed in relief when he found Sabre standing at the base of a huge tree, that was really the entrance to the tunnel. "You're back," he said, biting his tongue to leave it at that.

"I am," Sabre concurred. She made no attempt to move closer.

Brax's stomach dropped and everything he and Draven had just talked about flew out the window. Something was wrong. Of course. Just as he had predicted. It was like a self-fulfilling prophecy – his worst fears always came to fruition. Still, he held back his questions. "I was expecting you yesterday."

"I took an extra day to think about a few things," came Sabre's flat response.

"What kind of things?" Brax queried.

Sabre pushed away from the tree, absently patting Styx when he trotted over to her. "Like what I'll do when he comes for you. Or Jinx. Or Gage. Or even that fucktard of an angel of yours."

"What do you mean? He? He, who?" Brax was doing his

best to follow but felt like they had started in the middle of a conversation instead of the beginning.

"I was stupid to think a little warning by way of skin carving was going to keep them away," Sabre said, seemingly more to herself than to Brax. But then she looked up, those sugarplum eyes of hers locking onto his. "He will come for you."

Brax shrugged, trying to appear confident and unaffected, but Sabre was worrying him. He promised, "And I'll be ready."

Sabre shook her head sadly. "I don't think so. You're not ready for this. Not ready for the likes of *him.* I mean, that fucker was right in front of me, and I still couldn't stop him."

"Fucker? Are you talking about Carlisle? I thought we covered this. You can't physically harm him, Sabre," he countered, suddenly feeling exhausted.

"Not Carlisle. X."

Brax reared back. "Wait ... You found the elf?"

"He found me," Sabre corrected him darkly.

"Where? When? Are you okay?" He moved in to look her over, only for Sabre to back up maintaining space between them. He took a deep breath, trying to keep his impatience and temper at bay.

"He was at the veil. He killed poor, stupid Alba. Lucifer was nowhere in Hell, by the way. Nobody knows where he is," Sabre tacked on.

"Okay. Alba, who I don't know, is dead. Lucifer, who I

also don't know, is missing. And you met X. Am I following?" Brax did his best to sum everything up when all he really wanted was for Sabre's face to show a little animation. To show a little love.

Sabre nodded her head, face still expressionless. "You are. The elf doled out a few nuggets of random information, which are probably really important in the grand scheme of things, but which I don't really give a shit about anymore. Because he also made some not so veiled threats about you and the others. He also pointed out how ineffectual I'm going to be to protect you and Mikhail because I'm trippin' so badly."

"You are not tripping! Gods, Sabre! You are no weaker now than what you were before you fell in love with me," Brax all but shouted. Poor Styx hunkered low onto his belly, his great hammer of a tail thumping nervously against the ground.

"Don't you get it, Brax? I failed. Again!" Sabre yelled back. "He was right there in front of me, just like Carlisle. And I let him get away."

"He escaped, Sabre. You didn't *let* him do anything. It doesn't make you a failure. Not capturing X when you were alone without backup does not make you a failure," Brax told her firmly. Her resulting laugh, full of scorn and disdain, had his hackles rising.

"Yes. That is exactly what it makes me. He's going to come after you. He's going to come after *all* of you. And you know what? I can't be here to see it. I'm just not strong enough for that."

Brax felt his fangs elongate and a snarl rumbled in his throat. "What are you saying?"

"I can't stay here, Brax. I can't be with you. And it's not all because of the threat of an Ace gunning for you either," Sabre revealed. She continued on before Brax could question the Ace comment. "I've been kidding myself. My life as a created angel is not my own and never will be. I was sent to Purgatory as a child for one specific purpose, and it wasn't to fall in love," she delivered the blows to Brax's heart with a flat voice. "I am a guardian. I am a shield. I am a tool. You said so yourself."

"I did," he acknowledged. "But –" Sabre cut him off.

"I am all those things for someone who isn't *you*, Brax. It's Mikhail I am bonded to – not Mikhail's *brother*. It's Mikhail I'm indebted to – and will be for the rest of my life. Mikhail has to come first," she said.

"What? Since when did this become a competition with my brother?" Brax demanded confusedly. He was trying his best to keep up with the argument. And also keep his lunch down because he felt like he was going to throw up. "I've never once said I have a problem with you being his guardian. I understand that. It's a non-issue."

"It's a non-issue *now*," Sabre retorted angrily. "Now, when you're not in the same space. When I'm not torn between wanting to be with you and protect *him* at the same time. But what happens when we're faced with that, huh? Who do I choose? It has to be Mikhail, Brax. Not you."

Draven voicing the same concerns just minutes prior weighed heavily on his mind, but he brushed them aside, fighting to find the answer Sabre needed to hear. "We'll deal with it when it happens. I have faith in us." But he felt her slipping farther and farther away from him. Even though they were mere inches apart. "Besides, I don't need your protection. I just need *you*. I need your love."

"I do love you, Brax. I won't ever deny that. But it isn't enough. Hell, it's not even *right*. I would kill anything that harmed you. I would die for you," Sabre told Brax with the seriousness of a vow. "But that is supposed to be reserved for your older brother." She then added in a thready whisper, "Not that it's going to matter when an Ace storms the palace gates."

Brax grabbed her biceps and gave her a small shake. "Did you hear what I said? I don't need you to kill for me. I'm more than capable of doing that myself. But if you think so little of my abilities, I'll remind you that I have a guardian angel of my own. I don't need another one." But she clearly wasn't listening. She shrugged him off and took a few steps backwards. "Don't even think about running from me, Sabre. I'm warning you," he growled.

Sabre raised her chin, flipped him off, turned, and sprinted to the tunnel entrance.

"I don't fucking think so," Brax roared, giving chase. He

caught up to her within a few strides. She was fast and canny, but she was also hurting just as much as he was. Whether she wanted to admit it or not. He tackled her to the ground, fighting off her flailing arms and legs. The blows rebounded off his legacy, causing no physical harm. But the wounds to his heart, and to his soul? Those were another matter entirely. He finally managed to pin her arms above her head, straddling her in the dirt. The wench had the audacity to try to bite his nose off when he lowered his head to hers.

"Calm the fuck down!" He snapped his own teeth at her, aware his eyes were glowing like hellfire. "You want to talk about being weak? That's what this is, this *fear* that you're feeling right now. It's a weakness. You're running from me. Me! Do you really think I'm going to let you go?" he demanded. "You are *mine!*"

"Get off me! I'm not sticking around to watch you get slaughtered. I'm not giving Mikhail the chance to break us up," Sabre shrieked into Brax's face. Her breath was coming in short pants and her chest was rising and falling rapidly.

The whole thing was so out of character for her that Brax was beginning to get worried for a whole other reason other than their relationship status. "Sabre ..." he gentled his voice and his grip on her arms. "Will you listen to yourself? You're saying you would rather walk away now than give us a chance because you're scared of what might happen in the future."

"Scared? This isn't me scared, Abraxis. This is me terrified. And confused. I'm a predator who lets her prey escape. I'm a guardian angel in love. What the fuck was I thinking? There is no way this was ever going to work out." Sabre practically wheezed when she drew in her next breath.

Brax moved off her quickly, worried he'd squashed her lungs or something with his weight. He was no small man. Her breath began to come in faster pants, yet she appeared to find it impossible to fill her lungs. "Sabre? What's going on?" She didn't answer and Brax threw his head back, yelling, "Draven!"

Draven dropped from the sky in a flurry of white feathers a few seconds later. Reaching out a hand, he laid it on Sabre's pumping chest. He swore. "She's having a panic attack."

"A panic attack? Impossible," Brax automatically refuted the claim. Sabre wasn't susceptible to panic attacks. She was too hardcore for that. Too confident. Still, he pushed Draven closer to her. "Fix her!"

Draven shook his head, looking apologetic. "It's too late for that. But she'll be fine," he assured Brax.

Looking down, Brax realised that Sabre had already passed the fuck out. He fell backwards from his haunches onto his arse, staring at her beloved, pale face. "What a mess."

"I'll say," Draven agreed, looking at Brax with recrimination. "This is not what I had in mind when I told you to say hello."

Brax flashed his fangs at the angel. “Go to Hell, Draven. She wants to leave me.”

“Perhaps you should let her,” Draven suggested, placing gentle, healing hands on Sabre’s forehead.

Brax lost what little control he had been hanging onto and grabbed Draven by the front of his shirt. “I will *never* let her go. She is *mine* ...”

Draven calmly pried Brax’s fingers off one by one, telling Styx he was a good boy from where he was watching the pathetic show with sad, anxious eyes. “Well, if that’s the case, you have nothing to worry about. Do you?”

15

The following day, Brax wasn't feeling so sure of himself. All of his growly alpha proclamations of *mine* didn't amount to shit when he had no idea where his woman was. Or what he was going to do to repair their mutual damage.

He was sitting at the long, stained wooden bench in the warehouse where he had first introduced himself to Sabre. Gage's home was the epicentre for illegal street fighting in Purgatory. Back when he had first met Sabre, he had been revolted with such a place. Not because of the violent acts that took place there, nor the number of lives that were taken there. No, he had been ashamed because his father had dedicated so much time to eradicating organised crime. Mikhail had done a good job of holding it at bay during his reign, and Brax had played an active role in policing it. But then, that had all ceased when he had been crowned King. With his blatant disregard for his people, the criminal underbelly had re-emerged. Gage's establishment was one of many and felt like a lighthouse shining its bright lights directly onto Brax's failures.

But what had made it all worse at the time, was that he hadn't given a shit. All he'd cared about was hiring Sabre so he could get his revenge on the person who had ruined his life, and the lives of his family members. It was blind luck that things had been moving in a positive direction, rather than circling the drain. Mikhail was not dead. He had found the love of his life in Sabre. He had new friends and family. But none of that was really thanks to him at all. Sabre was the one responsible for it. *She* was the one making it all possible. Why couldn't she see that? Why couldn't he *make* her see that? Instead, he was tackling the woman and giving her panic attacks.

I'm just not enough for her, he thought, now at a point that was beyond even depression.

"I thought I might find you here," Gage said.

Brax whipped his head up to find Gage walking towards him with Jinx and Eric in tow. Draven had been sitting silently at one of the small tables. His guardian would not allow him to sulk in private, but at least Draven *had* been allowing him to sulk. "How?"

Gage shrugged, moving behind what amounted to his

bar. "Whenever men have female troubles, they always seek out a bar."

"There's no booze here," Brax pointed out, more than a little resentfully. He could really use a drink.

"Semantics," Gage responded.

"So ..." Jinx began, sitting next to him on one of the high stools. "Sabre finally did it, huh?"

Brax grunted, not really in the mood to discuss his love life with a teenager. But he also didn't want to be rude. It wasn't Jinx's fault that his relationship with Sabre was going down the toilet. "Did what?"

"Fucked up," Jinx and Gage answered simultaneously.

"I don't know if it's her so much as me," he admitted. "Maybe I'm not right for her, not the type of male she needs."

"You are exactly what she needs. Do not let *her* self-doubts become *your* self-doubts," Jinx all but commanded him. "You are her perfect complement. Her balance. She needs you, Abraxis."

"I used to think so," he admitted. "I thought I could help her. I thought we could help each other. You know, fill in each other's cracks. The Heavens know we both have them. But that was stupid. I mean, that would be co-dependency at its finest, right?" Brax laughed scornfully at himself. "And we all know Sabre won't let herself depend on anyone."

"Hey," Gage said, tapping Brax on the arm. He waited for Brax to make eye contact before he continued. "What you call co-dependency, I call family." He shrugged, dark eyes reflecting the dull lights overhead. "There's nothing wrong with depending on people. Or being dependable for that matter. And that's what you are. Dependable."

"If I'm so dependable, why can't I help Sabre?" he asked, not expecting an answer.

"Who says you have to? What makes you think that's your job?" Jinx fired her questions at him. "You told her that you loved and accepted her just as she was, that she didn't need to change. Did you mean that?"

Brax opened and closed his mouth a few times, a little dumbstruck. Jinx was making a fine point. "I meant it," he confirmed.

"Uh-huh, then why are you banging on about filling in cracks and having a cry instead of going out there and slapping some sense into an insecure, head-fucked assassin?" Jinx wanted to know.

"Umm ..." He looked over his shoulder at Draven, pleading for help with his eyes. But Draven must have thought this was a teaching moment or some such bullshit because he merely lifted a single shoulder.

"Well? Answer the woman, Abraxis," Draven prompted. "We're all waiting."

"I don't know," Brax finally admitted, glaring daggers at his guardian. "Because I'm a moron?" he suggested, taking a stab at it. "Though, I'll remind you I *did* tackle her to the ground yesterday and go all fangy in her face. I asserted myself."

Jinx snorted, verifying, “That you are. A moron, I mean. And as for the ‘crack’ nonsense and not being good enough pity party that you are intent on throwing yourself, I used to think the same thing. About myself. And do you know who snapped me out of it?”

“Uh, yourself?” he guessed. “Because you are a wise and noble queen?”

Jinx smiled at him, pinching his cheek. “Nice sucking up. But no. It was Sabre.” Her mood turned melancholy, and she turned her face away, her gaze distant as if she was seeing something no one else could. “When Sabre first found me, I told her not to bother trying to save me. I told her I was broken, that I had cracks everywhere. And do you know what she said?" The question was rhetorical because she continued on without waiting for an answer.

"She told me cracks were a good thing. That cracks allowed light to shine through. She told me she'd never seen anyone shine as brightly as I did when she found me, filthy and abused, in that brothel. And I should celebrate my cracks, I should be proud of them. Because that's how light gets *out*. And that's how light gets *in*. Through cracks, through holes, through *wounds*."

Jinx smiled small, her expression filled with both pain and joy. "Sabre then said she had no cracks. That there were no chinks in her armour. And so, nobody would ever see her shine – or fill her with light." Jinx turned her now eerily glowing eyes to Brax. "But she was wrong. You're her crack. You're her chink. You're her light, Abraxis."

Brax swallowed, averting his eyes. Sabre didn't need him to fill in what she was missing. "She needs me so she can shine," he murmured, more to himself than anyone else. The revelation made him angry because that had been his goal from the moment he had met her. But somehow, he had allowed Sabre to talk him out of it. "How did she do that?" he then muttered, thumping the bar with his closed fist.

"She's tricksy," Gage supplied.

Brax looked up at the zombie. "She *is* tricksy," he agreed, thrusting a finger in Gage's face to emphasise his point.

"Don't give up on her," Gage then added.

"I would never do that. I may have insecurities, but I would never give up on Sabre. I will never let her go," Brax vowed. "And I won't allow her to push me away again either."

"Good," Jinx praised, smiling like a proud mama.

"The only problem now is, how to convince her of that," he said. Nobody responded and Brax figured the well of wisdom had run dry. Until a male throat cleared.

"Uh, I have a suggestion."

They all turned to Eric, Brax cursing silently in his head. He had all but forgotten the young vampire was there. He would never have spoken of such things or exposed so much of his raw emotions had he noticed that Eric was sitting quietly at one of the small round tables. He liked the kid, he really did. He had an innocent, vulnerable vibe about him that made people want to be around him. Including Brax. In fact, Eric reminded him of Zagan when he had been young, younger than Eric was now.

Zagan had always been their mother's favourite, but he hadn't always been a spoiled brat. Brax felt some guilt thinking ill of his dead baby brother, but the practical side of him reminded him that dying didn't change the actions of the living. And while he'd been alive, Zagan had been a party boy – and a selfish one at that. Brax had loved him of course, fiercely. And he could admit that he had been one of the many people who had indulged Z. As had Mikhail.

As the last-born triplet, Z had been smaller than both Brax and Mikhail and had been rather sickly for a while as a child. He never did reach the heights or weights of Mikhail or Brax. As a kid and a young teen, Z had been happy, easy-going, and playful. He had loved to make jokes and was very affectionate, always hanging off someone. Eric was much the same, Brax had noticed. He thrived when he was given affection, soaking up the attention like a sponge did water.

Yes ... Brax thought now as he looked at Eric, who ducked his head shyly under the continued scrutiny. *He definitely has a 'little brother' vibe*. And it made Brax want to step into the role of big brother all too readily.

Was that why he had been ignoring the teen? Because he made Brax feel something he didn't want to? Something that caused pain and grief, but also the potential to feel fulfilled in the unique way of an older sibling once more? Brax winced, feeling like a dick. He'd been punishing the kid because he brought out feelings that had died with his younger brother. The others had embraced him with open arms, including Sabre. Though she was cautious, she had still liked him enough to vouch for him and give him a chance. And now, Brax decided, he was going to start doing the same.

"Eric," he said, gesturing him over, "what are you doing over there? Come and sit with us."

Eric looked surprised, even going so far as to look behind him as if there was another vampire called Eric in the empty warehouse. He approached the long bench tentatively, sitting quickly next to Jinx, who gave him a warm smile. The kid smiled back, looking shyly at Brax.

Yeah, I feel like a dick, Brax decided, sharing a look with Draven. Draven nodded back, easily able to read Brax's thought process. He knew why Brax had been hard on the new addition, and also agreed with him putting in the effort now.

Draven stood up and made his way closer as well. "You've done well," he assured Brax, patting him on the back.

Not yet, he thought to himself. *But I will.* Out loud he queried, "What's your idea?"

"It's probably silly. I didn't mean to overhear, and I don't want to butt in. I wasn't eavesdropping on purpose," Eric said in a rush, his sentences running into each other.

"Relax," Brax rumbled. "I know that. It's all good. I genuinely want to hear your idea."

"Yeah," Jinx added, giving Brax a teasing wink. "He needs all the help he can get with Sabre, trust me. That woman has a harder head than a gargoyle."

Everyone laughed at that, including Brax, because it was true.

"Well, I thought maybe you could get her a gift," Eric suggested. "Chicks dig gifts. And, well, it doesn't sound like she's had many of those." He shrugged his still-thin shoulders. "I know I haven't."

"A gift?" Brax repeated. He thought about it for a moment and knew for a fact Sabre wouldn't have had the opportunity to be given gifts before. Knowing his brother, he was sure Mikhail would have made some effort to do so over the years. But it wasn't like Sabre could keep anything personal or of significance in the den when she was undercover. Although, she did have a secret evil lair, as she liked to think of it, here in the warehouse. It had dozens of objects that Sabre had squirreled away over the years and secretly coveted. There was likely a thing or two from Mikhail, and even Jinx and Gage in there.

He turned to her friends. "What do you think? Would Sabre like a gift? What would I get her?"

Gage shrugged, clearly thinking it over. "She doesn't

respond to gifts very well. At least, she hasn't in the past. But it's not like it can do much harm. As for what, I have no idea. A weapon?"

"That would suit her," Draven readily agreed.

Brax was about to agree as well when he saw the look of pain on Eric's face. "What? What's with the look?"

"Dude, no," was Eric's reply. "Just no."

Brax scowled, crossing his arms over his chest. "And what is wrong with a weapon? Sabre loves them. So much so that she sleeps with them. It's a little disturbing now that I think about it," he added, causing Draven to roll his eyes and Jinx to giggle.

"Of course she loves weapons. She's a killing machine. But that's not all she is," Eric pointed out. "And that's kind of the point of your whole deep and meaningful, girl talk here. I promise you, it's the heart of the issue for her – what has her so churned up and inside out. She's trying to reconcile the past Sabre with the present Sabre. Then, there's the future Sabre to worry about. It's a lot, man."

Brax opened and closed his mouth a few times, staring at Eric before he was able to speak. "That was a very effective verbal spanking."

Eric's eyes widened, and he held up his hands. "No, no, no, I wasn't trying to spank you. I ..." he broke off, face turning red when everyone laughed.

"Relax, that isn't what I meant. I just mean you summed up our entire relationship issue in just two sentences. Maybe you should be a shrink," Brax teased, causing Eric to blush further.

"Besides, the way I hear it, Brax is the one spanking Sabre," Jinx informed everyone. "Though, I believe she's planning to turn the tables very soon. I'd be on high alert for that if I was you," she told Brax.

"My ears," Draven said, touching them. "Are they bleeding?"

Everyone laughed, Brax giving his angel a healthy shove. "You're hilarious. You're *all* hilarious. And you, Eric, are apparently wise beyond your years. So, come on, tell me what to get her."

Eric levelled his grey eyes on Brax, gaze direct and serious now. "I'm not going to do that. That would undermine the whole point. Get her something that will speak to *all* parts of her. Something she's always wanted but never had. And something that she can take with her into tomorrow."

Brax inhaled deeply, nodding his head. "Okay. I'll do that. Thank you," he said quietly.

Draven reached up and patted Eric on the shoulder. "You're a good addition to the family. Welcome aboard."

Eric ducked his head, but not before Brax saw the sheen of tears in his eyes.

16

Sabre was sitting on the sparkly bedspread in a pink, lacy nightgown, listening to Celine Dion as she ate chocolate by the kilogram. She was miserable, pure and simple.

After giving Brax the old heave-ho, and humiliating herself by hyperventilating until she passed out, she had retreated to her secret lair of rainbows and sequins. She consoled herself that she had done the right thing. Mikhail *was* her priority. Brax *was* in danger because of her. She *was* fucking useless. But she didn't feel comforted. She felt like shit.

Groaning, she fell onto her back, throwing her hand over her stinging eyes. Back in the day, when things hadn't been complicated by love or lust, she would simply hack someone up to release her frustrations. But now she was eating her way into a sugar coma, dressed in frills and she *still* didn't feel good. Hell, she had even brought out the big guns and watched a rom-com. But she didn't feel like she had made the best choice for the good of everyone involved. She felt like she had made a horrible mistake. She felt like she was missing something.

"I *am* missing something," she said out loud. "My heart."

"You can have it back if you want."

Sabre sat up so fast her head spun. Looking towards the door, she found the object of her misery – and her joy. Brax looked as shitty as she felt. She was just petty enough to feel good about that. "How did you get in here?" she demanded cattily, instead of throwing herself at his feet and crying like the little bitch she was.

"I opened the door. It wasn't locked. And it's not really a secret lair, remember?" he replied dryly.

"It's secret if you don't know it's here," she returned. Even Carlisle had been unable to access it throughout the years.

Brax looked around, no doubt taking in the messy chaos of colours, cushions, blankets, and weapons. "What have you been doing in here? It looks like a demented clown vomited."

"I've been having a pity party and nursing my broken heart," Sabre replied, scowling at him.

Brax's yellow eyes came to rest on Sabre, moving up and down her body. "That explains the chocolate smeared all over your face. And like I said, you can have your heart back. Or you can fix it. Or whatever cute analogy is going to cover the situation."

"Brax..." she began.

"Wait," he interrupted her. "Don't say anything yet. Let me go first."

Sabre bit her lip and nodded. She scooted her butt over, making room on the bed beside her. He sat down, eyeing the fluffy blankets like they were about to jump up and attack him. "They're just blankets, Brax."

"Is that what they are? I thought maybe you had gone and skinned a unicorn or something," he muttered, picking up a cream throw rug with pastel stripes and tossing it onto the floor with a shudder.

Sabre gasped. "I would never skin a unicorn. Their fur isn't as soft as it looks. It's deceptively coarse."

They looked at each other before bursting into laughter and it wasn't long before Sabre found herself crying against Brax's strong chest. He held her tightly, his muscular arms better than any security blanket she could ever hope to find. He was real and strong and solid, his heart beating a steady rhythm underneath her ear. She found herself bewildered about how she had thought to ever give him up. "I think I lost my mind for a minute or two yesterday ..."

Brax drew back so he could see her face but didn't release her. "I think I did too. I'm sorry."

Sabre shook her head, her hair long enough on the top

now to flop into her eyes. She pushed it back. “No, I’m the one who’s sorry. I’m sorry I keep second-guessing you. And us. And myself. I don’t know why I keep doing that.”

“Because your life is in a time of great flux right now. Because you have more to lose than ever before. Because you are justifiably afraid of the future. Because I keep patting you on the head and telling you it’s all going to be okay, brushing off your concerns and hoping you’ll just get over them. But it doesn’t work that way. Fears *fester,*” Brax said.

“Yes,” Sabre nodded her head. “Yes, to all of that. That’s how my mind has felt recently – like it’s been festering. Add in Carlisle and X threatening to take you away from me ... I haven’t been the best version of myself.”

“Neither have I,” Brax whispered as if he was in a confessional. “I think that’s what scared me the most. We love each other. My soul has claimed you as my mate. We should bring out the best in each other, right?”

Sabre frowned, watching Brax’s face closely. She had thought they were well on their way to some serious make-up sex. But did Brax still have doubts? Wasn’t this the big post-angst scene where they reaffirmed their undying love for each other? She said as much.

Brax smiled at her, and it reached his eyes. “Oh, this is definitely that scene. And the make-up sex is going to be mind-blowing. But it’s been brought to my attention that we don’t need to keep trying to prop each other up all the time. We’ve been doing that just fine for ourselves for years now.

We're still just Sabre and Brax. We can be a team but still be individuals. That means you're allowed to be scared and you're allowed to feel anxious. And I'm allowed to be insecure about my current kingly position as well as the mate to the most self-sufficient female in all of Purgatory."

"We're allowed?" Sabre asked, double-checking for permission.

"Yep."

Sabre sagged against Brax once more. "Thank fuck for that. So, all this? All the fear and the pain and the anger? It's all normal?" It didn't really sit right with her that something that felt so damn horrible was normal, but what did she know.

"It's normal. Teething problems. Growing pains. The post-honeymoon period," Brax ticked each item off his fingers. "Plus, a certain tiger promised me I was your crack. I'm going to let you shine, Sabre. In every way."

Sabre stilled, recalling the day she had found Jinx and telling her that it was her imperfections, her broken pieces, that allowed her light to break free. She had meant every word. "You're my gaping wound, my biggest vulnerability. But it's not a bad thing. It's a good thing," she told Brax.

"Sure," Brax readily agreed, grinning cheekily at her. "Because gaping wounds will always be a good thing to you."

Sabre grinned back, admitting, "I do like visceral soft tissue trauma."

They were both still smiling when their lips met, content

to move them slowly and bask in finally feeling *free.* Just as Sabre was about to push Brax's t-shirt up, he pulled away. She pouted a little, pointing at the mattress. "This is the part where we get our freak on."

"I have my freak flag handy, I assure you. But first ..." He pulled a small box out of his back pocket. "I got you a gift."

Sabre found herself shocked. Again. "A gift?"

"Hasn't anyone ever given you a gift before?" Brax asked, placing the prettily wrapped box in Sabre's lap.

Sabre looked down at the box, really thinking about her answer. Jinx and Gage had given her gifts here and there over the years on occasions like her birthday. But she had tried her best to not make a big deal out of it. Likewise, whenever Mikhail tried to give her something, she had typically threatened to hurt him. Because gifts made her feel hella awkward. "What's it for?"

"Eric suggested a gift might be more useful than words under the circumstances. Turns out the kid is rather astute," Brax said.

"Eric recommended a bribe?" She was surprised.

Brax's brow wrinkled and he shook his head. "It's not a bribe. Not really. I mean, sure, it's definitely an, *I'm sorry,* and an, *I love you,* gift. But it's also more than that. I wanted you to have something you could carry with you always. So that when we're apart, and those insidious fears begin to creep back in, all you need to do is look down. And you'll see this," he tapped the box with his forefinger. "And it will remind you of who and what you have waiting faithfully for you at home. Always."

Brax took the box from her lax fingers, pulling the bow off and opening the lid. Sabre felt her breath catch in her throat and her hands rose to cover her open mouth. Nestled in black crepe paper was a key. But no ordinary key. It was about an inch and a half long and as wide as her thumb. It shined dully with a matte finish and was kind of grey-looking at first glance, but she could make out the rainbow of colours when the light hit it just so. The rounded end was embedded with three beautiful yellow stones that matched Brax's eyes to perfection.

She picked it up with a shaking hand, finding that it was attached to a strong chain. She ran her fingers over it reverently, her eyes flicking to his. "Is this made out of the same material as your exoskeleton?"

Brax shrugged. "I think so. It sure looks like it, doesn't it? I dug this out of the royal vault. I remembered my father showing it to me once. He told me he was keeping it safe for me, that I would find the perfect person to give it to one day." He smiled, looking happy but also nostalgic. "It's rumoured to have belonged to the very first Queen of Purgatory. Cerberus had this made for his mate. So I guess if anyone could have fashioned a key from vibramantium, it would have been him."

"It's ... incredible," Sabre said thickly.

"It's not just really old," Brax was quick to explain,

looking adorably nervous. "It's also symbolic like I said. As in, you hold the key to my heart, or my happiness, or my future, or ... uh, everything really." He exhaled, those gorgeous peepers of his locking onto hers. "It's stupid, isn't it?"

"It's not. It's really not," she assured him. "I love it. I love you." Then she threw her arms around him and kissed him. He kissed her back but she didn't allow things to get carried away. She wanted to try on her new gift first. Pulling away from his tasty lips, she stood up and held the chain out to Brax. "Will you put it on me?"

Brax took the chain and moved behind her. Sabre looked straight ahead, noticing they were in front of the mirror. Which meant she had a front-row seat to watching the tip of Brax's tongue stick out in concentration as he undid the clasp. He then draped the chain over her neck, not needing to move her hair out of the way because of the short pixie cut on the sides and back. He took the task of fastening the necklace seriously before he smoothed the metal against her skin. Sabre watched his hand move slowly from the nape of her neck, over her collarbone, and down into the hint of her cleavage where the key rested perfectly against her breastbone.

He told her softly, "These are yellow diamonds by the way. Between these and with the key being made from Cerberus's legacy, it should be pretty much indestructible."

"Like you," Sabre responded, her own voice quiet.

"Like my love for you," Brax corrected.

Sabre whimpered. If she'd made such a sound just the day before, she would have been mortified. But now, feeling the weight of the most perfect gift in the history of thoughtful gifts, against her skin, right next to her heart, she simply went with it. Reaching back, she pulled Brax's arms forward and wrapped them around her waist. Her back was still to his chest and their eyes remained locked in the mirror as Brax's hand moved slowly and sensually up her ribcage before cupping her breast. Sabre arched into the touch, wanting him desperately, yet feeling no urgency to move to the bed.

"I like you in pink," he told her as he began to peel the thin straps from her shoulders. "It brings out the colour of your eyes." He then laid a series of kisses along the slope of her neck. "My sugarplum."

Sabre gave her head a small shake. "That is still the worst nickname for me you could have possibly chosen."

"I think it suits you perfectly," Brax retorted, pushing the nightgown down and off her body completely. The satin material pooled at her feet even as Brax thumbed her nipples, watching her all the while in the mirror. He nibbled on her shoulder and smiled at her. "See, sweet."

Sabre scoffed, not worried she would break the intimate spell they were under. "You're delusional."

"And you're mine," he stated.

"Fact," she granted. Then she turned around and helped

Brax out of his clothes, appreciating the small things like kneeling at his feet to untie the laces on his boots. And the feel of the hairs on his thighs under her fingernails when she raked them up and over his legs. Being able to touch him like that was a privilege and an honour.

Trying to swallow down the demon-sized erection he was sporting is also a privilege, she decided, licking her lips. Just as she was about to go to dick-town, Brax stepped back. Sabre arched a brow at him. "Where do you think you're going with that?"

Brax took a couple of steps back until he reached the bed. He smiled at her before replying, "Heaven."

Sabre groaned and palmed her face with her hand where she still knelt on the floor. "You are so cringey. Are you always going to be this corny?"

"Do you like it?" Brax questioned in return, holding his hand out to her.

Sabre didn't hesitate to take it, allowing him to pull her up and position her on her back in the centre of the bed. She sighed when she felt his now-familiar weight settle against hers. "Yes," she eventually answered, "I like it when you're corny."

"Then, yes. I'm always going to be this way." He kissed her, their shared passion making itself more known as their tongues tangled and rubbed against each other.

Sabre lay pliant when Brax entered her, his muscled body that looked so impossibly large, fitting hers to perfection.

She moaned, biting her lip, a gasping, "*Yes,*" escaping from her parted lips.

"That's right," Brax growled from above her. "This is your place, isn't it? Underneath me, stretched wide for my cock."

Sabre didn't even bother trying to reconcile the romantic words of just moments before with the erotic dirty talk of the now. Brax was like that; a contradiction. She simply nodded, more than willing to agree with anything he was saying if it meant he continued the very thorough fucking he was giving her. His hips moved back and forth in a steady rocking motion that surely rivalled those of professional strippers. He didn't slam against her roughly, nor did he increase his pace. But over the next thirty minutes, he systematically destroyed every remaining barrier between them. Because as his hard dick continued to slide in and out of her, his eyes remained locked on hers. He stared at her as they made love, their breaths mingling, their moans all but harmonising.

When she felt her core begin to tingle and clench involuntarily, Brax grabbed her hair in a secure grip, forcing her head still when she felt the urge to look away. He denied her any escape from the devastating intimacy. Sabre licked her lips, her mouth dry and her will all but shot.

"Don't close your eyes. I want to see you go over," he informed her, his body maintaining its steady speed and intensity.

The relentless drive was too much, the pleasure too overwhelming, and Sabre felt herself shatter. Her nails did their best to dig into the hot skin of his back and she pushed up with her own hips, grinding her clit against Brax's pelvis as best as she could. She bit down on his shoulder, feeling his inbuilt armour rush to the surface, as she shuddered her way through her release. Brax's hoarse shout from above her was like music to her ears and she continued to clench her inner muscles, drawing the pleasure from him as surely as he had done from her.

Brax rolled them, hauling Sabre onto his chest as they caught their breath and basked in the afterglow. She was almost asleep, lulled by the gentle, large hand he was running up and down her spine, when he spoke up.

"I wish I could get a tattoo."

Sabre tipped her head up so she could see his face. "You do?"

He shrugged. "Sure. For one, this is sexy as fuck," he said as he ran his hand over the black words on her back. "For two, I think matching tattoos are cute."

"Couples with matching tattoos? Lame, Brax," Sabre replied to her geeky boyfriend.

Brax just smiled and kissed the tip of her nose. "Lame? Says the woman wearing the key to my heart around her neck. I'll just take this back, shall I?"

As he reached for the clasp at the back of her neck, Sabre caught his wrist and pushed him back with force. Pinning his hand to his own chest she scowled at him. "Keep your hands away from my key or I'll cut off your fingers and shove them up your arse."

Brax grimaced, even as he stayed relaxed and docile beneath her. "Lovely imagery. Horrible threat," he praised. "And definitely a time when I'm glad the gift from my bloodline prevents you from following through."

Sabre thought about it for a moment, her gaze roaming over his perfectly unblemished skin. "Forget tattoos," she finally said, coming to a realisation of what kind of marks she wanted to see on her man if she were able to. "I'd be happy with seeing my teeth marks on your skin. Maybe a hickey or two."

Brax groaned, hips pushing up. "Gods, yes. I would love that."

Leaning down, Sabre kissed her way her over his shoulder and up to his neck. She nibbled a little, feeling his pulse beating frantically beneath her lips. When she bit down, her teeth met with a hard, impassable shield, just as they had when they'd been in the throes of passion. There was a pang of disappointment, she wasn't going to lie. She suddenly understood why Brax liked marking her up so much. So that the world knew she was taken. So that the world knew she belonged to someone. She wanted to do the same to him. Something of what she was feeling must have shown on her face because Brax cupped her cheeks, his lovely eyes locking onto hers.

"You don't need to mark me for me to be yours. Or for people to know that I'm yours," he assured her.

"I know," she responded, kissing his thumb as it stroked her lower lip.

Then he grinned, a mischievous look replacing the serious one. "Especially with you threatening to dance in the entrails of anyone who so much as looks at me."

Sabre grinned back, feeling amazing once more. He had a good point. "What can I say, violence is my love language."

"And it's a language that I love," Brax guaranteed.

"That's a lucky thing," Sabre acknowledged. Then said, "We really will be okay."

"I know it. I *feel* it. But more importantly, I *trust* it. I trust *us*." He cupped her face between his warm palms. "I also trust Mikhail. He isn't going to mess this up for us."

Sabre swallowed noisily before licking her suddenly dry lips. "I can admit to still being uncertain about the whole Mikhail thing. Because I used to trust him, too. I still do in nearly every way. But he ordered me to kill him, Brax. He was the first and only person for a very long time whom I was allowed to love. And he forced me to murder him with my own hands. The trust is a little strained," she said, being brutal in her honesty.

Brax's eyes flashed, his inner beast chiming in with its thoughts. They were not pleasant. "We'll figure it out. I have your back."

"And I have yours. Always."

17

The following day, Brax was feeling rather pleased with himself. He and Sabre had made love twice more throughout the night before they had finally slept in the rainbow covered bed, surrounded by fairy lights and glitter in Sabre's studio. He could well see the secret room as being their little getaway place whenever they needed to escape the palace.

Looking up, he saw Sabre talking with Jinx, Eric, and Gage. The yellow diamonds in the key pendant flashed in the sunlight and could be seen easily by all. Brax was more than a little satisfied. Marriages and thus, wedding rings, weren't really a big thing in Purgatory. There were too many cultures, beliefs, and traditions to focus on just one narrow idea of commitment. But he appreciated the idea of a symbol of that commitment more now. Sabre's reaction had been just about perfect and everything Brax had been hoping for. His eyes locked with Eric's, and he gave the vampire a nod in thanks. Eric smiled back, his fangs flashing in the morning light.

In between orgasms, Sabre had recounted her interaction with X in detail. Brax could easily understand why she had returned from the trip so raw and stressed. The elf was a real piece of work. Having confirmation that his nemesis gained pleasure out of the pain Brax and his family had been suffering over the course of two generations now, had his rage rising to the surface. They had all agreed it was time to put the elf into his grave. But before they did that, they were going to have to dig more information out of him first. The breadcrumbs X had tossed at Sabre were as intriguing as they were confusing. Like Sabre, Draven knew the history of Purgatory rather well. But he wasn't an expert on the Fore-bearers. As far as Brax knew, *nobody* was an expert.

"Other than Lucifer," Brax groused to himself. "Maybe."

"What about me?"

The deep male voice came from directly behind Brax, and he spun, leading with his foot. His steel-capped boot met with nothing but air as a man Brax had never seen before leapt quickly backwards. He spread his arms out to the side, his claws unsheathing, wondering if he could slice at the dark-haired man's jugular before he could move again. He had been very fast.

"Whoa there. Hold up. I come in peace," the man said.

Brax didn't believe him at all. The man practically had fuckery stamped across his forehead. The way his eyes twinkled and the dimpled smirk gave him away. "I don't believe you," Brax retorted, growling a little.

"Holy shit! Brax, don't kill him. That's Lucifer!" Sabre's shouted, running over.

Brax turned disbelieving eyes on his woman. "Say what now?"

Sabre nodded her head and patted Brax on the chest. "True story. This is the King of Hell."

Brax didn't sheath his claws but he also didn't lunge at the interloper. He watched the way Lucifer's eyes latched onto Sabre though. And he didn't like it one bit. The angel was too damn good looking to be assessing his woman with that much intensity.

"Popping up like that is a good way to get yourself killed, Your Majesty," Draven drawled from behind Lucifer. He had moved just as quickly as Brax had upon hearing the stranger's words.

Brax smirked a little because Draven really didn't like it when people snuck up on him. He also took exception to people showing up without an appointment. Draven was a stickler for good etiquette. And Brax could tell by the way his guardian was gripping the hilt of his sword, that he wanted to do more than just verbally reprimand the King of Hell.

Lucifer glanced over his shoulder. "You must be Draven." His very light, pearl-like eyes travelled over the other angel from head to toe before he grinned. "Sabre has described you perfectly."

Draven immediately glowered at Sabre. "I bet she has."

Lucifer laughed, the sound annoyingly pleasant to Brax's ears. There was no denying the man was attractive with his dark hair, light eyes, broad shoulders, and height. But there was also something else about him that was ... alluring, almost.

"He's the Devil, darling," Sabre whispered into Brax's ear as if she'd read his mind. "He supposed to be charming."

Brax grunted, not bothering to reply. *I don't think the guy is charming,* he assured himself.

"What are you doing here, Luca? And are you okay? Alexis said you just took off. We were worried." Sabre inquired of the Devil.

"Luca? The fuck kind of nickname is that? And what's this *we* business?" Brax grumbled, his hands flexing once more. He received an elbow to his ribs from Sabre for his efforts.

Lucifer watched the exchange with apparent amusement. "I'm fine. I heard you were looking for me. After discovering my dead doorman, I figured opening a portal directly into Purgatory's royal palace would be the wisest and most expedient course of action."

"Alba wasn't my kill," Sabre quickly spoke up.

"I know. Alexis filled me in. It's like everything is one big clusterfuck right now ..." he trailed off, noting the new jewellery Sabre was sporting. "What's this? The key to your chastity belt?" Lucifer asked, reaching for the chain around Sabre's neck.

Brax snarled savagely, knocking the King of Hell's hand away before it made contact with Sabre or the necklace. "Touch that and die."

Lucifer's opalescent irises flashed for a moment, his body going rigid before he nodded once and relaxed somewhat. Though he still looked cautious, he held up his empty hands. "I get it. Sabre is yours. No sharing."

"You got that fucking right. Mine," Brax growled, reeling Sabre into his side with his arm, still not taking his eyes away from Lucifer.

"I think I just had an orgasm," Jinx's voice cut through the tension as she stepped up beside Brax. "That was so hot."

"Same here," Sabre murmured, squirming a little.

Brax looked at the two women and rolled his eyes, feeling most of the jealous tension leave him. He knew Sabre and the other angel were good friends and had never been anything *but* friends. What's more, Lucifer was a good ally to have, so Brax checked his ego and held out his right hand. "I'm a little possessive," he conceded, not going as far as an actual apology. It wasn't like he was sorry.

Lucifer glanced at the outstretched hand, then at Sabre,

before he finally smiled and held out a hand in return. He shook Brax's hand firmly but not in a battle of strength kind of way. He didn't squeeze the shit of Brax's hand, nor did he try to incinerate him with his angelic powers. *If he still has those,* Brax thought to himself. It was assumed that Lucifer was a fallen angel, and as such, had no Grace left. But the fact that he could open a doorway between Hell and Purgatory belied that. He made a note to ask Sabre about it later.

"It's all good," Lucifer declared, releasing Brax's hand. "Besides, I'm pretty sure I just orgasmed too."

The wink the man tossed him caused Brax to choke on a laugh. "No wonder you and Sabre get along so well. You're both deviants."

"Abraxis ... I'm the Devil," Lucifer reminded him. "Deviancy is kind of my cup of tea."

"Why do I get the feeling you're going to be a joy to get to know," Brax wondered sarcastically.

"Oh, I'm just full of all kinds of joy," Lucifer guaranteed. "It's odd that we haven't had the opportunity to get to know one another before now. I knew Maliq. He was a good man. I know Mikhail a little. Also a good guy."

The last vestiges of defiance left him when he heard Lucifer speak well of his father and brother. The angel's faculties were clearly dubious, but he wasn't without taste. "Thank you. They were. I mean are. Mikhail still is anyway," he corrected his tense. "I think."

"Anyway, why did you come knocking on my door?" Lucifer asked, looking at Sabre.

"We were kind of at a dead end as far as locating where the bad guys went. I was feeling a mite annoyed with the situation and was hoping you would have some information or some way you could assist us. But that was before Alba got sliced and diced and I was accosted by the mystery elf himself."

Lucifer's dark eyebrows rose and he looked concerned. "Right. Alexis said the bad guy had approached you. Ballsy."

"I wish I'd been able to de-balls him," Sabre muttered, sounding disgruntled.

"He got away, I take it," Lucifer commented.

Sabre nodded. "Yeah, just vanished into thin air. I'm pissed about it. But he did give up some information. Something I'm almost positive you'll be able to shed some light on."

"I'll give it my best shot," Lucifer told them.

Brax believed the guy. He screamed honesty, which was weird given where he lived. Styx chose that moment to walk over and drop a large centaur thigh bone at Brax's feet. He then sat his butt down and stared at Brax in expectation. He sighed because there was no way he could resist those puppy eyes. "Do you two have this?" he asked Sabre and Lucifer. "Poor Styx is feeling a little neglected." He bent over and picked up the bone.

Lucifer looked taken aback. "You're going to go and play

fetch with your dog while Sabre and I discuss potential theories for the assassinations of the royal line?"

Brax narrowed his eyes. "I hear judgement in your tone."

Lucifer held up his hands in front of him and backed up a step. "No judgement here, man. I happen to love hellhounds. And centaur bones," he added.

Brax narrowed his eyes on the devil for a moment, wondering if Lucifer meant that literally. For all he knew, the guy did indeed eat centaurs. Who knew what went on in Hell. He had never been there. He could well believe the hellhound comment though. They were endemic to Hell. Even as he watched, Styx leaned against Lucifer's legs demanding to be patted. The angel obliged, rubbing Styx with his fingernails so the hound could feel it through his tough, leathery hide.

"I'm glad that's settled then," Brax said before turning to Sabre. "Ask the hard-hitting questions, babe. Fill me in later." He then yanked her face to his and kissed her with a passion bordering on obscene before sneering a little at Lucifer. He threw the weighty bone into the garden, watching Styx take off after it, and walked away from Sabre and her friend. He gestured at Draven, Jinx, Gage, and Eric, who had all been shamelessly watching the show.

"Move along," he ordered them. And much to his surprise, they did so easily enough. Brax knew Sabre would tell him everything she learned from the conversation. Besides, she was the best person to do it. Not only had she been the one to speak with X, but she and Lucifer had a shared history. Although he was more than willing to get to know the irreverent male further, something told him Lucifer would be more willing to open up to Sabre if it were just the two of them.

"I'm proud of you, you know."

Brax jolted, Draven's words sounding from right beside him. Draven, of course, had stayed with him when the others had wandered away, giving Sabre and Lucifer a modicum of space. "Huh?" he asked, unsure what Draven was referring to.

"I'm proud of you," Draven repeated. "You're learning, adapting. I know you think you're not good at this type of thing – liaising, meetings, political intel – but you are. You would have made a great king, Abraxis. If your father were here, he'd tell you the same thing."

The words meant more to him than he could say, so he nodded his thanks instead. But he did want to address that last part. "Maybe I would have ended up being a great king. But I'm really fucking glad I don't have to."

"Understandable," Draven said.

As Styx brought him back the bone to throw again, Brax knew the time for Mikhail to come home was fast approaching. And he was both pleased and relieved. Purgatory needed its king as much as Brax needed his brother. "Depending on what Lucifer can add to the status quo, we're going to have to get Mikhail back from Earth."

Mikhail had been acting as rebel leader, Hound, and staying safely tucked away on a whole other plane of existence. At least in that, Brax could admit his brother had acted intelligently.

Draven concurred, "I agree. Are you and Sabre prepared for that?"

"We are," Brax replied simply, gazing at her once more. She looked up immediately, plum eyes smiling into his amber ones. "We can handle anything."

"I see she liked the gift," Draven noted, after clearing his throat. "You didn't, ah ...?"

Brax rolled his eyes, fighting with Styx over the bone for a moment before he managed to yank it out of the hellhound's strong teeth. He flung it as far as he could, watching a happy pup take off after it like a bullet. "No, Draven. I didn't tell Sabre it was you who suggested the key pendant. Trust me, it was beneficial for me to take credit for that."

Draven shuddered, loosening the top button of his shirt. "Stop. I beg you. Do not be sexually suggestive in my presence, please."

Brax laughed, slapping Draven on the back. "Whatever. But seriously, I had forgotten all about dad showing me that necklace until you brought it up."

"He wanted you to have it," Draven reminded him again.

"I know. I recall that now. Those crazy visions of his ..." he looked at Sabre, speaking more to himself than to Draven.

"I wonder if he knew all along that Sabre would be the one for me. If he knew all this crap was going to happen ..."

He wondered if he owed his father for his soulmate. Or whether he should be cursing his father's name for allowing the royal line to descend into ruin.

18

"Way to make a good first impression," Sabre said dryly, punching Lucifer on the shoulder.

"Ow," he whined, rubbing his arm. "And what do you mean? I was nothing but my usual, delightful self."

Sabre rolled her eyes and scowled at her old friend. But she couldn't deny she was amused. "That old chestnut? I hate to break it to you, Luca, but whoever said you were delightful was lying through their teeth."

"Nobody can lie to me," Lucifer reminded her, his chest puffing out with pride.

That was a good point, Sabre admitted. And one that could well prove useful in the future. "Thanks for coming," she began. "I need to pick your brains."

"My brains? But not my balls, huh? Not based on Abraxis's reaction," Lucifer offered.

Sabre choked, turning wide eyes to the guy. "The fuck? Luca!"

Lucifer shrugged, his eerily pretty eyes focused on where Brax was playing with Styx and talking to Draven. "It's cool. It's not like we ever had a torch for each other. But I can't deny I was curious to see if a rumble between the sheets was in our future."

"It wasn't," she informed him flatly. "Say bye-bye to that disturbing fantasy."

Lucifer screwed up his face, looking constipated instead of upset. "I'll just have to content myself to sex with random, lonely strangers then."

"Why lonely?" Sabre asked, knowing they were getting distracted but curious as hell.

"The lonely ones are always the horniest. Duh," Lucifer replied flippantly. But then he added in a much softer voice, "And the lonely people are the ones most in need of affection." He shook himself off, shifting gears and getting serious. "Now, what did this X dude say to you?"

Sabre asked him, "What do you know about the Founding Fathers?"

Lucifer's usually smooth brow wrinkled when he frowned in her direction. "As in the Forebearers of the species?"

"Exactly those," she confirmed.

Lucifer shrugged, the frown remaining in place. "A lot, I guess. I was around when they were born or created. Why?"

Sabre breathed out. She had known Lucifer was old. But not that he was *that* damn old. "How old are you?" she blurted out.

He met her eyes, telling her, "As old as creation, essentially. As old as the first sin."

Seeing something buried in the opalescent depths, Sabre didn't press him – even though she was dying to ask what the original sin was. She had a feeling it wasn't anything as mundane as eating an apple. She refocused on her companion as he listed off the seven bloodlines.

"Demon, angel, vampire, shifter, fae, dragon, and human. Each species originated from a single being. No matter how the bloodlines have mixed throughout the generations, the genetic legacy of the progenitor remains true."

Sabre's ears perked up. "Wait, you said *legacy*."

"That's right," Luca confirmed.

"Legacy, as in the one seen in the royal triplets?" she pressed.

He nodded. "Just so. The royal lines of Cerberus are the direct descendants of the original demon to crawl out of Hell. That's why Cerberus's powers were so nifty. And why there are so many types of demons around these days. His genes had the ability to evolve like crazy."

"X said the same thing," Sabre revealed. "About Cerberus

being the first demon. It sounds important. It *feels* important. But I just don't know why. Do you?"

"Honestly? No," Lucifer denied. "I have no idea why it would matter. No clue as to why it would have such dire implications and be so significant that the Heavens are chiming in."

Now it was Sabre's turn to be shocked. "The Heavens? What are you talking about?"

"That's where I was when I went AWOL. Top floor," he said, pointing to the sky.

"You were in Heaven?" She knew Lucifer could technically go there. He could open any veil to any plane. Plus, he was an angel, fully imbued with Grace. But he despised the place as well as everyone in it. He had vowed never to go there again. Or so she had thought.

"Trust me, it wasn't my idea to go there," he told her, looking like he'd sucked on a lemon.

"Who did you see? What did they tell you?" She wanted to know who would be brave enough to yank Lucifer into Heaven.

"Loki," Lucifer replied readily. "And he didn't tell me much. It's hard to take that guy seriously, you know that. But I will say, he was acting more intense than I had ever seen him."

"Loki, now that is interesting ..." she trailed off, remembering how Mikhail had said a few months ago that Loki had been the only God willing to talk to him at the time.

Mikhail hadn't expanded much because he hadn't thought it was relevant or important. But she made a note to question her charge further about the specifics next time she saw him. Which was looking to be sooner rather than later now.

"Anyway, he was going on about the guardians guarding shit, and how if too many dragons kept crossing into the afterlife, there was going to be more treasure for the pirates."

Sabre's gaze sharpened, as did her brain. "Dragons? He mentioned dragons specifically?"

"Sure did. Apparently, they're falling off the perch in high numbers lately."

"X and Carlisle are responsible for that, according to a source of mine. And we know they are responsible for killing Maliq, the uncles and the cousins. And Zagan of course. Dragons and Demons – two out of the seven species," Sabre noted.

Lucifer nodded, clearly following her reasoning. "We know Cerberus was a Forebearer. What do you want to bet that all the dragons being targeted are direct descendants from the original dragon bloodline?"

"I think that's a losing bet," Sabre murmured, spinning a throwing star on her hand just to give her something to fidget with. They had made a breakthrough. She knew it. "X is killing off the descendants of the Forebearers."

"I agree," Lucifer concurred.

"What the fuck for? And he can't seriously want to eradicate every single bloodline from all seven species, can he? That would have to be an awful lot of people," Sabre said.

"I can't help you with the *why* but I can maybe help you with the number," Lucifer offered. "Souls are kind of my thing, remember? Besides, I'm not so convinced regarding the scale. Take dragons, for example, they're an endangered species as it is. If their genetics were traced back, I'm sure there would be less than a handful directly related to the first dragon."

"You're right. The same goes for the Cerberus line as well. Sure, there are a bunch of cousins around the place, but the number of them from the direct royal line – the ones born with *legacies* – there aren't many of those left." Sabre was getting all tingly. Not in the same way as she had the previous evening when Brax's head had been between her legs. But it was a good tingle, nonetheless. "My assassin tingle," she whispered shakily. "It's back."

Luca eyed her more closely. "Your death tingle was missing? Since when? No wait, let me guess ..." he looked pointedly across the garden at the current king.

Sabre followed his gaze, catching her throwing star between her thumb and middle finger, and using her pinky to spin it around and around. "You don't like Brax." The thought was rather outrageous. *Everyone likes my guy. He's likeable.*

"I didn't say that, so don't be giving me your side-eyes, Sabre," Lucifer cautioned her. "I like him just fine so far.

I'm just concerned that he might be a little too nice for you ..."

"That demon has a beast riding his soul and has been the General of the Demon Horde for fifty years," Sabre defended her man's badarsery.

"That demon is currently rolling around in the grass with a giant puppy," Lucifer retorted dryly.

Sabre looked over at Brax once again only to discover that he was indeed on the ground with Styx. The hellhound was currently on Brax's back, pinning him to the grass face-first, as Brax pretended to be eaten alive. He was screaming, rather shrilly, and as they listened, Sabre heard him say, "Noooo! Oh, someone please save me. I'm being eaten alive by a hellhound. Argh!"

Sabre snorted, shaking her head. But it was with pride rather than embarrassment. Brax was all kinds of awesome. She turned back to the King of Hell. "Brax *is* a nice guy. I don't know what possessed him to hook up with someone like me. But he wakes up every morning and *chooses* me. And I'm so very grateful."

Lucifer looked apologetic and sheepish. "I didn't mean it as a slight against either of you. I just worry that he's going to be too soft for you in the long run."

Sabre looked at her old friend, following his reasoning. Hell, she'd just had a real-life panic attack because she'd been worried about her own softness. But she had never been anxious about Brax for the same reasons. She spoke quietly, so nobody else would overhear. "That's just the point, Luca. I am the darkness. He is the light. I need him to be my softness. I don't need a throat-slitting, macho man. I need a reluctant demon king who will hug me at night and joke with me. I need a man who will point out all of the things he loves about me. I need a mate who will help me retain my humanity. That's Brax. And that makes him stronger than anyone I've ever met."

Lucifer wrapped an arm around her waist, leaning his head against Sabre's as they continued to watch Brax's antics. "I get it now. And I'm more than a little jealous. Congratulations."

"Thank you," she whispered.

Styx was now sitting with his huge heavy butt on Brax's lap, his dark blue tongue lolling out and a very happy doggy grin on his face. Brax, noticing their regard, blew her a kiss. She didn't blow him a kiss back, but she did smile. A smile just for him. "I really am in love with him."

"I can tell," her companion assured her.

"By the way, if you had seen how Brax held me down with those lower mandible fangs of his and reamed me from behind last night, you wouldn't think he was too soft in any department."

Lucifer choked, pulling away from her and looking at her askance before he burst out laughing. He slapped her on the back, saying, "Damn, girl. That man really is good for you. Look at you, cracking jokes and being all horny. If I had known you were into that kind of thing, we could have been doing that ourselves years ago."

Sabre rolled her eyes, not bothering to reply. For all of Luca's flirtations, she knew he didn't see her as anything more than a friend. "I'll update the gang with all of the tingle-inducing goss. But before that, can I reciprocate and help you with your detoured souls?"

"Alexis mentioned that, huh?" Lucifer replied neutrally.

"Yeah. Weird," was all Sabre said.

"Super weird. You know me, I don't mind inflicting some lovely torture on rotten souls. But I'm not a fan of slicing and dicing virgins," he grumbled, looking angry.

"Is it linked with X?" Sabre queried.

Lucifer shrugged his shoulders, reaching up to rub the back of his neck. "We'd be pretty naïve to think it's not. Coincidences are for morons."

"And we're not morons," Sabre agreed, holding out her fist. The Devil didn't leave her hanging, bumping his knuckles against her own "Definitely not morons," she repeated, the thrill of an impending kill coursing through her system.

Death was coming soon; she was sure of it.

She hadn't realised she's spoken aloud until she heard Lucifer say, "It is." Unfortunately, her stabby endorphins were squashed in their infancy when the King of Hell tacked on, "But whose death?"

19

Sabre stalked her prey from the shadows. She was in a tree, high up above the ground, perched precariously on a leafy branch. She hardly breathed as she watched the man below her. She really hoped he wasn't going to do anything stupid because going toe to toe with him would be a challenge.

A fun challenge, she thought. But also a complicated one. It was almost midnight, but a full moon made it easy to see the expression on her mark's face. The usual handsome features were pinched with worry and disappointment. She saw the moment he decided to act, and she cursed silently, hoping she could get out of this with no blood spilled.

She dropped from her branch, her wings expanding to catch the air and ensuring she landed with nothing but a whisper of sound, blocking the male's path. He jolted hard before he cursed and pulled out a switchblade fast – extremely fast. She had to give him credit for that. When he had the nerve to lunge at her with it, she slapped it out of his hand and jumped on his toes. It was the only thing she could think to do that wouldn't cause serious injury under the circumstances.

Hopping on one foot, Draven cursed. "Damn it, Sabre. What the hell do you think you're doing? He's getting away."

Sabre risked a quick glance over her shoulder, seeing the cloaked figure disappearing into the darkness of the secret tunnel to the palace. Draven tried to get around her, but she blocked him with her wings. "Let him go."

"Are you mad?" Draven hissed. "He's a mole, a spy, a plant. He's a fucking traitor!"

"I'm aware," Sabre responded mildly to Draven's rage. He must be legitimately furious if he was using words like *fucking*.

"If you're so aware, then why are you letting him escape?" Draven demanded.

Draven dodged to the right, almost slipping past her when he yanked on her wing. Sabre gritted her teeth, reminding her trigger finger that Draven was not for killing. "I don't want to hurt you, Draven. Not really. But if you touch my feathers again, I'm going to give you pain."

Draven yanked on his hair, releasing an inarticulate bellow of fury. "Great. He's gone. He's likely going straight to Carlisle or X. This could have been our one chance to follow him and discover their locations. This whole thing could have been over by sunrise."

"I think that's a vast oversimplification of the possibilities," Sabre retorted, moving out of Draven's path when it appeared he was no longer going to follow Eric. "Just find the bad guys and exterminate them within hours when you haven't been able to achieve that in *years.*" She wasn't trying to antagonise the other angel further, but she wanted to make sure Eric had enough time to get away before Draven inevitably tried to track him.

"Sabre, get out of my way," Draven issued the demand with forced calm.

Sabre pretended to think about it for a moment before she shook her head. "No." She saw his eyes flick to his switchblade lying nearby on the ground. One body roll and he'd be able to scoop it up. "Just let it go, Draven."

He whipped his head up, blue eyes blazing. "Let it go? Like you just let Eric go? What are you thinking? Are you on *their* side, Sabre? Have you been one of them all along?"

Sabre dug deep for inner peace, but there was none to be found. She had never felt so insulted in all her life. She jabbed Draven in the nose before her brain even computed what she was doing. Blood sprayed immediately but there was no gross yet satisfying crunch that came hand in hand with a broken nose. She wasn't sure if she was glad or disappointed. "I hate Carlisle with a passion you will never understand. I was *never* on his side."

Draven gripped the bridge of his nose with one hand, holding it tightly for a few tension-filled minutes, while his other hand cupped his nostrils. When the blood flow turned into more of a bloody trickle, he wiped his hands clean on his pants. He looked a little like a Jackson Pollock painting. He then took a single, aggression-laden step in her direction. Sabre braced herself for a good, old-fashioned angelic death-match but needn't have bothered. Because her best friends didn't listen to a word she said.

"Don't even think about it, Draven," Gage warned, stepping out from behind a tree. He was holding a baseball bat and looked like a total zombie badarse in his fatigues.

Jinx moseyed over from the clearing, a bow with an arrow already notched in her hands. "Just chill, Draven."

Mercy then popped up from behind a bush like some kind of horned, demonic daisy. He pointed directly at Draven with a very long, razor-sharp claw. "What they said."

And last, but not least, Phaedra returned to her full size, startlingly close to Draven's side. "Draven, please. Just listen."

Sabre firstly fought back her gag reflex upon seeing her pixie pal touch Draven's arm and his resulting blush. Then she had to fight back her annoyance at the Musketeers in front of her. "I told you I didn't need back-up," she grumbled at them.

"You're not the boss of us, Sabre," Jinx informed her primly.

Sabre let out an aggravated sound before responding. "I'm not the boss of Brax either, yet he isn't here. I know he stayed in our room, trusting me to handle the situation like I promised I would."

Mercy snorted rudely, his huge biceps bulging as he crossed his arms over his chest. "We're not looking for you to fuck us like a rabid chipmunk later, either. That's the only reason Brax is being a good boy and staying put. I guarantee it."

"I don't fuck like a chipmunk," Sabre refuted, but she gave it some thought. "Or do I? How do chipmunks fuck?"

"With wild abandon," Gage supplied.

"Oh, well, maybe I do," Sabre permitted, filing a mental note to search the internet later for chipmunk porn.

"You're all in on this?!" Draven's incredulous shout broke through the silly ramblings.

"In on Sabre doing the best thing for everyone involved? Yes, we are," Phaedra replied.

Draven clenched his jaw, breathing heavily through his mouth because his nose was no doubt blocked with blood and swollen. "Sabre, explain yourself. If you *please.*"

With her annoying friends watching her back, Sabre stared off into the distance where Eric had disappeared. She was not an imbecile, nor was she a bleeding heart. She knew a plant when she saw one. She had known from the very first moment she had seen Eric that he was working for Carlisle as a spy and reporting back to the incubus. She also knew what it was like to be forced into an unwanted job.

She turned back to Draven and told him, “We're not following Eric because we're giving him a chance.”

“A chance? A chance at what? To stab you in the back?” Draven countered.

Sabre huffed, bending down to retrieve the folding knife from the ground. “I'm not scared of my back being stabbed. I face my opponents head-on. If I'm going to be stabbed, it’ll be in my heart. Or maybe my eye. Or my ear. Or –”

“I get it,” Draven rudely interrupted her. “Gods, you are so irritating. I just want to smother you with a pillow.” He then began to pace back and forth, ignoring the snickers from his audience.

Sabre couldn't blame him for feeling frustrated with the situation. What he’d said was true. They could absolutely have followed Eric and perhaps discovered where their greatest enemies were located. They could have progressed a few squares on the chessboard that night. But she wasn’t thinking about the line of Cerberus or legacies or even Mikhail just then. She was thinking about being a kid whose choices were crap, shit, and shittier. When those were the only choices presented, the least damning option was still nothing but turd.

Draven stopped moving, watching Sabre closely now. “Seriously, Sabre. Help me understand your reasoning here.”

She studied Draven for a moment, noting his good looks,

his nice, classy clothes, and his all-round golden boy persona. She couldn't deny it had been hate at first sight when they had met each other. Draven was everything she could have been, once upon a time, if life hadn't thrown a huge curveball at her. It was hard to look at his perfect face every day and be reminded of that. Things had thawed between them somewhat since she and Brax had gotten serious. Still, they were acrimonious at the best of times and would likely continue to be, no matter how used to each other they became. But when she finally answered him, it was with sincerity and truth.

"I want to give Eric a chance to come to us of his own volition and tell us the truth. I don't want to follow him. I don't want to beat the secrets out of him. I just want him to 'fess up."

"He's been living at the royal palace for weeks now and he hasn't slipped yet. Why do you think he'll come to you now? And why do you even care?" Draven wanted to know.

"Because he's just a kid, Draven!" Sabre shouted, waving her arms around. "Eric is just a kid that has somehow been dragged into a shitty situation. I want to give him a chance to prove himself. I want to give him a chance to *save* himself."

Draven regarded her intently and she fought the urge to squirm. She knew he could read emotions, but also knew he had a strong moral compass and would never invade her privacy like that unless it was absolutely necessary. So, when he spoke again, she knew it was because he had read her face and her voice, rather than the churning emotions inside of her.

"You want to give him the chance nobody gave you," Draven said quietly.

Sabre nodded her head, afraid to open her mouth for a second. "Yes. That's what I want, though it's not completely accurate. *Most* people didn't give me a chance. But one person did; King Maliq. He looked at a traumatised, violent, fallen angel and handed over his firstborn son. Yes, the bond I felt for Mikhail was immediate and intense, but I could have denied it. All my programming told me to deny it. But Maliq looked at me and saw the scared kid, not the monster in the making. And I wanted to make him proud. That's what I see when I look at Eric – just a terrified teenager. He doesn't have to become an arsehole. He can just be ... Eric."

"And if it backfires?" Draven pressed.

"Then I take full responsibility," Sabre said.

"It's not going to backfire, Draven," Jinx joined the conversation. "He's a good guy that has been making some poor decisions. All we want to do is give him the opportunity to make a better one."

Draven stared into the distance where Eric had disappeared for a long moment before his shoulders finally lost their rigid hostility. He slumped, sighing, before meeting Sabre's eyes once more. "We give him a chance."

The relief she felt was physical and she told herself to keep it together long enough to get back to Brax. She nodded to her friends, who nodded back and began to disperse. She held out the switchblade to Draven, a peace offering. He didn't hesitate to take it back, tucking it into the back pocket of his now ruined pants.

She turned to walk away, to go back to Brax where he was no doubt pacing a hole in the floor in their bedroom. But she paused and looked back over her shoulder. "Thank you, Draven," she said sincerely.

As she walked off, praying she hadn't made a huge mistake with Eric, she was sure her ears were tricking her because she could have sworn she heard a very quiet, "You're welcome, Sabre."

20

"Tell me again why we're walking into the forbidden forest at sunset like a bunch of tools?" Brax asked nobody in particular as he trudged along in the semidarkness. Heading blindly into a magical forest that was rumoured to be haunted and all kinds of weird was not his idea of a fun time.

"Because, when Eric went out last night, he heard that something strange was going on in the forest and wanted to check it out," Jinx reminded the crabby Brax. "I, for one, am pumped. I've been wanting to investigate this place for ages. I mean, it's a *forbidden forest*. How cool is that?"

Brax groaned and rolled his eyes, looking at Sabre who was walking beside him on the narrow path between the trees. "Why is she so perky?"

Sabre's lips twitched as she replied, "Because she's a

tiger. Tigers love trees. And forests. This is like her dream playground."

"She couldn't have dreamed up a playground with more natural light?" Brax muttered, his eyes constantly scanning his surroundings.

Jinx poked Brax in the back. "Don't be such a grump. You didn't have to come. *None* of you had to come," she added, gesturing to their usual, eclectic group of companions. "Right, Eric? We could have checked it out with just the two of us."

Eric's eyes were also continually moving, Brax noted, and he looked very pale. "Are you okay? You look a little off," he noted, when Eric didn't reply to Jinx.

"I'm fine!" Eric practically shouted. He grimaced and lowered his voice when he next spoke. "And it needs to be all of you for this. Not just Jinx."

Jinx shrugged, unconcerned, and looped her arm through Eric's. "Whatever. I think the rumours of people using this place as a secret hideout are really cool. I mean, it could even be Carlisle and that evil elf. Wouldn't that be crazy? If they have been hiding so close to the palace the entire time – practically in plain sight?"

"Oh, yes. Crazy," Draven agreed, his tone heavy with sarcasm.

Brax nudged him to shut him up. If Draven couldn't be as convincing as Jinx, then he shouldn't say anything at all. They had all agreed to the same terms. When Eric had announced at breakfast that day that he had heard about potential campers hanging out in the forbidden forest that bordered the edge of the palace grounds, Brax had known the vampire had made his choice. He had been more disappointed for Sabre than for himself. Still, he had also been betting on Eric stepping up and doing the right thing. He didn't think he was a bad kid. But it seemed whatever hold Carlisle or X had on him was too much and he had made his choice to set them all up.

Brax was pissed off about his enemies being so close to his home that he welcomed the upcoming battle, regardless of Eric being a traitor. Glancing to his left, he saw Eric looking at Jinx's animated face, fear flickering over his features. Eric clearly cared about Jinx, at the very least.

"We're like a really bizarre mashup of the fellowship of the ring," Jinx said, laughing at her own joke. "Unlikely heroes making their way through the unknown terrain to –"

"Wait!" Eric said suddenly, pulling Jinx to a stop. "Don't go any further."

Brax saw Sabre close her eyes, her shoulders slumping a little in relief. He knew she hadn't been looking forward to killing the young vampire. He also knew she still would have done it. If Eric had betrayed them and walked them all into danger, Sabre wouldn't have hesitated to decapitate him.

"What's wrong?" Brax asked, wanting Eric to say it.

"It's a trap," Eric revealed, looking frantic.

"Really? A trap you say?" Brax drawled, crossing his arms over his chest, and looking around at his friends ... his *family*.

Eric nodded hard. "Yes. I'm sorry. I've been lying to you from the beginning. I'm not some helpless tween vampire in need of a home. I mean, I am, but that's not *all* I am. I'm also a thief and a spy. Carlisle has been using me. And this merry little trip into the creepy forest is a trap." His words were rushed with barely a breath or a full stop added, but they all got the gist of what Eric was saying.

"Wow," Brax widened his eyes and looked at his companions. "What a shock."

"Yes," Sabre agreed deadpan. "I am shooketh."

Eric looked around at everyone only to find them all staring at him, seemingly unconcerned. "Why don't you look more surprised?" he asked.

"Because we're not," Draven said. "We knew."

"What do you mean you knew? That I was a spy?" Eric looked like he was about to have a heart attack. "Since when?"

"Since always," Jinx told Eric kindly. She rubbed his arm in comfort. "It was kind of obvious, sweetie. I mean, trying to steal Sabre's car? That wasn't exactly subtle."

Eric's mouth fell open and he stared at everyone again. "If you knew, why didn't you say something?"

"Because we were waiting for you to pick a team," Sabre told Eric seriously. "And you just did. Which also means you just saved your own life." Then she set off walking again, the rest of their crew following behind.

"Wait. No. Why are you still walking? Didn't you hear what I just said? It's a trap. Carlisle and his cronies are in there," Eric exclaimed, running in front of them and blocking their way.

"Good," Sabre declared, a healthy bloodlust shining in her eyes and ramping up Brax's inner beast. "I've just about had enough of his shit. It's time he got dead."

Eric held his hands out in front of him. "You don't understand. It's not just Carlisle or that shifty elf. There are heaps of others in there too. It's going to be a slaughter."

"Yeah. A slaughter for *him*," Brax vowed. He could already feel his gums tingling in anticipation of his fangs bursting forth, ready to rip Carlisle's head off.

"Abraxis, please," Eric pleaded. "I am so sorry for the part I played in this. I know you probably don't trust me anymore, but please listen to me. I don't want to see you get hurt."

"Eric, I can see how remorseful you are about this whole thing. But trust *me* when I say that *we* are not the ones who are going to get hurt." And with that, Brax let out a shrill whistle. Rustling sounds came from all around them, shadowed forms emerging from the darkness of the trees. "Have you met my Demon Horde?" Brax asked Eric. "The largest army in all of Purgatory."

"Holy shit," Eric exclaimed, looking at the dozens upon dozens of soldiers stepping into the dim light.

"That's right. This isn't a trap for us. It's a trap for that shithead, Carlisle," Sabre promised Eric. "This is not *our* slaughter. But his."

Eric gulped. "Okay."

Brax levelled a look at Eric and Jinx in particular but cast a sweeping glance over Gage, Phaedra, and Mercy as well. "Now, when the fighting starts, I suggest you fall back with a few of my lieutenants. They will protect you."

"Excuse me," Jinx scowled at Brax. "We talked about this. Or rather, we *argued* about this already. I'm not sitting this one out. I can fight."

"Yeah. And I'm fighting too," Eric said bravely, standing tall next to Jinx. "I need to make it up to you."

"Oh, we'll be talking about this more," Brax promised, his eyes boring into the vampire. "You're not off the hook just because you decided to confess right at the last minute."

Eric nodded, meeting the current king's eyes without flinching. "I understand."

"Okay then," Sabre clapped her hands sharply. "If we're all finished, could we get on with the bloodbath now?"

Before she could stride off, Brax yanked Sabre to him by her leather corset and planted a steamy, hard kiss against her lips. "Don't get dead," he warned her. "You won't like what that would do to me." Then he strode into the trees ahead of her.

Unfortunately, his desire to walk boldly into the line of fire and start killing everything that moved didn't exactly go to plan. All the chatter with Eric had obviously alerted the bad guys to their presence – and to their plan. Several of Brax's soldiers were already engaged in hand-to-hand combat, more joining the fray by the second. Sabre stopped next to him, and he spoke to her but didn't look at her because his eyes were too busy seeking his prey. "Stick to the plan, okay? You and Draven take X, and I'll handle Carlisle."

"What if I accidentally shank Draven instead of the elf? Will you still love me?" Sabre teased.

Brax laughed roughly. "You already punched him in the nose. He owes you. I'm more worried about *him* shanking *you*." He wasn't really, of course. Draven wouldn't hurt Sabre, no matter what she did. Because hurting Sabre would hurt Brax, and Draven would never do that.

"Just so," Draven concurred, overhearing their conversation. "Sabre could do with a good shanking."

Sabre snorted. "Good luck with that. I see X," she gestured across the way with her flail. "Shall we?" she invited Draven, literally skipping off before either man could comment.

Draven pinned Brax with a serious look, communicating without needing words. Brax nodded and his friend returned the gesture before he followed Sabre to a smirking, gleeful looking elf. Brax knew it was hard for Draven to leave his side. He knew it went against everything in the angel's nature. But Brax was skilled and all but indestructible thanks to his legacy. Sabre had stressed exactly what they were up against in the slender package of X. An Ace. Brax felt better knowing that the two warrior angels were fighting their common enemy together. And as for him, he had a burning rage to wipe Sabre's 'Master' from existence.

He joined the fray, stabbing people here and there, breaking bones and cracking skulls. All the while, weapons and projectiles bounced off him, causing him nothing more than mild annoyance. He did his best not to focus on where he could see Sabre and Draven with their magnificent wings out, facing off against a pack of shifters. X was nowhere to be seen now. He also forced his eyes away from Jinx and company because dividing attention in the middle of a warzone was asking for trouble. Plus, he knew his civilian friends were well covered by his Horde. Despite not wanting to be babysat, Brax had still commanded Hugo, Shiloh, and six others to shadow Jinx, Eric, Gage, and Phaedra. He was less concerned for Mercy. He was a pain demon and no doubt in his element.

A sweet smell tickled his nostrils and he spun, following the scent like a bloodhound. Only a few things smelled good on a battlefield. And one of those was a sex demon. Brax found Carlisle predictably being a coward and hiding behind some dense, strange, purple bushes. He stayed quiet, watching the assassin den master for a moment. Carlisle looked to be sweating as he eyed his cronies falling like flies. From what Brax could tell, it looked to be a mix of professional assassins, mercenaries, thugs, and common criminals.

"Wow, scraping the bottom of the barrel for reinforcements, huh?" Brax commented, revelling in Carlisle's unmanly yelp as he spun to face him. "My Horde will have these pathetic goons holding their own livers in no time."

"King Abraxis," Carlisle sneered at him, appearing to gather himself. "Hiding behind your army I see. Too cowardly to face me without them."

Brax's brow rose as he looked around. It was literally just him and Carlisle in the small space. He spread his arms wide, standing unflinchingly in the open. "I'm not hiding behind anyone. Bring it." The incubus's pheromones hit him with the force and finesse of a sledgehammer. Annoyingly, Brax felt his dick give a single twitch behind his zipper. He knew it was a physiological response to what amounted to a toxin in the air, but it still made him want to hurl. "Your sex gas could use a little more oomph," Brax informed Carlisle blandly.

"Fuck you!" The incubus shouted.

"You see, that is the opposite of what will be happening here. Because your fuck fumes won't work on me any more than they worked on Sabre." Brax flexed his fingers, his claws extending with slow deliberation. Likewise, his sharp fangs came out to play. "The thought of you trying to roofie my mate displeases me, Carlisle."

"She always was a frigid bitch," Carlisle spat out.

The sounds of the battle were already decreasing, and Brax knew his army was doing what it did best – demolishing everything in its path. He was itching to see how Sabre and Draven were doing, as well as the young ones. Which meant he really wasn't in the mood to draw out the death of the pile of shit in front of him. He was half tempted to simply knock the incubus out and lock him away in the palace dungeon so he could do a little bloodplay with him whenever he was feeling frustrated or angsty. But Sabre wouldn't be free of him, or the Blue Devil Den, until Carlisle's heart stopped beating.

"It's time for you to die now." And so saying, Brax moved forward swiftly, grabbing Carlisle by the shoulders and holding on tight. The other man swore and struggled, looking like an ant stuck in honey with his arms pinned to his sides. He was going nowhere. But Brax did allow him to slash at him with the blades now protruding from the tips of his shoes for a moment.

"That's a nice idea," Brax admitted. Carlisle's eyes widened in horror when Brax's kneecaps didn't slice open but instead were shielded by his funky armour. "Oh, sorry, were you expecting to see my patella?" Brax inquired courteously.

"What are you?" Carlisle wondered, staring at Brax's normal tanned skin through the cuts he had made in the combat pants.

"You didn't know about this, huh? I figured your buddy, X, would have let you in on the whole legacy secret. He seems to be in the know," Brax taunted.

Brax then changed his grip, releasing one of Carlisle's shoulders – but not before he yanked it forward with all of his might. The pop that rang out was as satisfying as the scream of agony that left Carlisle's lips. "Oops, I seemed to have dislocated your shoulder. And here I was trying to rip it off altogether. Well, if at first you don't succeed ..." he trailed off, getting another solid grip.

"Wait!" Carlisle yelled, spittle flecking his lips. "I have information. I can be useful."

"Are you really trying to deal your way out of this? You stole Sabre's innocence. You tortured her, ordered her to kill, you *coveted* her. For over a century." Brax leaned in close and snarled in Carlisle's face. "There is nothing you can say or do that will save you from me."

Carlisle tried to headbutt Brax, but he telegraphed the move so much that Brax didn't even need his vibramantium. He simply moved his head out of the way. "Pathetic," he growled, before using his fangs to rip off the den master's right ear.

Carlisle squealed and cried, practically hyperventilating. Blood poured out from the hole in his head, and Brax spat the ear out, disgusted and done. He just wanted Sabre to be free. He placed his hand on top of the blond head in front of him and then *squeezed.* It wasn't the most efficient way to kill a man, but it was decidedly painful. Brax kept up the steady pressure, his claws digging into flesh. It took perhaps two minutes of his ever-tightening grip for the blood vessels in

Carlisle's eyes to rupture, making the sclera look red. When the tormented screams turned to pleas and then whimpers, Brax decided he'd better end it before the incubus passed out and missed the grand finale.

"Go to Hell," Brax ordered. He gave one last squeeze to the already dented skull in his grip, roaring his triumph when Carlisle's head suddenly popped like a ripe melon left out in the sun too long. Blood and brains went everywhere. Brax kicked the body at his feet, shaking incubus pulp from his claws, then made his way back to where the main fighting was. He wanted Sabre to see what a headless Carlisle looked like.

A feminine scream of fear rent the air, and Brax looked up just in time to see Eric take a bullet to the heart after jumping in front of Jinx to protect her.

"No!" Jinx cried out, falling to her knees and pressing her hands over the rapidly welling hole in Eric's chest.

Brax launched himself at the man who had fired the gun, king-hitting the piece of filth in the temple. He made a strange, garbled sound before he fell to the ground in a crumpled heap, half of his head caved in. Looking around, Brax noticed that only a few creatures were still engaged in battle. Most of the fighting was over. Dropping to his knees beside Jinx, he was quickly joined by Gage and Draven. He wasn't sure where the angel had come from, but he was endlessly relieved.

Draven placed his hands over the bullet hole in Eric's

chest, a shining light emanating from him. But only for a brief moment. Too brief.

"Draven?" Brax asked, already knowing the answer. Because Eric's eyelids were no longer fluttering, and his chest was no longer pumping up and down with his painful breaths.

"I'm so sorry," Draven stuttered a little.

"No!" Jinx cried, giving Eric's body a small shove. "It's not fair. He saved me. Did you see? He saved me! Please, Draven, help him."

Draven held up his hands, now covered in Eric's blood. "I can't heal the dead."

Brax ignored Jinx's heartbreaking sobs – something that hurt to do – in favour of searching for his mate in the chaos. Because, although Draven couldn't help the dead, Sabre fucking could.

21

When Sabre sought out her friends after the fighting was over and X had, of course, disappeared into thin air again, it was to find them all piled around a lump on the ground.

She felt her blood chill and her eyes moved wildly over the people still standing or sitting, trying to calculate who was missing. Brax stood up abruptly, making eye contact with her and she just knew someone was dead.

"It's Eric!" Brax called out; his voice hoarse but still booming.

Sabre felt sick to her stomach but still flew across the distance between them. Landing next to Brax, she asked, "Dead how? Is his head still attached to his body?"

Brax nodded, gripping her cold hands between his own.

"Yes. He was shot in the chest. His heart must have been hit because he bled out within seconds. His body had no chance to try to regenerate."

Sabre nodded, taking in all the information with relief. As long as a body had all of its appendages, she could drag a soul back into it. "Back up," she ordered the crowd. Nobody moved away from the rapidly cooling body on the ground, so Sabre put a little more force into her voice. "Everyone move the fuck out of the way!"

Gage glanced up sharply, relief all but seeping from his pores when he saw her. He grabbed onto Jinx and tugged her away from Eric a little. "Here now, Jinx, it's Sabre. She's going to fix everything, okay? Sabre is going to make it all better."

The lump in Sabre's throat grew and her palms began to sweat. That was a lot of pressure right there. She cast a quick look around, not seeing Carlisle's body anywhere but knowing Brax had been successful in his goal. She had felt the soul-deep bond to the sex demon snap the moment his life had been extinguished. Later, she promised herself, she would get all the lovely, grisly details from Brax. But for now, she had a vampire to resurrect.

Kneeling down next to Eric, Sabre reached over and closed his eyes. "Ah, Eric. This is the type of thing I was trying to avoid. I'm sorry," she told him.

She scooped Eric up as much as she was able to, holding

him close to her chest. Her wings fanned out and wrapped around his lifeless body until the pair of them were cocooned in red and gold. She closed her eyes and reached out metaphysically for her Grace. It was a deep well of power buried in her very soul, both vibrant and magical. Drawing on it, she stepped out of her physical body and simply stared at the image she made on the ground, surrounded by blood, bodies, and grieving friends.

"Messy," she murmured. "Death is always so messy."

Nobody responded to her words of course. Nobody could hear her where she was – unless you were a lost soul. Her astral form existed between worlds and between realms. It wasn't the same as stepping through a veil or a portal. Her physical body had nothing to do with it. It was all about her soul.

"What the fuck?!"

Sabre spun around, seeing Eric's astral form goggling at their feather-shrouded bodies in Purgatory. "Eric, hey ..."

"Wait ... is that me? And is that you? Am I dead?!" Eric practically shrieked.

Sabre winced, the sound of his voice echoing in her skull as it bounced around in there. "Take a chill pill, Eric. Yes, that is you ... and me ... and you are very dead right now."

If it was possible for a non-corporeal soul to turn pale, that's what Eric did. He went so white, that his astral form flickered a little. He moved forward and attempted to touch Sabre's physical wing that was almost obscuring him from view, but his hand passed straight through it. "I'm dead!" he yelled again.

"Eric! Get a hold of yourself. Seriously, you teenagers are so dramatic. You're going to be fine," she told him.

"I am?" Eric gasped, his gaze focused on all the red shiny stuff on the ground under him.

"Yes. You are," Sabre said with confidence. "You're going to take my hand and I'm going to shuffle us back into our bodies, okay?"

"Shuffle ...?" Eric repeated, no longer even blinking.

"You're in shock. That's pretty normal for people in your situation. But I don't want to fuck around in here for too long. Fresh is best when it comes to resurrecting a soul."

Sabre moved her astral form closer to Eric's, unable to resist running her fingers over Brax's furrowed brow as she passed him. There was no way he could feel her or see her. Only the dead had access to her here. But he still cocked his head to the side, looking around as if he could *sense* something. The thought of Brax being able to sense when her non-corporeal soul was near him made her heart go pitty-pat.

Shaking off her sentimental thoughts, Sabre grabbed Eric's hand. It felt real and solid. Then she led him back to where their physical bodies were huddled together. She placed her hand on her own bowed head and delved for her Grace once more.

"Oh, wow, you are so beautiful," Eric whispered reverently.

Sabre smiled, knowing the radiant picture she made when she used her angelic powers. Her wings glowed red and gold, light emanating around her until it covered her and her charge completely like a magical igloo. Looking at her physical form, she could even make out a golden ring above her head.

"Is that a halo?" Eric all but wheezed.

Sabre rolled her eyes. "Yes, it's a halo. Resurrection angels have real halos. Now, come with me." She shoved Eric's soul at his body, observing him long enough to ensure his heart started beating and electrical impulses were going to his brain once more. Then she simply stepped into her own body.

When she next lowered her wings, it was to find the entire Demon Horde staring at her with awe and veneration. She hoped they would conveniently forget what they had just witnessed. Resurrecting people tended to be something she did without an audience. She now felt decidedly uncomfortable. Clearing her throat, she looked down and saw Eric's lovely grey eyes blinking back at her. "Hi. Welcome back."

She was then engulfed by multiple arms and legs as people tried to hug her and Eric at the same time. Sabre pushed them all away, scooting backwards on her butt to escape the love fest. "Fucking hell, they're like the tentacles on a kraken or something," she said, shuddering. She yelped when she was picked up by strong arms. "Brax ..."

"Sabre ... that was the most miraculous thing I have ever seen. You ... you're a miracle."

He kissed her with so much love that she knew he was wrong. *Brax* was the miracle. Not her.

22

"How are you feeling?" Sabre asked, looking down at Eric where he was lying comfortably on Brax's lounge in his private quarters.

Eric touched his chest where the bullet had entered him even though there was now no evidence of any wound. He shrugged his shoulders, answering, "Fine. I've never felt better."

"I'm so glad," Sabre said, meaning it. "And listen, saving Jinx's life at the cost of your own has more than proved your loyalty to us. But I still think it's about time you gave us an explanation. Don't you?"

It was technically the morning after their little shindig in the forest, simply for the fact that it was now after midnight. But the sun hadn't risen in the sky yet and Sabre knew everyone was still reeling from the events of the previous few hours. Brax, Draven, Gage, Jinx, Eric, and herself had retreated to Brax's suite of rooms only about an hour ago, after listening to dozens of post-battle reports. Phaedra and Mercy, along with Hugo and Shiloh, were handling things with the Horde and all those dead bodies now lying around the forest.

Including Carlisle's, Sabre reminded herself, casting a quick look at Brax. She could still make out the blood underneath his fingernails that he said was from popping her arch-nemesis's head like a grape. She wished she could have seen it, but the absence of the constant itch to return to the Blue Devil Den was also reward enough.

"What were you doing working with Carlisle? Who are you really?" Brax prompted Eric when he continued to sit in silence.

Eric fiddled with the blanket Jinx had placed over him when she had insisted that he lay on the lounge and take it easy. Physically he was fine but getting killed and then brought back to life again could be very overwhelming. Eric finally looked up, his expression was nervous, resigned, and apologetic in equal measures. "I just wanted answers. Carlisle said he would give them to me if I could get close to you."

"Answers? So, you're not one of the outside assassins who accepted the hit on Sabre?" Draven pressed, and Sabre couldn't help but give him a chin lift. That had been her assumption as well.

"An assassin? Me? No," Eric stated, shaking his head. "Carlisle bribed me, is all."

"Bribed you for information? About what?" Brax wanted to know.

Eric looked at Brax, his face open and earnest. "My brother."

Sabre frowned, trying to follow along. "Carlisle has your brother?"

"Yes. No. Maybe? I'm not sure," Eric spoke quickly, looking flustered and sounding pained. "Carlisle employed my brother. He was on a job for Carlisle when he went missing. I just want to know what happened to him."

"I know all of Carlisle's employees like the back of my own hand. There were a few vampires bound to the Blue Devil," Sabre allowed, "but none that looked like you and none who claimed to have a younger brother." She didn't outright accuse Eric of lying to them, but it was close.

Eric was quick to shake his head. "He wasn't a vampire. And he didn't live at the Blue Devil Den. He is – was – an outside contractor who Carlisle would hire on a case-by-case basis. Joda was from the Memnar Guild."

Sabre sat down on the lounge next to Eric's hip so she could listen more carefully. "Start at the very beginning."

"Most of what I told you about myself wasn't a lie," Eric promised, looking at Jinx. Only after Jinx smiled at him and patted him on the leg did he continue. "I *was* orphaned pretty much at birth, and I have no idea who my parents were. My brother found me on the streets when I was twelve. He's not technically my brother. But he became one, you know?" Everyone nodded, knowing full well the bonds that united a family were more than just by birth and blood. "Anyway, I was starving and tired and just kind of done with life, so I attempted to pick this random dude's pocket."

Eric paused and Sabre took a second to feel pissed about a twelve-year-old being 'done with life'. She shared a look with Brax, knowing they were on the same page and that Eric would never want for anything ever again. "Your brother?" Sabre guessed.

"Yep. It was Joda. He caught me of course. Which, given he was a master manipulator and thief, was easy for him. But I didn't know that at the time. Instead of beating me up or reporting me to the authorities as I thought he would do, he took me in. And then taught me everything he knew about stealing, spying, grifting," he shrugged, "that kind of thing."

"Wait, so when you tried to steal my car, you weren't faking it? You really are a thief?" Sabre asked, narrowing her eyes when Eric flashed her a cocky grin, typical of a teenage male.

"Oh, I'm a thief alright. And I could have been into your car in under ten seconds if I really had wanted to. Like I said, Joda was a member of the Memnar Guild. I never officially was, but I lived there for over four years. I picked up a few things here and there."

"The Memnar Guild is known for their top-rate thieves, right?" Jinx questioned, looking at Gage.

Gage nodded, confirming, "Most definitely."

Because he was heavily entrenched in organised crime, Gage knew almost as much as Sabre did about the reputations, employees, and clients of the biggest criminal employers in Purgatory. "Have you heard the name Joda before?" she asked Gage.

Gage thought about it for a moment before shaking his head. "I don't think so. I do know a bunch of guys from the Memnar Guild though."

"Only I call him Joda. He's a really private guy. With good reason. His supernatural status is what made him so popular," Eric said, looking around at everyone.

Sabre noticed how he kept switching between present tense and past tense when he spoke of his brother. No doubt, not knowing what happened to him, whether he was dead or alive, was the driving factor behind Eric agreeing to spy for Carlisle.

"I haven't seen him in eighteen months or so. He took a job for Carlisle, and he never came back." Eric ducked his head, hiding his face from the compassion swirling around the room.

Sabre may have been trying to figure everything out, but she *did* believe him. "And you think Carlisle knew what happened to him?"

Eric's jaw clenched along with his fists. "He had to know.

He kept a very close watch on the people who he employed. Whether they were bound to him or not."

"That's true," Sabre acknowledged. "He was a fastidious, untrusting bastard."

"Yeah, well now his head is nothing but pulp," Brax grumbled, leaning over and kissing Sabre on the forehead before he turned back to Eric. "So, Carlisle bribes you, says he'll tell you what happened to your brother if you work for him, even set up a trap for Sabre?"

"In a nutshell ... yeah. At first, I wasn't going to, I've never liked Carlisle. What I told you about him before – about me using him for blood? That was also true," Eric confessed, a blush of shame staining his cheeks. "But I owed it to Joda to find out what happened to him. He was the first person to ever give a shit about me, you know?"

"Yeah," Jinx said quietly, picking up Eric's hand and holding it in hers. "I know exactly what you mean." She shot Sabre a warm look of affection.

Eric smiled at Jinx, looking relieved that she empathised with him. He made no attempt to move his hand. "I didn't have any loyalty to Carlisle to begin with. I only wanted information. So, when I figured out you were all good people, I didn't tell him anything accurate. But I was still torn about confessing my sins to you and sticking with Carlisle. I know my brother is probably dead. I'm not naïve. But the not knowing is worse than having all the gory details." He paused, looking each and every one of his new friends in the eye. “I'm sorry.”

Sabre brushed off his apology with a wave of her hand. “Pfft, please. There's no need to apologise. I happen to be one of the biggest liars in all of Purgatory. Besides, you came to us with the truth eventually.”

“Which you already knew,” Eric said, looking at Brax.

Brax nodded and smirked. “Which we already knew. But it doesn't make your admission any less valuable or appreciated. Now as for your brother, I just so happen to have a lot of contacts, what with me being the king and all,” Brax added drolly. “What’s his real name and his supe status? I’ll use my royal resources to see what I can find out for you.”

“Really?” Eric sat up on the edge of the lounge cushion, looking hopeful.

“Of course,” Brax said.

Eric’s eyes lit with excitement, and he spoke quickly. “The name he went by at the guild, and what he used during jobs, was Jedediah.”

Gage whistled low, drawing the attention of the room. “Now that is a name I've heard of. He’s one of the best thieves in Purgatory. He can break into anything without leaving a trace. And there are never any witnesses. Hell, nobody even really knows what he looks like.”

“Yeah, well,” Eric said, looking sheepish as he rubbed the back of his neck. “There's a good reason for that. It’s because nobody *does* know what he really looks like. Including me.”

"What do you mean?" Jinx asked, looking confused.

"Joda's best-kept secret, the one he never told anybody, was that he was a skinwalker. Carlisle knew though, and so did a bunch of the other crime bosses. It's why he was so popular."

Sabre froze, her gaze immediately seeking out Brax's. Her internal antenna was going haywire. Months ago, they had tossed around the theory that the person who ordered the basilisk to bite King Maliq had been disguised to look like the giant hellsnake's master. It hadn't really progressed, because they had been so focused on finding Carlisle and X. But now they had proof there was a skinwalker in Purgatory, taking private contracts. Add to that he was currently missing – or more likely, *hiding* – and it was too much of a coincidence for Sabre.

"How old was he? Your brother." Sabre asked, all but holding her breath for the answer.

"Oh, way older than me," Eric disclosed. "He already had his first one hundred years under his belt before I even met him. I know that much. He'd been with the Memnar Guild for over eighty years and had a good reputation established at least fifty years ago."

"So, he was working in the business forty years ago," Brax commented, looking tense and clearly thinking about the death of his father.

Eric nodded. "Yes, easily."

Brax looked at Sabre directly. “Tell me you're thinking what I'm thinking.”

“I most definitely am,” she assured him, positive their thoughts were in harmony.

“What are you both thinking? How does Joda being in the Guild specifically for forty years have anything to do with him going missing last year?” Eric wanted to know.

“Had he worked for Carlisle before?” Sabre asked instead of answering his questions. She had to get more pieces of the puzzle before she could figure out what the completed picture would look like.

“Yes,” Eric confirmed. “Many times before. Carlisle had never cheated him out of anything in the past, which is why he didn't hesitate to take the last job when Carlisle contacted him about it.”

“When exactly did Carlisle contact him this time, do you know?” Sabre pressed, feeling all tingly.

“About one week before Joda went missing,” Eric said.

Sabre moved some pieces around in her mind, asking, “And that was about eighteen months ago you said?”

Eric held out a hand and wobbled it from side to side in the classic gesture for *kind of.* “It was a little less than that. If you want the exact date, the job was supposed to be for six hours on a Saturday night at Club Inferno. It was January sixth of last year.”

Fuuuuck, was all Sabre’s mind was capable of thinking for a moment. Because then, *right* then, was when she knew without a shadow of a doubt who the killer was. She knew who was responsible for trying to take down the throne. She knew who was responsible for killing so many of Brax's family.

Sabre licked her lips and stood up slowly, watching Brax carefully. She could practically see the wheels turning inside his head as he processed the latest information. She noticed Draven was moving closer to his charge in small increments as well. The guardian angel just made it to his side before Brax flipped his shit and went fully demonic. His claws extended whip-fast from under his cuticles and looked sharp as razor blades. His fangs erupted quicker than Sabre had ever seen. They were also far longer, rising so high that they pressed into the skin on the outside of his upper lip, just under his nose. The growl rumbling in his chest was something even Styx couldn't rival, and his eyes shifted from the amber she adored to a blood red. And if all of that wasn't enough, his armour decided to get on board with the whole demonic display.

Sabre watched in stunned disbelief as Brax's legacy from Cerberus charged over his skin from head to toe. All of his exposed skin that Sabre could see was now covered with the hard, scale-like shield – including his face. Sabre had thought it was only a defence mechanism, and as such, was a passive ability. But the way the individual scales rose and fell with every growl rumbling from Brax's chest made her think that perhaps there was more to it than that. In fact, covered as he was now in the indestructible plating, he looked almost as if he were a shifter. She wondered what would happen if she – or anyone – were to touch him right now.

Unfortunately, she didn't have to wonder for long because Draven chose that moment to talk to Brax and place his hand on the beast's arm.

23

Brax literally saw red.

The moment his brain caught up with the words he was hearing, and the very second the internal maths equation he had been doing was answered, he lost his ever-loving mind. His heart wanted to reject the conclusion, but his mind overrode that folly. He knew. He just knew.

Rage, grief, and pain rose inside of him like never before and he closed his eyes, riding the wave of emotion. He felt his claws pierce his skin and his armour rush to the surface in a strange, bold, new way. When he opened his eyes, everything was red and black instead of normal colours. His breaths fell heavily from his nostrils, huffing and puffing as his chest seemed to expand. He looked down to see his scaled exoskeleton rising and falling in perfect synchronisation with his heartbeat. *No, not with my heart. With my emotions,* he realised. His armour was responding to his thoughts and feelings, instead of acting in response to a threat like it had always done before.

"Brax, can you hear me?" Draven asked from where he was standing very close and looking at him with great concern.

Brax wanted to roll his eyes at his guardian. *Of course, I can still hear.* But he wasn't interested in hearing anything just then. The only thing he was interested in was finding the murderer and ripping him to shreds.

"I don't think he's listening," Jinx said. She gripped Eric's hand tightly and the pair of them backed up until their backs hit the far wall.

Brax would like to think he would never hurt them. But right then, at this particular moment, he couldn't be sure.

"Abraxis!" Draven's voice cracked through the air like a whip. "Snap the fuck out of it. Or I will do it for you. Do you understand me?"

It was a command, clear and simple. But it was one that Brax's inner beast didn't like. At all. He growled deep in his chest, the individual plates of his armour standing to attention and vibrating in the air. He knew what Draven was alluding to. He was going to use his empathic powers to dial down Brax's rage. But Brax wanted to revel in the simplicity of his ferocity, so he snarled again, hoping the pesky angel would take the hint. He didn't.

"Fine," Draven spat out, "be that way."

As Brax watched Draven reach out his hand, he heard Sabre shout, "No!" Her warning came half a second too late. Draven's palm landed on Brax's arm. But instead of his emotions decreasing in response to his guardian's divine powers, they increased. Exponentially. A bright spark flared to life between Brax and Draven before the angel jolted like he'd been hit with a thousand volts of electricity. He flew backwards, landing heavily against the wall. He did not get back up.

The sight of Draven being hurt, and because of *him* no less, penetrated the madness in his mind a little. He blinked rapidly, noting that the red haze from his vision was gone. But his legacy was still covering his entire body and he still felt more than a little unhinged. Looking guiltily at Draven, who was now being tended to by Gage, Brax felt shame and fear. What if he'd killed Draven? His legacy from Cerberus had never presented itself in such a way, and he hadn't known it could be used as a weapon instead of merely a defence.

Trying to make the new weapon recede, he took a couple of deep breaths. But it did sweet fuck all. Before panic started setting in, he turned to the one person he knew he could count on to fix him. *"Sabre ..."* Her name was garbled thanks to the sheer length of his lower canines, but he knew she understood him.

Sabre, for her part, looked very chilled. Like there was nothing out of the ordinary going down in her living room. She had a small smile on her face, and her beautiful mauve irises moved over him from head to foot. “My, my, my, look at you. And here I thought you were a sexy beast before,” she all but purred.

Brax choked on a laugh, shaking his head, appreciating her attempt at normalcy and humour. He didn’t know if she was bluffing though, just to get him to calm the fuck down. So he looked more closely at her face. What he found there eased his heart and had his legacy receding immediately. He saw acceptance – no fear, no disgust – just acceptance and understanding. *And maybe a little horniness,* he added. Sabre loved him no matter what he did or what he looked like. That would never change.

When she grinned at him and started walking toward him, he took a hasty step back, holding out his hands to ward her off. “Stay back.”

“It's okay,” Sabre soothed, not stopping her forward motion. She grabbed onto one of his hands, turning it over. “See?”

Looking down, Brax discovered that his hands and arms were now nothing but tanned skin. He touched his face and neck, relieved when his fingers weren’t met with vibramantium. “Sabre ...” he tried again.

Sabre flew into his chest, her arms wrapping around Brax's body in a strong and steady hug. "I'm here," was all she said. "I'm here, and everything's going to be okay. We're going to fix this."

It was exactly what he needed to hear at that moment. He crushed her in his embrace for a few seconds, gave her a quick kiss, and then released her so he could rush over to Draven. "Gage ...?" he questioned the akuji shakily, scared to know the answer.

"He's okay," Gage stated confidently. "He has a heartbeat and he's breathing just fine. He's just knocked out. I think he hit his head pretty hard against the wall."

Brax sagged in relief. He couldn't believe he had hurt his own angel.

"He's going to be just fine," Sabre said, standing next to him where he was kneeling on the ground. She ran her fingers through his hair as she continued, "Besides, even if he *was* cactus, I could have dragged his soul back into his body. I would have fucked around with it first of course," she admitted. "But ultimately, I would have put it back into his meatsuit."

"I know you would have. Sick bitch."

Brax's head whipped around at the sound of Draven's voice. "Draven ..."

Draven groaned, wincing when he touched the back of his head. "It's just a bump. Don't fret, Brax."

"I'm so sorry," Brax choked out.

"Come here," Draven urged, holding his arms out wide.

Brax leaned against his best friend's broad chest, accepting the hug gratefully. He didn't care if it made him look like a pussy. Both of them needed the grounding the touch wrought. After a moment, he helped Draven up and over to the lounge, arranging him on it so his head was on a soft pillow and he had a warm blanket over him. "Gage, would you mind getting some ice from the freezer, please?"

Sabre watched the care and consideration Brax showed for Draven. She noticed the shaking in his hands and the stoop to his shoulders. Brax's entire demeanour told her just how much the incident had scared him. There was no doubt as to how deep their bond was. Nor how much love the two men shared. Instead of being jealous or feeling threatened, Sabre was warmed by the knowledge that Brax would always have someone to watch his back.

Although, she speculated silently as she eyed Brax's skin, *perhaps he won't need as much back-watching as he used to, given the revelation of his armour.* She knew that fascinating discussion was going to have to wait because there was an even bigger elephant in the room that they needed to address first.

"Zagan."

The one word, spoken from Draven's lips, sent the temperature in the room plummeting down to subzero. Sabre watched Brax closely, looking for signs of an impending meltdown. His lips were pressed tightly into a thin line, and his jaw was clenched hard enough to crack his teeth. But there were no other indications that Brax was morphing into the Tin Man again.

"Yes," Brax bit out. "Zagan."

"Umm, does someone maybe want to fill in the ignorant among us?" Eric said, raising his hand as if he was in a classroom. He and Jinx were still huddled together over by the doorway to the bedroom, but they tentatively made their approach back now.

Draven and Brax simply stared at each other. Sabre waited for one of them to speak, but it was Gage who stepped up instead. "Zagan is the name of your younger brother. Do you think he's the one behind all of this?" he queried.

"Yes!" Brax spat out the damning word.

"Why?" Gage pushed, totally unflappable under the glares of a demon king and a guardian angel. Gage was shorter, and nowhere near as heavily muscled as Brax was. But the special armed forces soldier he had been in his first life still shone through in his bearing and attitude. "Isn't he dead?"

"Apparently not," Draven was the one to respond this

time, though his eyes were now closed, and he had a hand covering his eyes where he still reclined on the lounge.

"Does this have something to do with that funky thing your skin just did? That was wicked cool, by the way," Jinx offered.

A fleeting smile crossed Brax's face and the affection he had for Jinx was plain to see. He took a deep breath and then rolled his neck, the resulting cracking sounds echoing around the room. Sabre cringed a little. For all her gory deeds, she wasn't a fan of the sound knuckles or other joints made when they popped. But it seemed to have done Brax some good because he looked a little less tense and murdery now.

"That thing is my legacy from Cerberus," Brax explained. "You know how the ruling king always has triplet sons?" Gage, Eric, and Jinx nodded in unison. "Well, that's not all we won in the genetic lottery due to being his direct descendants. Cerberus, as the original gatekeeper of Hell and rumoured to be the first-ever *demon* to crawl from the depths of Hell, had three distinct and very powerful abilities," Brax continued to a rapt audience. He held up one finger, "One: he had an impenetrable armour that would rush to the forefront whenever he was injured or threatened."

Jinx's bi-coloured eyes rounded in awareness. "Just like you." Brax nodded. "You know, I wondered how you got out of that battle at the den all those weeks ago without so much as a scratch on you. You were rather hands-on, after all. I thought I saw something that day when you were fighting but I wasn't sure ..."

"It's a very closely guarded secret," Draven spoke up once more. "Whenever he fights in the army, he wears long sleeves and long pants. Some of his most trusted lieutenants know of course, but overall, it's a secret that has been successfully kept from the wider population for hundreds of years."

Brax held up two fingers now. "The second superpower is the gift of accessing all gateways, including teleportation. This is what Mikhail inherited. He can cross the veil as well as journeying to the separate planes including Heaven, Hell, and Earth."

"Wow. Handy," Gage said. "If I'm following correctly, that means your younger brother, Zagan, received the third power Cerberus possessed."

Brax nodded, looking more exhausted than anything else now. "The third legacy he left to his descendants was the ability to shapeshift. That's not uncommon in and of itself," he admitted. "But it's what exactly Cerberus could shapeshift into that made his ability unique. And that was pretty much anything living."

Eric's eyes widened and he worried his lower lip with one pointy vamp fang. "He was a skinwalker ... wasn't he?" Brax dipped his head once in confirmation. Eric's breath escaped in a rush. "Okay, so your younger brother was a skinwalker too. I still don't get why that caused you to go all batshit-rage-machine before. Like Gage said, wasn't Zagan killed?"

Draven made a move to get up and Brax quickly held out a hand to him, gripping him securely and helping him sit up straight. The look on Draven's face said he was in pain still, and he made no move to stand up. But he volunteered to explain, pulling Brax down next to him on the lounge. Brax leaned rather heavily into Draven's side, even though it was the angel who was the physically injured one. But Sabre knew that some of the deepest hurts could never be seen on the surface. Draven patted Brax on the leg in a very paternal manner, making Sabre aware of how badly she wanted to be alone with him. But she knew he needed this time with Draven first, and perhaps even this time to speak the truth and hear it out loud.

"The date you mentioned when Joda went missing," Draven began, "is the day Zagan was assassinated at Inferno."

"The same nightclub Joda was supposed to be working? I do remember hearing about that, of course," Eric said. "But I didn't really give it much thought. I didn't really care." He winced and looked at Brax. "Sorry, man. I didn't mean it like that. I –"

"It's fine, Eric. I get what you mean," Brax put a halt to Eric's ramblings. "Why would you care about the death of the Royal Playboy when the one and only member of your family was suddenly missing?"

Draven continued, "Brax and his father shared the same trait. We know that King Maliq was killed by a basilisk. It is one of the only creatures with the ability to pierce the genetic armour. They can only be controlled by their masters. Jinx hypothesised that it could have been someone that *looked* like the demon lord and *sounded* like the demon lord. Rather than the arsehole guy himself."

"A skinwalker," Eric stated. "I'm following you. But Joda wasn't a killer. I mean, he didn't take on jobs that were assassinations. He stole stuff. He lied a lot. He provided alibies for clients. That kind of thing."

"I admit, when you first said your brother was a skinwalker and how long he had been under the employ of the Memnar Guild, my initial thought was that Joda was our killer. Or at least somewhat associated. I don't *do* coincidences. But when you mentioned the date that he went missing, it made sense in a whole different way."

"Unfortunately, it truly does," Draven agreed, sighing tiredly and leaning back. "Zagan was the one to shapeshift into the demon lord and command the basilisk to kill his own father. It all makes so much sense – from a horrible perspective, of course. We always wondered how the killer could get inside the palace and pick off the uncles and the cousins one by one. It was because he was already *in*."

Brax didn't contribute anything further to the conversation. He was staring straight ahead, hardly even blinking, but

Sabre knew he was listening to every single syllable uttered. She wanted to ease his pain so badly.

"What does this have to do with Joda and the nightclub?" Eric asked, perhaps suffering from a mental block preventing him from reaching the logical conclusion everyone else had.

Jinx wrapped her arm around his slender shoulders ... and delivered the blow. "They think he was hired to impersonate Zagan, honey. That was his job that night. Zagan and Carlisle had obviously been in cahoots for a long time. A body double makes for a perfect cover-up. And a perfect proxy."

"Oh," Eric mumbled quietly. "It was *my* brother who was set on fire and killed that night. Not yours." His gutted eyes looked over at Brax.

"It makes the most sense," Draven muttered.

"How does any of this make sense?" Brax suddenly burst out, leaping to his feet. "I mean, why? Why would Z do this?"

"I don't know," Sabre told him, walking over and taking his face between the palms of their hands. "I don't know," she repeated. "But, I promise you I'm going to find out."

Brax crumbled, practically folding himself against her. She wrapped her arms around him and held him tight. She was furious beyond belief that his own brother would hurt him like this. Brax had been mourning the death of his brother for almost a year and a half, not to mention all the other family members taken because of Zagan.

He'll pay, Sabre vowed silently, her eyes meeting those of Draven's over Brax's broad shoulder. She saw the same seething determination in his eyes that she knew would be in hers. They were on the same page for once. And Heaven help the male who had just become a target of two battle angels.

24

"I promise to contact you if Brax needs you," Sabre told Draven. She received a nod and weary wave as Gage helped Draven down the hallway.

She closed the door quietly and took a few seconds to lean back against the door, closing her eyes. She had convinced Brax to go and get the bath started. It had been a struggle because he was stubborn and looking for a fight. Sabre couldn't say she blamed him. And if it turned out he needed an argument, or if he needed to spar in order to exorcise himself of his pain and anger, then she would happily do that. But for now, she believed a little softness – a little peace – would be better suited.

"Who even am I?" she wondered out loud. "*Softness!*"

Pushing away from the door, she stopped next to Styx on

her way through the living area. He had not been present for all of the revelations earlier, but he was looking sad and worried now. The large hellhound was picking up on the feelings of his master.

"He'll be okay, boy," Sabre told him as she gave him a solid pat on the head. "Brax is going to be just fine. But his baby brother on the other hand, now that's a whole different story," she said, her voice turning low and lethal.

Styx's intimidating growl rumbled in his chest as if he approved of what he was hearing. And he likely did, she thought. Hellhounds were savage beasts capable of great acts of debauchery and violence. They were also extremely intelligent and loyal. Styx chose that moment to nudge her hand with his head, giving it a lick, before he trotted off to his bed by the door. He laid down with a small moan, crossing his front paws and placing his head on top of them.

"You look like the very epitome of a puppy. Sure, go ahead and do that sad doggy eye thing, just to contradict my thoughts about hellhound depravity," she said to the contrary canine. The thick ridge above his eyes lifted comically as if he was raising his eyebrows at her and Sabre waved her hand at him, chuckling lightly.

She entered the bedroom and shut the door, not wanting any interruptions even from the lovely hellhound. She could still hear the water running so she knew the giant bath was still filling up. She began to strip as she made her way into the bathroom, peeling off her layers one by one. By the time Sabre made it to the marbled room, she was completely naked.

She stood watching the large demon as he lounged in the tub with the dragon head taps. It was massive and more than accommodated his length, which was just as well because she planned on joining him. He had his hand over his eyes but moved it when she stepped into the hot water. She held her breath, waiting to see what he would do. She was happily relieved when he didn't hesitate to pull her against him so that her back was flush with his chest. She tugged on his wrists and wrapped his arms around her chest, not satisfied until she was caught up in an Abraxis straitjacket.

“Why would he do this?” was his first question.

“I don't know. In fact, I have no theories whatsoever,” she answered quietly. “I didn't really know him at all. In the same way that I didn't really know you. Yes, I discovered Mikhail when he was a baby. And I made sure I had every opportunity to get close to him and get to know him. King Maliq made sure of that. He facilitated my getting into the palace, as well as finding ways for Mikhail and me to meet safely and discreetly elsewhere over the years. But I very deliberately stayed out of your path. And Zagan's.”

She turned her head a fraction, looking into his eyes. “Mikhail wanted to tell you about me. He really did. But I always talked him out of it. The more people who know a secret, the harder it is to keep."

Brax's muttered, "Mmhmm," vibrated through his chest and into her back. It also went straight to her core if she was being honest. She pressed her legs tightly together and told her libido to get a grip. It was not the time to get frisky. It was the time to be emotionally available for Brax. She could Venus flytrap his dick later.

"What about the stalking you did of me from afar? Gage and Jinx tell me you've had a thing for my derriere for years," Brax told her, surprising her with the humour in his voice.

She turned her head to meet his eyes once more. The yellow depths were shadowed with pain and confusion, but they also held amusement and love. So much love for the likes of her. *Oh yes,* she swore to herself once again. *I'm going to make Zagan pay.* And when she thought about how the news was going to impact Mikhail, she knew it was going to be a *double* dose of vengeance.

Mikhail had given up everything in order to protect what was left of his family and his royal heritage. He had given up his position as king, lost his standing with his people, gambled his relationship with his brother, abandoned his home, and even given up his very *life.* And all along, it was his brother conspiring against him. Sabre knew she had to tell him as a matter of urgency. She would do it in person as soon as she knew Brax was going to be okay.

There was a brief flare of guilt when she realised she was prioritising Brax's wellbeing over that of her charge. But the worry and anxiety she had experienced over the past few weeks about how she was going to balance the conflict of interests were no longer as sharp. It now seemed so simple. Brax was here with her now, and he needed her now. So, she would be there for him. When she was with Mikhail and *he* needed her, she would be there for *him*. There was enough of her to go around.

Love didn't have a limit – a maximum capacity. Sharing it around did not diminish it at all. In fact, it was the opposite. The more you loved, the more it expanded to accommodate those around you.

"Damn, girl. Check you out with the emotional growth," she mumbled, swirling the hairs on Brax's arms with her fingers.

"What's that?" Brax asked, giving her a squeeze.

Sabre explained her newfound emotive maturity.

Brax brushed a kiss against the nape of her neck, his feet tangling with hers under the water. "I'm so proud of you."

Her heart squeezed in her chest before it started to pound so loudly she figured Brax must be able to hear it – and feel it. Nobody had ever said those words to her before. Not Maliq, or Mikhail, or her ragtag group of friends. Brax was proud of her, and it was somehow just as life-altering as knowing he loved her. It meant he admired her, believed she was worthy and understood the momentous journey she had travelled from *then* to *now*. It was like saying, 'congratulations, all your dedication and sacrifice has paid off,' but in a more connected way. Pride was intimate because it was based on the relationship you had with the person.

With the knowledge that she had Brax's love *and* pride, came the realisation that she was going to make a promise. A binding promise. Something she thought she would never do again after circumstances forced her to do it before with Carlisle, *twice*. She knew it wouldn't be the same this time though. This time, she would be making a vow freely, with no reservations. And also with no agenda.

She took a deep breath, told Brax she appreciated his words, and then adopted an innocent expression. "And I have no idea what you're referring to about me stalking you." She pursed her lips, "And who says derriere?"

Brax snorted, his arms tightening around her for a moment before he said, "Uh-huh. Sure, you don't. What about that time you watched me trying on my ceremonial robes in my room? I don't wear anything under those."

Sabre gasped and sat up straight, pulling away from him and splashing water over the side of the tub. "Jinx told you about that? The little traitor!" she hissed. Brax laughed and Sabre was relieved he could still do so. Still, she had told Jinx that in confidence one night when they had been doing shots in the warehouse. The little tiger was going to pay.

"I was only twenty-one at the time, I believe. That was

rather pervy of you," Brax tsked. "Dirty older angel peeping at the younger, naked demon."

Sabre 'peeped' at him now with all of his tanned, wet skin, and taut muscles ... A young Brax had been intriguing and beautiful. But the mature man in front of her was the complete package. She finally admitted, "Okay, maybe I had a thing for you. But that was scary and confusing to me. I didn't know why I was drawn to you. So I buckled down even harder to maintain distance from you. It's why I hadn't even met Styx before. I was staying well away from anything and everything to do with you."

The amusement in Brax's eyes fled to be replaced with understanding. "I get it. I also know why you were drawn to me. The same way I was drawn to you the first time I saw you."

Of course he did, Sabre thought. "We'll figure this whole thing out."

"Yes," Brax agreed. "Together."

Always together. Then she moved in closer and touched her lips to his. The kiss was chaste by their usual standards, but no less intense. They kissed and stroked, hands running over slick flesh until the easy and the gentle became the fast and the frantic. Sabre soon found herself pushed back against the side of the tub, Brax's hard body between her legs. She clutched him by the ears as he tugged on a sensitised nipple with his teeth. Gasping, she arched her back, pressing herself against him even further, her ankles locking around his back. And just as she was about to tilt her hips to take him inside, Brax pulled back.

His cheeks were flushed, his eyes were glowing, and he was panting roughly. “Bed,” was all he said.

Sabre nodded, all too happy to obey.

25

Brax allowed Sabre to gently push him onto the bed. He didn't mind Sabre taking the reins under the circumstances. She didn't immediately join him and he took the opportunity to observe her as she stood boldly naked next to the bed.

Her short, black hair was so dark and shiny that it held a few hints of blue when the light hit it right. Her body was a masterpiece of perfection, from her strong shoulders to her toned calves. There wasn't a lot of softness to her body, she was far too disciplined for that. Her body was just another one of her weapons and she kept it well maintained, just like she would a gun or a blade. His eyes zeroed in on her small breasts and the mound between her legs, thinking, *well, there are two places where she is soft.*

"Thank you for tonight," he said when Sabre continued

to stand next to the bed watching him. "For handling the craziness like a boss. For taking care of me."

"I haven't finished yet," she said, the words like a promise. "And I'm just returning the favour. You've been taking care of me since we met. I didn't think I wanted anyone to take care of me. I didn't think I needed that. But I did. I do. Thank you."

"I love you," was Brax's simple response. As far as he was concerned, it was the only one that mattered. And it explained everything.

"I know," Sabre assured him. Then she smiled, her eyes lighting up delightfully. "I love you more."

He laughed, feeling another fragment of his newly broken heart lock back into place. "It's not a competition," he reminded her, thinking back to the first time they had expressed their feelings for each other.

Sabre rolled her eyes. "You keep telling yourself that, babe. Everything in life is a competition."

"And you're a winner," he told her, shaking his head and grinning.

"You're damn right I'm a winner," she agreed, smirking at him. Then her face softened. "I'm a winner because I have you."

"Sabre..." he murmured thickly.

"Ever since you gave me this," Sabre said, touching the key around her neck. "I've been trying to think of something I can give you in return."

Brax frowned and sat up, sitting on the edge of the bed now. "It's not about owing me anything. You don't have to give me anything because I gave you something. That's not how gifts work."

"I know that. But I want to," Sabre said with emphasis. "Is that okay with you, Your Majesty?"

Brax curled his lips in, fighting back his laughter. Sabre was very touchy sometimes, but it was hard to take her seriously when she was looking so adorably disgruntled, standing there naked with her hands on her hips.

"What's so funny?" she demanded, reading him well.

"Sorry," he said, a small chuckle escaping. "It's just ... you're so cute when you're mad."

Sabre narrowed her eyes. "Cute? Always with the insults ..." she muttered.

"I'm sorry," he apologised, adopting a serious expression. "I'll behave. You were saying ...?"

"I'm wondering if the mood is ruined now," Sabre commented, crossing her arms over her chest and inadvertently plumping her breasts.

He licked his lips, eyeing the subtle curves over the tops of her arms. Then lowered his gaze to her core, which was now conveniently located directly in front of his face. "Oh, the mood isn't ruined, trust me." His cock was standing up straight and tall, and it was impossibly hard. He wanted her. *Bad.* He was going to grab her and toss her down when he caught the look on her face. It was nervous almost. "Sabre? Everything okay?"

She licked her lips and nodded quickly. She took a breath and said, "My gift ..." She kept her eyes locked on his as her wings began to slowly unfurl from behind her back.

Brax froze, all deer caught in the headlights. "Sabre ..." he breathed, unsure how to react. He was spellbound.

Her wings continued to expand until they were stretched out on either side of her. She flapped them twice and Brax felt the displaced air against his face. The dull, artificial light in the room was enough to make the golden feathers shine, but he longed to see them glow in the sunlight. Her red feathers appeared darker than usual, more like red wine or a well-aged port. The contrast was striking and so fucking magnificent it literally took his breath away.

She let him look his fill for a moment before she stepped forward into the space between his legs and wrapped her arms around his neck. She bent her head down a little so their foreheads touched and wrapped her wings around his back, effectively wrapping them both up in a feathery cocoon. "Touch them," she urged.

Brax loathed to create distance between them, so he simply ran his hands up her back, stopping to feel where her wings protruded from her skin. It was odd because there was no open wound but there *was* a discernible attachment point. It was hard, but not like bone. More like how a deer antler was attached. Her feathers covered the hard nub, and he traced his fingers over the red and gold plumes reverently. They were very soft, and strangely, radiated warmth. The stemlike structure that ran down the centre of the feathers was very hard, but as he moved it a little, testing its strength, he found it to be slightly flexible. He was utterly fascinated.

When he sniffed at a large primary feather near his face, Sabre's amused chuckle met his ears. He looked up, finding eyes of plum dancing into his. He blushed, ducking his head. "Sorry, didn't mean to make it weird."

Sabre placed two fingers underneath his chin, tilting his head up so their eyes met. "You can touch my wings any time you like, and in any way."

Brax's brain went on the fritz for a moment, a visual of Sabre sprawled out naked on the ground with her wings spread out wide while he jerked himself off until he came all over her, at the forefront of his mind. His cock twitched and he felt pre-cum trickle from the tip.

"I have no idea what you're thinking about, but I'm going to need you to tell me," Sabre declared, voice husky.

Brax had to clear his throat twice before he was able to reply. "Sure ..."

"But first," Sabre said, "do you understand what it means when an angel makes a promise?"

Brax looked at her face, noting the seriousness had returned. He nodded his head slowly, replying, "I believe so." He understood the significance of Draven's vow to be his guardian. It had resulted in a life-long bond.

"I can't bite you and leave my mark on you like a shifter. I can't bind our souls together for eternity like a vampire. But I can promise to be yours. I can promise to love you and respect you and be there for you, for the rest of our days," Sabre told him.

His breath stuttered out and his heart pounded wildly in his chest. "Sabre ..."

She pulled back far enough to cup his face in her hands. "Abraxis, second-born son of the late King Maliq, second in line to the throne of Purgatory, descendant of Cerberus, I, Isrephel, claim you as my mate. I claim you as my partner in all things. I promise I will always belong to you. I promise you will always be mine."

"You promise?" Brax confirmed, voice wavering.

"I promise."

Brax didn't know if it was his imagination or a trick of the light, but he could have sworn her eyes flashed gold for a moment. A current of ... *something* ... moved between them and he placed a kiss directly over her heart. "Isrephel," he then whispered in wonder.

"That's me. At least, who I used to be. And maybe still am a little. Who knows. I think Sabre suits me better though," Sabre said.

Brax wasn't so sure, knowing Isrephel was a very old name. It was a Heavenly, *royal* name. "I like Sabre just fine. It *does* suit you," he told her, knowing what she needed in that moment.

Sabre swallowed audibly, looking relieved. Then her expression changed lustful just before she tackled him onto the bed.

Now that all the sap and all the formalities were out of the way, Sabre felt ravenous in her need. She climbed on top of a very willing Abraxis, held his erection up and dropped down onto it in one swift motion. Her breath caught in her lungs, and she felt like ants were crawling over her skin. She was on fire and ice cold at the same time.

She rode him hard, planting her hands on his shoulders for leverage. Back and forth, up and down, over and over until she couldn't think straight. The fierce look on Brax's face wasn't what she would call pretty as he frowned and grunted, clearly feeling pleasure with painful intensity. Sabre was right there with him. He grabbed her hips and slammed her down, his hips moving as well. The friction was too much to last and he came with a roar.

"Isrephel!" he bellowed.

As much as she didn't want to be called her angelic name in public, and as much as she felt more like Sabre, hearing the word on the lips of the man she loved as she was giving him pleasure, made her go a little mad. She lost control of her body – and perhaps of her damn mind as well.

She pumped herself wildly over his still bucking hips,

feeling the hot splash of his cum inside her. She bent forward and sunk her teeth into his neck, needing something more to grip, something else to anchor her body. She forgot all about his armour – and so, apparently – did his DNA. She felt his hot, slick skin give way beneath her savage bite. Her blunt teeth were very much those of a human, but they could do a lot of damage. She felt blood fill her mouth and bit down harder, frenzied and fuelled by instincts. Her wings beat wildly behind her but thankfully didn't cause her to lose her grip on his neck – or his dick. Rocking her hips a few more times, her orgasm finally hit her and she released her mouth from Brax's neck so she could scream.

By the time her body stopped spasming in ecstasy, her throat was sore from all the shrieking. She collapsed onto Brax's chest, her body twitching with aftershocks. It was almost too much and she didn't know whether she was feeling amazing or whether she felt like she'd been hit by lightning.

"What in the ever-loving fuck was that?" Brax demanded from beneath her.

Sabre licked her very dry lips, unsure how to answer. Her brain wasn't working. But when she tasted blood, she bolted upright, looking at Brax's neck in horror. "Oh, my fucking hell! What ... how?" she stuttered.

Brax reached up with a shaking hand to touch the wound on his neck. It came away bloody. He looked at his red fingers in stunned disbelief. "You bit me."

Sabre grimaced, looking at the nasty injury. "I think it's a little more than a bite. I kind of ... *chewed* on you."

They stared at each other for a moment before they started to snicker, and then laugh. Perhaps they were both a little hysterical. Once they had calmed and were holding onto each other, Sabre said, "But seriously, what happened?"

"I think you mated with me. Like, for real mated," Brax proposed.

"Angels don't mate," was her automatic response. But it felt like a lie.

"I think maybe they can, under the right circumstances. Much like a demon can create a bond by continued claiming," Brax explained.

"And the right circumstances would be ...?" Sabre questioned.

"I'm thinking something like a binding promise from a righteous angel, created in the Heavens themselves. And with their Heavenly-gifted name no less. Names hold power, just as vows do," Brax reminded her softly.

Sabre stared at the ceiling in silence. She didn't know if she was ecstatic or terrified. "Okay. Okay. We're mated somehow. I can deal."

"Are you sure?" Brax asked, looking at her in concern.

She took a deep breath and forced herself to calm down and really think about it. When she did, she realised she was indeed okay. In fact, she was filled with joy and wonder. Brax was really hers now. And she was really his. No matter what happened with the throne or Zagan or even the fate of the world, Brax wasn't going anywhere. Because she had lassoed him good and proper. The thought had her smiling.

Brax blew out a relieved breath. "And there it is, the look I was hoping for. You're happy."

"Very," Sabre promised him, giving him a kiss. Pulling back, she added, "But I am also sorry. Your neck is a mess. How come your shield didn't prevent this?" she wondered, running a finger over the still-oozing bite.

"My armour is automatic – self-determining," he reminded her. "Looks like my legacy has determined you're not a threat. Or at least, you're a threat that it wants."

"Cool," Sabre decided.

Brax laughed. "Very cool, indeed. It seems to be doing lots of cool things lately, like frying people. We're going to have to figure that one out, too."

"We will," she assured him, patting his arm in support. "But just let me check something first ..." she murmured, before retrieving a small ball hammer from underneath her pillow. She brought it down quickly on Brax's chest. He flinched, but he needn't have worried. His scaly exoskeleton rushed to the surface, blocking the blow. "Phew, that's lucky," she said, wiping sweat off her brow.

"I'll say," Brax agreed. "That would have smashed my sternum!"

"Your sternum?" Sabre questioned. "Who cares about your sternum. I was referring to my desire to stab you at any chosen moment. If your legacy stopped reacting to me all the time, it would seriously put a dampener on my fun."

Brax grunted and rolled to his back. "Of course. We wouldn't want to ruin your fun."

She was glad he agreed.

26

Sabre was nervous. She hadn't seen Mikhail in person for a long time, since before the big reveal to Carlisle. Kind of a lot had happened since then.

The last time she had seen him she had confessed that she did indeed love Brax and she wanted to pursue something with him. Mikhail had given his blessing, of course, because he wasn't an arsehole. But that had been before more shit had hit the fan. Now that the end game was in play, would things be different for him? It was too late, if that was the case because there was no going back.

She stood at the post office box in a shitty downtown alleyway, in the middle of the warehouse district. She had left her mark on it earlier in the day, her signal for needing to meet urgently. She knew Mikhail would open a portal exactly two hours later. A cold breeze ruffled her hair and she fought off the chill. The days were cooling and the nights were becoming longer. That wasn't necessarily a bad thing when you had a demon mate to share the nights with. Plus, now that she was free of the bond with Carlisle and the den, she had far fewer restrictions on her time.

She shook her head, more than a little bemused with how she had gained a new bond right when she had lost one. She again fretted, beginning to pace, as she wondered what Mikhail would make of that. The link with her official new mate was a different connection to the one between guardian and charge, but it was no less vital to her. She only hoped Mikhail's support was still there, and that he would be happy for her and also for his brother. It was a major development to inform him of, but it wasn't the only one – and not even the biggest. On top of that, she had to tell Mikhail that it was his triplet who was behind all the killings.

She, Brax, and Draven had talked that morning about the whys and hows. But they were largely drawing a blank. She had spoken to X twice now – at the veil entrance and then in the forest – and she knew he wasn't interested in the throne simply for the sake of being a king. That would have been too easy. Zagan was far too fucked in the head for that. His motivation had to have more significance. She was hoping Mikhail may be able to shed some light on the situation but knew it may take a while for him to calm down. Or even believe her. After all, their evidence against Zagan was circumstantial. They really had no proof that X was Z. It was based purely on timing. And gut instinct. She figured the gut of two angels and one demon was more than enough, but it may not be.

On her next turn, she drew up short when she noticed a small light in the air in front of her. It was nothing more than a white dot at first, but it slowly got bigger, expanding outwards until it was big enough for her to step through. It was a portal and very different to a veil. The fissure created by Mikhail was essentially a hole in reality, a tunnel between planes. He was one of a very few beings that could open a doorway that went both ways, and she didn't hesitate to step through.

The transition from Purgatory to Earth didn't feel like anything in particular. It was as easy as walking through a door. She stopped as soon as she stepped through and simply stared at the man in front of her. He was tall and muscled but not bulky or overly broad. His physique was more of a track athlete or a swimmer, rather than a body-builder. He had a bald head and bright green eyes, and a square jaw with several days' worth of beard growth. He was surrounded by about half a dozen people including the fae prince, who was responsible for keeping his true face hidden.

When Mikhail had first told Sabre of his plan to die and go undercover as Hound she had said no, of course. She had said no hundreds of times before they had finally agreed the best way to ensure he would be kept safe when she wasn't around was to alter his appearance. Thinking back to the time when he had hounded her with his plan until she finally acquiesced, that was the only time she could recall in their acquaintance that they had ever fought. It was the only time she could recall that she had ever truly been mad at him. She loved Mikhail, loved everything about him. That was, until the day he had ordered her to put a crossbow bolt directly into his heart.

She recalled looking down at his dead body, his blood flowing around him in a red river of betrayal, and she had hated him. And her hate for him had caused her to despise herself. There had been a heartbeat of time, a split millisecond, where she had considered not bringing him back. A punishment, if you will, for both of them. But her heart, and her duty, would not allow for that. They had reconnected, of course, and she had forgiven him as much as she had been able to. She didn't hate him anymore. But there was still anger there. There was still resentment. There was still *pain.* Mikhail had apologised repeatedly for the need to take such drastic action. But he had never once apologised for *ordering* her to do it.

Shaking off her thoughts, Sabre noticed that Mikhail was standing there with his head cocked to the side, studying her closely. She let him look, for once, not hiding her expression. He gave a chuff and opened his arms wide. That's when she cracked and all but flew into his arms, nearly knocking him off his feet. He wrapped them around her, and although he was in a different body, his hugs felt exactly the same. Mikhail had always been good at giving hugs. They held each other tight for a few moments, saying nothing, before she pulled back.

Mikhail placed his palms on her cheeks and looked at her closely. "Last time I saw you, you told me you were in love with Brax."

"I remember," she said.

Mikhail nodded and hummed. "And now I see it's more than that. You're his."

"I am," Sabre responded simply. When he didn't say anything else, she began to get a little nervous. Shoring up her courage, she asked, "Are you okay with that?"

Mikhail dropped his hands and paced back and forth. His guard of carefully selected loyal men and women watched him but made no move to intervene between the two of them. They knew better. "Is that okay?" Mikhail repeated. "Are you kidding? It's fantastic!"

And finally, Sabre saw the joy on his face. He was telling the truth. Her shoulders slumped a little, tension leaving her in a rush.

"I couldn't have found a better mate for Brax than you. You know, I always saw the way you looked at him. Like he was a juicy antelope steak, and you were a starving she-lion in the Serengeti."

Sabre gasped. "I did not!"

Mikhail chuckled, "Oh, you did. Trust me, you did. And it

was a way you had never looked at anyone before. I thought there was some potential there. I wasn't sure what Brax would make of you, of course. But I was hopeful."

"Hey!" she yelled, offended once again. Mikhail ignored her.

"I was worried maybe you would eat him alive," he continued. "But I knew out of everyone in the world, Brax would be the one person who could save you. I knew that you, after dedicating your entire life to saving others, would eventually need a saviour for yourself."

Sabre toed the ground, feeling embarrassed and humbled. To overcome the annoying sensation, she scoffed. "Saving others? I don't think so. Have you forgotten about the thousands of people I've killed? Including yourself."

"I haven't forgotten. I know exactly what you are, Sabre. You're an angel and a blessing, and I am so relieved to know that my brother isn't as slow as I thought he was. Because he clearly knows it too if he has claimed you."

Sabre had to blink quickly to dispel the moisture in her eyes. She'd be damned if she would cry in front of Mikhail and his lackeys. A smile kicked up the corner of Mikhail's mouth as if he knew exactly what she was thinking. *Which he no doubt does,* Sabre acknowledged silently.

"You have news?" he then prompted.

Right, back to work, she told herself. "I do."

Mikhail motioned her over to a seat in the corner of an open plan apartment. She wandered over and sat herself down by the window, looking out at the water in the distance. “You really do have a nice view here,” she commented.

Mikhail turned and ran his eyes critically over the view of Darling Harbour, Sydney, complete with the iconic Opera House and Harbour Bridge. It was a sunny day, and the water was sparkling with the reflection from the rays of the sun. It looked calm and quiet. But that was a deceptive impression because she knew the bustling city was loud and hectic. And the surface of the ocean also hid many turbulent secrets.

“It is a good view,” Mikhail agreed, “but I can think of a better one; Purgatory.”

“Well, you're a few steps closer to getting that view back. In fact, I think it's probably time for you to return.”

“What?” Mikhail quickly leaned closer, grabbing one of her hands. “What's been happening? What's going on? Is everyone okay? Last I heard, Phaedra said Carlisle was on the run and you were doing everything you could to find him. Did you succeed?”

“I guess it depends on your definition of success. Brax crushed Carlisle's head in his hand,” Sabre revealed. “Making his brains explode kind of like a busted water balloon.”

“Really?” Mikhail perked up at that, smiling a little evilly. “I wish I had seen that. You’re free of the assassin contract then?” Sabre nodded. He squeezed her hand saying, “Thank fuck. I definitely consider it a success.”

"Let's see, what else ... Oh, I know, Brax's armour did some funky thing and basically electrocuted Draven into unconsciousness."

"It did what?" Mikhail exclaimed, looking shocked.

Sabre nodded. "I know, weird, right? It overtook his entire body and made him look like some kind of sentinel-shapeshifter robot. It was hot. Plus, you should have seen the way Draven flew backwards. And the weird goat-fuck sound he made." Sabre sighed, reminiscing. "Good times."

"His armour did something other than defensive. I've never heard of such a thing," Mikhail said, looking intrigued but also a bit concerned.

"It sure did. We haven't been able to figure out how to make it do it again, but we think it's linked with his emotions."

Mikhail frowned. "How so?"

"Well ..." Sabre hedged, speaking more carefully now. "I think it has something to do with feelings of incredible rage ..."

"Ah, of course. Carlisle." Mikhail assumed.

Sabre cleared her throat, shifting a little uncomfortably in her seat. "No, not Carlisle."

Mikhail squinted at her a little before his breath caught in his throat. "You know. You figured it out, didn't you? Who?! Who is the fucker that has been killing our family – who killed our father and baby brother? Why did he do it?!"

"We don't know why," Sabre told him. "We've got a little

bit more to go on than we once did. Luca is helping with that."

"Lucifer?" Sabre nodded. "Okay, then. I don't need the why yet. But the *who* ... tell me now."

Sabre reached for Mikhail's hands once more. This time holding them between her own. Tightly. "My dear friend, I am so sorry. It is Zagan."

"Zagan," he repeated, face shutting down as if he had gridlocked his emotions. He tried to tug his hand free but she wouldn't let him.

"I know it sounds crazy. I know it's hard to believe. But it's him. At least we're pretty sure it's him. I –" but she didn't get to finish.

Mikhail snapped out of his stupor and looked at her sharply. He tugged with more force, pulling his hands back. "What do you mean *'pretty sure'*? Are you saying you don't know? You can't just make an accusation like that, Sabre."

"Hey," Sabre returned sharply. "Be careful with your tone. You don't get to sit there and tell me what accusations I can and cannot make in this war when I'm the one who has been on the frontlines the entire time."

"I've been helping," Mikhail gritted out.

"*Helping ...*" Sabre tried to keep the bitterness from her voice. "Fine. You have been helping. I acknowledge that. But you haven't been there for a while now, not the same way I have been. Now, if you are ready to listen, I'll tell you what we know."

Mikhail's jaw was clenched hard to match the hardened look in his eyes. It was a look she rarely saw directed at herself. But she wasn't backing down. *Perhaps I have more anger and resentment leftover than I thought,* she admitted to herself. She kept her silence – and his stare – until he slumped, scrubbing his hands over his face. She felt like a bitch. This was his baby brother she was talking about, and so far from left field. "I'm sorry."

Mikhail drew himself up, looking every inch a king despite his appearance and the setting. "No. I am sorry. I'm ready. Tell me everything."

Then she did.

27

Brax stared at the male in front of him. The bald head and the bone structure were of someone he recognised as Hound, the rebel leader.

He had only ever met with Hound a couple of times personally, and it was always in the dark. He had never been able to make out the other man's eyes. If he had, he would have been questioning his sanity long before now. Because the green eyes staring back at him from across the room were undeniably Mikhail's.

"Mikhail, is it really you?" he couldn't help but ask.

"It's really me," Hound replied gruffly. He motioned to a man next to him and he stepped up, waving his hand in front of Hound's face.

Before his very eyes, Brax's big brother appeared once more. The shaved head made way to brown locks much the same as his own, but with lighter highlights. His green eyes glowed with an unholy light, evidence of the beast riding his soul, much like Brax's. His face slimmed down some, losing much of the square jawline and gaining higher cheekbones. Mikhail's features were very symmetrical and he was more classically handsome than Brax was. Everything in his bearing from his straight shoulders and back to the way he held his hands gently clasped in front of him, screamed royalty. Mikhail was, in every way, a king.

Brax felt himself choke up because even though he had believed Sabre when she'd said Mikhail was alive, he had also seen his brother's dead eyes staring silently at the ceiling as his blood pooled around his cold body. They were images that Brax would never forget seeing. Mikhail as he was now, healthy and whole, did not erase the nightmare, and as happy and relieved and joyous as he felt, seeing his brother and the rightful King of Purgatory, he also felt anger and pain. So, when Mikhail's own eyes began to become suspiciously shiny and he opened his arms wide for a hug, Brax took the final two steps towards him and punched him straight in the jaw.

Mikhail went down hard, the circle of people around him glaring daggers and cursing Brax. "How the fuck could you?!" he snarled at his brother.

Mikhail said nothing for a moment. He remained on his arse looking up at Brax and wiggling his jaw from side to side. Brax knew it wasn't broken. Even in his rage, he had pulled his strength at the last minute. Yes, he wanted to hurt his brother, but he didn't want to dismember him.

"I'm sorry," Mikhail said with the same voice Brax had heard every day of his life except for the last grief-stricken twelve and bit months.

"Sorry doesn't fucking cut it," Brax told him. "What were you thinking?"

Mikhail got slowly to his feet, brushing off the hands that tried to help him and telling everyone to stay back. "I was thinking I wanted to save your life. That I wanted to save Zagan's life."

Brax snorted, sneering at his older brother. "Oh, yeah. That worked out so well for you, didn't it? I thought I was the last one of us left. We were born as triplets and I had to bury you both!"

Mikhail swallowed noisily, shaking his head and looking pathetic. "Don't ..."

"Don't? Really? You don't get to stand there and tell me what to do, Mikhail. You died. I grieved you. I thought you were fucking dead. And then Zagan was killed as well. With father and mother long gone, I had no one. It changed me, Mikhail."

And it had, Brax thought. He had always been easy-going and nice. Not especially flirty nor in love with the limelight like his younger brother, Zagan. But he hadn't been a grumpy recluse either. He had been friendly. He had been happy. The fact that he was a general for an army and had made a career out of being a soldier hadn't changed him in any profound way. He'd still had fun with his friends. He'd still played happily with his hellhound. But the loss of both of his brothers in such a short timeframe had taken those parts of himself away.

On top of that, losing the king and having to ascend to the throne – an honour Brax had never wanted – had changed him on a profound level. He had become angry, more than angry even. He had been so filled with rage that all he had been able to think about was vengeance. He stopped smiling. He didn't see his friends. He also didn't accept the responsibility of the throne, which meant that all the supernatural creatures of Purgatory had suffered as well.

The one bright spark in that miserable downward spiral had been hitting rock bottom, as strange as it seemed at first. Because it had led him to the narrowed-eyed woman leaning against the wall over by the windows. Sabre had her legs stretched out in front of her, with her ankles and arms crossed. She looked as if she didn't have a care in the world. But Brax knew better. He could read her. And not just because they were officially mated now, but because she let him *see* her. She let him see the *real* her. It was a gift almost greater than her love for him. And Brax vowed never to take that gift for granted.

Thinking back to how he felt when he had sought her out at the illegal fight club all those months ago, he couldn't say he would do it all again. Because the pain, pounding fresh and acute throughout his body once more, was a pain he never wanted to experience again. But he also knew he was happy and grateful to have Sabre, and that he wouldn't give her up for anything.

Sabre tipped her head at him and smiled, saluting him with one of her knives. He smiled back, knowing she could read him the same way he could her, and that she didn't fault him for being on the fence about turning back time. Looking back at Mikhail now, his brother looked weary but also more at ease. As if he knew Brax had been struggling with his inner demons and that he had now successfully reconciled them to some extent. It was true, but Brax wasn't willing to give an inch yet.

Mikhail looked at Sabre, gesturing to his already-bruising jaw. "Are you going to protect me?" Sabre simply flipped him the bird and Mikhail shook his head in mock disappointment.

Brax could clearly see the love and affection his brother held for Sabre. He was going to have to explore how he felt about having to share Sabre with his brother – not in a gross way – but in a guardian/charge way. He was more than familiar with the type of bond thanks to Draven, of course. But it was very likely still going to be an adjustment. Especially to the beast in his soul who was possessive as all fuck.

"Some guardian angel you are," one of Mikhail's flunkeys sneered at Sabre abruptly.

In the blink of an eye, Brax's claws were out and he had

them wrapped around the fool's throat. He backed the guy up until he hit the wall, squeezing with enough pressure for blood to trickle down the thin, pale neck. Leaning in close, he growled, "What the fuck did you just say?" The shifter's eyes bulged, and he gasped for breath. He was unable to reply even if he wanted to because Brax was choking the air out of him.

"Brax, how about you put the fox shifter down, hmm?" Draven said from behind him where he had been watching the proceedings with caution.

It had only been Sabre, Brax, and Draven to come through the portal to Earth a few hours after Sabre had gone to talk to Mikhail by herself. Brax understood why she had needed to see her charge alone first after so much had happened. And though it made him feel cowardly, he was relieved he hadn't been the one to tell his big brother that the little brother they both loved and helped raise, had been trying to kill them all.

When Brax didn't move, other than to curl his lips back, flashing his fangs, Draven sighed and turned to Mikhail. "Do you maybe want to step in here, my lord?"

Mikhail looked at the shifter in disdain and disappointment. "Why would I want to do that? It seems to me, that Foxy here could use a lesson in manners."

Brax felt himself thaw further. This was the Mikhail he knew and loved. His brother was loyal and protective first, above all else. Whether it was the richest person in the room or the lowliest servant, Mikhail was always on the side of right. He always stood up for the person who was wronged. He fought for the downtrodden and he sought justice. Brax was glad to see that hadn't changed.

The shifter managed to gasp three words out, "But my lord –"

"Silence!" Mikhail's voice lashed out like a whip. "You insulted my guardian. My best friend. You have done good work for me, Timothy, and I appreciate it. I really do. But if you ever speak about Sabre that way again, in my presence or anywhere else, I will kill you myself. Do you understand?"

Timothy looked on the verge of tears, having displeased his master, and Brax let him go. No doubt the little fox shifter thought to gain points and look like a hero or a tough guy to his peers. When in actual fact, he just looked like a douche. Brax felt warmth from behind him and turned to find Sabre at his back. She smiled and wrapped her arms around his neck.

"My hero," she practically purred and then proceeded to maul Brax's mouth.

Brax responded in kind, heedless of their audience, and in fact revelling in it. He wanted to stake his claim in front of everyone, including his brother. When they finally pulled apart, Brax glared at his brother, his eyes flashing.

Mikhail held up his hands in surrender and rolled his eyes. "Yeah, I get it. Sabre is yours. You can relax, little brother. I have no issue with your claim on my guardian."

Sabre huffed, "Wow. I'll say, that is very magnanimous of you, Mikhail."

Brax covered his snicker with a cough. He was gratified to see that Sabre took no shit from her charge. Releasing Sabre, he walked back over to his brother. They stood looking at each other in silence for a moment before Mikhail spoke up.

"I'm sorry. Do you think you can forgive me one day?"

Brax was happy to hear the apology. And even happier to hear that Mikhail had realistic expectations. He didn't expect Brax to forgive him right now, at this moment. Forgiveness would take time. Healing would take time. For all of them. Still, his brother was standing before him, healthy and whole, and Brax was so very grateful. So he simply nodded his head and this time dragged his brother into his arms.

The two demons held each other tight patting each other on the back, not saying anything because there was nothing more to say. Before he released his brother, Brax spoke quietly into his ear. "Yes. I will forgive you one day, Mikhail. I'm sure I will. But first, you're going to have to make things right with Sabre. Because as much as you injured me – as much pain as you cost me – the mission you tasked Sabre with was even more painful. She's bleeding, Mikhail. You can't see it from the outside but she's bleeding out internally. You made her *kill* you."

Mikhail dropped his forehead against Brax's shoulder and Brax accepted the king's weight gladly. His brother nodded his head, and it was enough. He knew words were likely clogged in his brother's throat. He eventually released the slightly shorter man and asked, "Now what?"

"Now ..." Mikhail said, green eyes flashing and a predatory growl rumbling in his chest. "We *hunt*."

Brax felt an answering growl rise from his own throat. He nodded decisively, agreeing, "We hunt."

It didn't matter that they were hunting their own baby brother.

It didn't matter that it was going to break something integral inside of them both.

They were going hunting, and Heaven help anyone who stood in their way.

EPILOGUE

"Okay, so check it," Jinx said, leaning companionably close to Draven. "After shredding her underwear like a beast in heat, if you notice her lady-box is naked and smooth like she's recently tortured herself with hot wax for hours, it means she wants your face on it. And by *it* I mean-"

"I know what you mean!" Draven burst out, feeling his face burn like an inferno.

"I mean the lady-box, the pussy palace, otherwise known as the pearl purse ..." Jinx continued doggedly.

Draven felt his eyes widen. "The pearl purse?!"

Jinx hummed, "It's been known to be called that."

"By who?!" he barked out.

"By people with an actual sex drive," Jinx smirked at him.

Draven dropped his head in his hands, muttering, "Dear

Gods, why did I think it was a good idea to ask you about this?"

"Because you want to lose your V-card and you knew I would tell you the truth and give it to you straight," Jinx answered. "Now, speaking of giving it straight, the clit is not a turntable, and you are not a DJ. There's no need to rub it back and forth so hard she gets friction burns. There's also no need to slap at it with your dick." Jinx levelled bi-coloured eyes full of seriousness in Draven's direction and shook her finger at him. "I know the clit looks like a love-button but please resist the temptation to whack it with the force of your love-stick."

Draven felt his love-stick shrivel with every word Jinx spoke. Did men really slap their penises against lady bits? *Why?!* he wondered, though he wasn't crazy enough or stupid enough to ask out loud. He was already in a nightmare of untold horrors. He didn't want to make it worse.

"I don't want to whack her with anything. I just want to ask Phaedra out on a date. That's it," Draven said, trying his best to contain the situation. "All of the, err, sexual advice is appreciated but premature."

"Premature ejaculation is quite common. Don't feel bad about that," Jinx said, patting Draven kindly on the arm.

Draven's jaw dropped and his back stiffened. "I assure you; I have no issues in that department." He paused, thought about it for a moment and then slumped. "At least, I don't think I do. What if I do?" Dear Gods, he was starting to panic.

"Draven, relax. I'm sorry, I shouldn't mess with you. I think it's wonderful that you want to take Phaedra on a date. She's really great. Don't worry about the rest of it for now. Deal with it as it comes along. I doubt she'll try to jump your bones on the first night. And you're a gentleman, so I know *you* won't try it," Jinx said kindly.

"I *am* a gentleman," he confirmed, sounding stuffy even to his own ears. He studied the lovely young werecreature in front of him, noting the cheekiness and fun in her eyes but also the endless kindness. She had a bearing that belied her years, wisdom and grace shone through even when she was attempting to give him a heart attack. Jinx always had a kind word and an intelligent answer for every situation. It was why he had sought her out. He should have anticipated that her fun side would make an appearance.

He relaxed enough to bump her shoulder with his own. Leaning in close, he whispered, "I'm a gentleman but I'm also a *man*. And that pixie is *fine*. So it's good to know all of the above. Thank you."

Jinx's eyes widened and she covered her mouth with her hands, giggling. She then bumped his shoulder in return and wagged her finger at him. "Draven! You bad boy, you. It's always the quiet ones ..." They laughed together for a moment before Jinx continued, "Phaedra has been an indentured servant for years. Serve *her,* spoil *her* for a change and you can't go wrong. Just treat her like the treasure she is. You'll do just fine, Draven."

Draven smiled at Jinx. "I think *you're* the treasure, my dear Jinx. Thank you."

Jinx huffed, looking away. "Tarnished treasure, maybe. I'm no prize, Draven."

"You'll find someone who knows your worth," Draven murmured, reminding himself he had a code and not to take away the pain he could feel emanating from her in waves. "And if you don't, you have a lot of people on your side willing to teach them a lesson."

Jinx smiled, bopping Draven on the nose. "You are so sweet. But trust me, I can handle my own lessons."

"I don't doubt it," Draven replied, having seen how competent Jinx was with his own two eyes.

"Thanks to Sabre," Jinx pointed out, a sparkle in her eyes.

Draven grunted, refusing to comment.

Jinx laughed. "Come on, admit it. You like her. It's just the two of us here," she gestured to the open space of the warehouse. Gage and Eric were currently mopping up blood on the far side, but they weren't within earshot.

"I will do no such thing," he promptly rejected the idea. It was worth it to hear Jinx laugh once more. It was also a matter of pride. Plus, the other angel was underhanded and duplicitous, he wouldn't put it past her to pop up out of nowhere like some kind of afrit just as he spoke those damning words. "I will store up my courage and ask Phaedra if she would like to join me on a date."

And then hyperventilate about all the other disturbing, yet interesting, things Jinx had talked about, he added silently.

"Excellent. I want to hear all about it. And I won't tell anyone, you have my word. Not even Sabre," Jinx promised.

"I don't doubt your word for a minute," Draven told her honestly. "Thank you, Jinx."

"You're welcome. Go get 'em, tiger," she said with a wink.

Draven laughed and was about to reply when he froze. He was being watched. Looking over his shoulder he saw Sabre standing a few metres away glaring at him. He glared right back, noting the healthy glow in her cheeks and the absence of shadows in her eyes. He approved.

"What are you doing here, butt face?" Sabre asked as she sauntered closer.

Draven's lips curled in disdain, and he narrowed his eyes. "None of your business, you horrible shrew. What are *you* doing here? I thought you were supposed to be with Brax and Mikhail."

Mikhail had returned to the palace just that morning. In secret, of course. They were still working on the finer details about how to reintroduce him to society whilst keeping him and Brax safe from their younger brother. Draven had left his charge in the more than capable hands of his mate, not that he would admit it out loud, so the two brothers could have some time to reconnect in private. And so he could ask Jinx some dating advice. But if Sabre was here, who was watching over the two royal men?

"They are ensconced in Brax's rooms with Styx and a million guards, including Phaedra, Mercy, Hugo, and Shiloh. They are completely safe. They wanted real alone time, with no one lounging in the corner like some kind of creep, pretending not to hear every single word." Sabre shrugged, touching Jinx on the arm with casual affection when she came to a stop next to her. "They can handle themselves anyway. They're big boys now. Unlike some ..." she added, casting him a scornful look.

Draven stepped away, giving Jinx a small bow. "Thank you, Jinx. I appreciate your time and advice. I will head off and wait outside the door in case I'm needed." He would feel better if there was at least one guardian angel in the royals' vicinity, despite the pair being capable.

"You're welcome. Any time. Oh, and Draven, it's probably worth practising a little. You know, solo, just to check your ... stamina," Jinx told him with a straight face.

He immediately turned and walked away, praying Sabre didn't see the blush staining his cheeks.

Jinx watched the angel flee, a snicker leaving her throat.

"What was that all about?"

Jinx looked at her friend and saviour for a moment, really

drinking in the changes. Sabre had always been a confident woman. It was hard not to be when you were one of the baddest badarses in Purgatory. But since meeting Brax she practically glowed with strength and purpose. She was sure of her place in the world.

Love will do that to a woman, Jinx supposed. She doubted she'd ever get a chance to find out for herself. She wasn't deluded, she knew exactly what she was. The moment any potential partner found out about her time in the brothels, they would drop her like the filth she was.

She tried her best to keep her face expressionless, not wanting to receive a lecture about how fabulous she was. She knew her friends meant well and that they believed everything they said, but it was hard to hear sometimes. It was also hard to live with constant contradictions in your mind, she acknowledged. Because, on the one hand, she loved who and what she was. She was proud of her accomplishments and loved her life. But on the other hand, she struggled with intrusive thoughts, her memories like anchors on her feet, weighing her down.

Focusing on Sabre, she replied, "Nothing. And don't push, I won't tell you."

Sabre shrugged, leaning back against the bar to watch Gage and Eric across the way. Jinx smiled to herself because that was it – just a shrug. Jinx had told her not to push and Sabre wouldn't. She was truly the best. Jinx loved her for more reasons than just because the angel had saved her from Hell. They watched Eric lapping up the attention of Gage as the pair talked, cleaning the area from the most recent round of fights. She was glad her new friend had all these excellent role models around him. It would make him, just as it had made her.

"So, how are things with the brothers?" Jinx asked, doing her best to keep the urgent curiosity from her tone.

She was more than a little disappointed to discover that her crush, Hound, was really Mikhail, the rightful King of Purgatory. She'd harboured high hopes of pleasure-filled nights with the rebel leader, but that was no longer an option. Not that Mikhail wasn't good looking – he was. She had seen pictures of him and had even seen him from afar a few times. But she had never met him. Sabre had kept her relationship with Mikhail top secret. Even from her and Gage.

"They're getting there. It helped that Brax was able to punch Mikhail in the head," Sabre acknowledged. "Healing takes time. Thankfully, they *have* time."

"And what about Zagan? That is so fucked up," Jinx added. It was still hard to believe, even to her.

Sabre sighed, looking tired. "They are prepared to do whatever is necessary to find and stop him. We need answers, but he also needs to be held accountable for his crimes. I know they plan to eventually kill him ..." she trailed off, looking troubled.

"You have a problem with that?" Jinx asked, surprised. Sabre usually loved all things killing-related.

Sabre shook her head. "No. I heartily approve. But it will hurt them. Irreparably. Mikhail and Brax aren't like Zagan. They are skilled and understand duty and are willing to uphold their responsibilities, even when they suck. But they are good men. They have a conscience, a soul. Zagan lacks that. He's an *Ace.* Killing his brothers means nothing to him. But, Mikhail and Brax? Killing Z will hurt them in ways they may not ever recover from."

Jinx watched her friend closely, forming a conclusion within seconds. "You plan to kill him yourself."

"They've been through enough," was all Sabre said.

So have you, Jinx thought silently. And in that moment, she vowed to take this burden from her friend. Taking Zagan's life would not affect her at all. But it could affect Sabre, even if she didn't think so.

Would Brax be able to look at his mate with the same love and devotion if she killed his baby brother? Jinx thought he could, because he was a stand-up guy. But she wasn't willing to take the risk. Sabre deserved Brax and Jinx would be damned if he would be taken away from her. Besides, it wasn't like Jinx had anyone to worry about alienating. She had no partner. No mate.

And never would.

The Reluctant Royals continues in book three,

Reluctant Rebel

About the Author

ALL ABOUT MONTANA

Montana is an Aussie, self-confessed book junkie. She writes paranormal and urban fantasy romance with fun, sex, sarcasm, and magic. She has a soft spot for broody male leads that need a little redemption, and feisty female leads that can kick butt. Because Montana believes variety is the spice of life, she writes all kinds of relationships with all kinds of letters – MF, RH, and poly with MM. She is a scientist by day, a writer by night, and a reader always!

- Join her Facebook group here: Montana's Maniacs
- Email Montana here: montanaash.author@yahoo.com
- Visit her Website here: http://www.montanaash.com/
- Or check out the links below.

Also by Montana Ash

Montana has a chunk of books out in the wild, including multiple series, solo titles, boxsets, and co-written works.

For a full list of all of Montana's books, please check out her website:

http://www.montanaash.com/

Or seek her out on any of her social media platforms.

Or any book retailers.

She is everywhere!